A Warrior's Promise

A Warrior's Promise

ROSANNE BITTNER

Copyright © 2018 by Rosanne Bittner.

All Rights Reserved.

No part of this book may be used or reproduced in any manner without prior written permission from Don Congdon Associates, Inc.; the agency can be reached at dca@doncongdon.com.

This is a work of fiction. Names, characters, places, and incidents are either the products of the author's imagination or are used fictitiously, and any resemblance to actual persons, living or dead, business establishments, events, or locales is purely coincidental.

By payment of required fees, you have been granted the *non*-exclusive, *non*-transferable right to access and read the text of this book. No part of this text may be reproduced, transmitted, downloaded, decompiled, reverse engineered, or stored in or introduced into any information storage and retrieval system, in any form or by any means, whether electronic or mechanical, now known or hereinafter invented without the express written permission of copyright owner.

The reverse engineering, uploading, and/or distributing of this book via the internet or via any other means without the permission of the copyright owner is illegal and punishable by law. Please purchase only authorized electronic editions, and do not participate in or encourage electronic piracy of copyrighted materials. Your support of the author's rights is appreciated.

Although wrongs have been done me I live in hope. I have not got two hearts... Now we are together again to make peace. My shame is as big as the earth, although I will do what my friends advise me to do. I once thought that I was the only man that persevered to be the friend of the white man, but since they have come and cleaned out our lodges, horses, and everything else, it is hard for me to believe white men any more.

      MOTAVATO (Black Kettle) of the Southern Cheyenne

Are not women and children more timid (weaker) than men? The Cheyenne warriors are not afraid, but have you never heard of Sand Creek? Your soldiers look just like those who butchered the women and children there.

      WOQUINI (Roman Nose) – Cheyenne –
      to General Winfield Scott Hancock

(Both of the above quotes from *Bury My Heart at Wounded Knee,* by Dee Brown)

Damn any man who sympathizes with Indians!... I have come to kill Indians, and believe it is right and honorable to use any means under God's heaven to kill Indians... Kill and scalp all, big and little; nits make lice.

      Col. John Milton Chivington, Leader
      of the Colorado Militia in 1864

I saw the bodies of those lying there cut all to pieces, worse mutilated than any I ever saw before; the women cut all to pieces...With knives; scalped; their brains knocked out; children two or three months old; all ages lying there, from sucking infants up to warriors...By whom were they mutilated? By United States troops...

John S. Smith, Congressional Testimony
of Mr. John S. Smith, 1865

(From internet article regarding the infamous Sand Creek Massacre in Southern Colorado, November 28, 1864)

From the Author:

The 1860's brought danger, death and grave losses to the Cheyenne Nation in the Territory of Colorado. One of the most infamous Indian haters in history, Colonel John Chivington, led the Colorado Militia on killing raids against peaceful Southern Cheyenne in the early 1860's, ending in the Sand Creek Massacre, one of the most horrific slaughters in that shameful era of Colorado's history. The primary sources for the real historical events in this book are *The Southern Cheyenne*, by Donald J. Berthrong, University of Oklahoma Press, 1963; and *The Fighting Cheyenne*, by George Bird Grinnell, University of Oklahoma Press, 1955.

This book is a work of fiction; however, mention is made of real characters who were involved in the Sand Creek Massacre.

A Warrior's Promise is the continuing story of a half-breed man torn between his white and Indian worlds, and the young woman who gave her heart to him in my novel, *Capture My Heart*, available from Amazon.com.

Chapter One

Mid-October, 1864...

The foothills to the west splayed downward in a cascade of deep green pine and bright yellow leaves that danced against the white trunks of aspens.

"Look at all the color, Peter," Claire told her husband. "And the sky is such a deep blue." She moved an arm under his and rested her head against his shoulder. "I love this time of year. The only problem is it means more snow will be coming over those mountains sooner than later, enough to keep us from making these trips."

"We are lucky the snow from last week's storm melted," Peter answered. "I just hope we get these supplies to Colorado Springs before another storm hits. There is already a lot of snow on top of Pike's Peak." He snapped the reins against the rumps of four work horses that pulled the heavy freight wagon he drove. STEWART FREIGHTING was painted on the sides of his and the two wagons that followed, but that name would soon be changed, now that Claire Stewart had married him. They'd been so busy re-locating the business from Denver City to Fort Collins that there just hadn't been time to repaint the wagons to read MATTHEWS SUPPLIES, after Peter's white name, Peter James Matthews.

A stiff wind made a sudden rush across their path, and Claire pulled the collar of her woolen coat around her neck against its chill. She snuggled closer to her husband. "Let's hope for the best. The mountains seem to be in charge of the weather this time of year."

Peter turned to glance at the red curls that sprang from under his wife's knit hat. He grinned and kissed one of them. "This is our last trip. In your condition you shouldn't even have come along on this one. We are risking a snow storm, and this is your first child. Just riding in this wagon is in itself too much for you."

Claire felt the flutter of life in her belly, a life that had been planted there by her husband of only eight weeks...planted before they even were married. Then she only knew him as Two Wolves, the Indian scout who'd saved her life from a raid on her supply wagons. Through their ensuing flight from danger she'd fallen in love with the man, not the Indian, not the white man, but just the man.

"God gave us this baby, and nothing is going to go wrong," she declared with complete confidence.

She turned to look back at the other two drivers, giving them a wave. It had not been easy finding men who would work for her, now that she'd married a man of mixed blood. The hatred of most Colorado citizens for the Cheyenne ran deep. A hatred stirred mostly by lies and misunderstandings. She leaned close and kissed Peter's cheek.

"I know staying in one place will be hard for you," she told him. "You'd rather be riding free on the open Plains and spending time with your relatives among the Cheyenne."

Peter shook his head and snapped the reins again, watching ahead as he spoke. "I would rather be right here with my beautiful wife and the mother of my child," he answered. "I said I would live the white man's way for you, and I do not break my promise. You wish to save your father's business, and so I will help you. But the traveling is too much for you. Most of the supplies from your store in Denver City should be at our new store by the time we get back."

"It was so nice of Major Ansley to send men to Denver City with wagons to load what was left at my father's old supply store."

"Ansley is a good man."

"The settlements around Fort Collins are growing fast and will constantly need supplies," Claire said, excitement in her voice. "We will have plenty of business, and after this shipment we can pay for the new inventory coming from Omaha."

Peter nodded. "I want to get out of the freighting business and just run the store. With all that is going on with the Cheyenne, and you carrying, these trips have become too dangerous. We'll be just fine without making any more deliveries."

"I'm just glad you'll be working beside me when we get settled," Claire told him. "I don't think I would have lasted much longer in Denver City trying to run the business alone. I just wish you didn't need to continue helping Major Ansley with more scouting expeditions." The wagon bounced hard, and Claire grabbed his arm tighter. "The Indian haters and Colorado Militia have become more dangerous now than the Indians themselves, thanks to all the lies they print in the *Denver Post*."

"Most of those stories come from the self-righteous John Chivington," Peter answered with obvious anger. "And thanks to Governor Evans, the Colorado Volunteers have free reign to kill Indians for no particular reason, like hunting animals. It is all political. Building the militia is the governor's way of showing he is protecting Colorado citizens. Even after what you and I went through proving there are some whites who deliberately make up stories about raids, the hatred continues."

Claire felt her husband's ire through the tense muscles of his arm. She glanced sidelong at his profile...full lips, a chiseled jawline, straight nose and dark eyes. Today he wore cotton pants instead of buckskins, a blue paisley shirt and leather vest under his sheepskin jacket. His hair was tied into a tail, and he wore one silver earring and a silver-and-leather necklace. Always well-armed, he wore a six-gun and a knife at his side. A shotgun and a Winchester rifle were positioned in slots next to the seat.

She smiled inwardly at knowing she needn't worry about Indian attacks now, because her husband was friends with and even had relatives among the Southern Cheyenne and spoke their language. In fact, she often called him by his Indian name, Two Wolves, for he had been all Indian when she met him...when he saved her life more than once...when against all reason they fell in love. He'd been schooled in Chicago after soldiers tore his white mother and him away from the Cheyenne when Two Wolves was just a little boy. His mother had loved his Cheyenne warrior father, but whites couldn't understand that.

I can understand it, Claire thought. If her husband's father had been anything like Two Wolves, brave and protective and loving and handsome and skilled, it would have been easy to love him.

After his mother's death, Peter had returned to his roots in Colorado, living with the Cheyenne but realizing their way of life could not last. He dearly wanted peace for them and had decided the best way to accomplish that was to work as a peacemaker between the Cheyenne and the U. S. Army, which was why he spent part of his time scouting for Major John Ansley, who was in charge at Fort Collins and who had become a good friend and father figure.

Claire knew her husband suffered inside over the plight of the Cheyenne, while at the same time realizing they could never survive the old way. Too many still didn't realize that, and his heart ached for them.

"I know it hasn't been easy adjusting to this new life, Peter, and I love you all the more for it."

"It is not difficult as long as I have you in my arms at night, *Maeveksea*. I made a vow in the name of *Maheo* and in front of a Christian preacher to love you and take care of you for the rest of my life. I will keep that vow. That is my life in your belly, and I will love and protect you and our child forever."

A shadow moved over them. Claire looked up at an eagle that soared above them, its wings still as it simply floated on the wind. To Claire it was an omen to her husband's promise. She loved the Indian name Peter had given her...*Maeveksea*...Red Bird. Two Wolves loved her red hair and thought her tiny like a bird. Everything about him was gentle and loving and honorable, but she'd seen him physically battle other men, and few cared to challenge the warrior he could be when necessary.

She shifted in the seat and wrapped her woolen coat closer around her neck. In all her years of growing up motherless and helping her father with his freighting business, she'd worn boy's pants and never cared much about her looks...until Peter came along. The way he'd looked at her the first time he saw her in a dress was all it took to awaken the woman inside and make her want nothing more than to be beautiful for a man. Impractical as it was on these trips, she wore a dress this time. Until the Indian Two Wolves made her a woman in every way when he claimed her virginity, she'd not realized how pleasant being a full woman could be.

"We should make camp soon," Peter spoke up, turning to signal the other two drivers. It was then he noticed them, riders coming, ten or twelve of them. He reined the horses to a halt and slammed on the wagon brake.

Claire turned to look. "Who are they?" She was experienced enough in traveling the wide-open plains in these dangerous times that she knew several men riding together could mean trouble. "They look like they mean business, Peter."

Peter squinted, then stiffened. "Colorado Militia," he answered with a hint of disgust. He quickly wrapped the reins around a post before grabbing his Winchester. "Let me do the talking."

Chapter Two

Claire clung tightly to the side-bar of the wagon seat, her heart racing. Everyone knew how unreasonable and unpredictable the Colorado Militia could be, especially if John Chivington himself was with them. And dressed like a white man or not, Peter was obviously Indian. The law allowed any citizen to shoot down an Indian if that Indian seemed to be threatening him, stealing from him or trespassing on his property, but eye witnesses and stories behind the headlines told of a militia that needed little reason at all to attack and kill.

The riders came closer, ordering the wagon drivers to halt even though they had already done so. Claire had seen pictures of John Chivington, a big, bearded man with glaring dark eyes that betrayed the evil behind them. She was relieved to see he was not among these men who circled the wagons, their apparent leader riding closer to Claire and Peter. He held his chin in a haughty pose, as though to make sure they understood how important he was. Stringy blond hair stuck out from under his floppy leather hat, and his sunburned face was partially covered with a several-day-old beard. His blue eyes were bloodshot and puffy, the kind of puffiness that comes when a man drinks too much. At the moment, those eyes were full of hate. His military jacket was dirty, and two buttons had popped open due to a paunchy belly.

"State your business!" the man barked at Peter.

"My business is none of *your* business," Peter answered. "You can see we are driving freight wagons and doing nothing wrong."

"There isn't an Indian alive who isn't up to something wrong," the militia men answered. "I asked you a question, Indian. Answer it or suffer the consequences!"

"Consequences?" Peter positioned his rifle across his knees. He glanced back at the other two drivers, both white men whom he trusted. One of them was Hubert Huff, a farmer who'd lost everything, including his wife, in a raid on his farm by white men dressed and posing as Indians. His testimony regarding that truth had saved Peter from a hanging only a month before in Denver City. Hubert didn't trust the Colorado Militia any more than Peter did. He climbed down from his wagon, rifle in hand.

"Stay put, Mister!" one of the soldiers told him as Hubert headed for the lead wagon.

"We're just takin' a load of supplies to Colorado Springs," Hubert answered. He kept walking.

"It is okay, friend," Peter warned. "Just stay where you are."

Hubert stopped in his tracks but kept his rifle ready and watched the volunteers with distrust.

Peter glared at the scruffy man who'd been giving the orders. "It is as Mister Huff told you," he explained. "My wife and I own a freighting business and are hauling supplies to Colorado Springs. This is our last load before moving to Fort Collins, where we will open a supply store."

"Your wife?" The leader glanced at Claire. "That white woman is your *wife*?"

"I most certainly am!" Claire answered defiantly. "This man is Peter James Matthews, and he's my husband."

Peter reached over and grasped her arm, squeezing lightly in a warning not to say anything more. "Now you know my name. My Cheyenne name is Two Wolves, and I spend part of my time scouting for Major John Ansley at Fort Collins, so I, too, am with the Army."

"Is that so?" The soldier moved a hand to his sidearm. "I'm First Sergeant Millard Craig, and mister, you look familiar."

"He sure does!" one of the other volunteers shouted. "He's that Breed that almost got himself hung in Denver City a month or so ago, Sergeant. Remember? I was there. You were there, too. He called himself Two

Wolves and worked out of Fort Collins. He's the one responsible for the hanging of that businessman, Vince Huebner – claimed Huebner led white men posing as Indians on raids against whites. He's a damn troublemaker."

Peter's fingers tightened around the trigger of his rifle. "Vince Huebner got *himself* hanged, for being behind those raids on innocent white people, his own kind!"

"And that woman is Claire Stewart of Stewart Freighting." The second volunteer sneered the words, looking Claire over as though she were filth.

"Claire *Matthews!*" Claire reminded him, refusing to show any shame for marrying an Indian.

Sergeant Craig leaned closer. "You're no wife," he sneered. "You're an Indian lover and a *whore!*"

Claire took a deep breath and straightened more in her seat as Peter squeezed her arm even tighter. He kept his eyes on Craig in a glare that made the sergeant move back a little. Claire was terrified Peter would let his temper get the better of him. If he did, he would most certainly be shot down before her eyes, even if he managed to kill one or two of the soldiers.

"You will not speak such things about my wife again, or before you can get your gun from its holster, I will be on you and break your neck!" Peter told Craig. "That is a *promise*, no matter what happens to me after that!"

Claire could hardly take a breath. Everything grew quiet then as the two men faced each other off. Sergeant Craig pulled his horse back a little, obviously seeing that Peter could probably do exactly as he said he could. He swallowed, pretending no fear, but Claire could see it in his eyes. She'd seen Peter in one-on-one battles more than once. He was not a man to challenge.

"That's enough!" Huff spoke up, walking closer in spite of being ordered not to.

Sergeant Craig glanced his way. "Orders I get from Colonel John Chivington give me the right to shoot you down just for being an Indian lover," he warned.

"And right now, I'm *proud* to call myself an Indian lover! You have no right stoppin' us. We've done nothin' wrong. We're on a legitimate delivery, and all of us here are white. Peter there is half white and well-schooled. Your business is supposed to be protectin' white folks, not stoppin' and threatenin' the ones who ain't doin' nothin' wrong."

"The man is right! Ride off and leave us alone!" The words came from the second driver, Klas Albertsson, a big Swede few men cared to tangle with just because of his size.

"Shut up, foreigner!" another one of the solders growled at him.

Craig kept his eyes on Peter. "The woman here that you call your wife says you're well-schooled. What Indian school did you go to?"

"I didn't. I lived in Chicago for several years and was schooled there with other white children."

Craig nodded. "So, if that's the case it's a sure thing one of your parents was white and went back home. Most white men who take Indian wives stay out here, so I'm betting it was your *mother* who was white, and she was rescued and sent back home. She was raped by some damn Cheyenne filth and lived in shame the rest of her life!"

"Oh, my God," Claire whispered, aching for Peter. She could feel his black anger in the way he continued to grip her arm. "My mother was saved from Pawnee Indians when she was still a young girl. She was raised by the Cheyenne, and she willingly wed my father. When white soldiers raided their camp and killed him, she *grieved* for him! And if you make one more insulting remark about either my wife or my mother, you will not see another sunrise!"

The sergeant sniffed. "You're pretty uppity for bein' half Indian! And I remember now. You and that woman with you came to Denver City and accused Vince Huebner of heinous crimes and got him hung. During his hearing you admitted to killing a white man at Fort Robinson for attacking your woman there, which means that however you pretend to live now, you're a goddamn Indian at heart, Peter James Matthews... or Two Wolves... whatever you want to be called. I could kill you right now just for being *part* Cheyenne."

"The law says you cannot shoot down an Indian unless he is doing something wrong!" Claire spoke up. "These men with us have already become good friends and can witness what you do here today. I am the one who managed to get Vince Huebner hanged for what he did, because some of his men attacked my wagon train and I heard them talking about Vince. I knew something had to be done, and I'm the one who insisted on going to Denver City and letting people know the *truth*! I and these men here will see that you get the same punishment Vince did if you shoot my husband for no good reason!"

Peter let go of Claire's arm and swung one foot over the side of the wagon as he set his rifle aside. He held out his arms. "Now I show no weapon, so you cannot say you are threatened. But I tell you now, I need no rifle or pistol or knife to take care of the likes of you! Shoot me if you think it is the right thing to do. But I tell you now that if you try to pull your sidearm, you are a dead man. I will break your neck before you get off a shot!"

"You had better believe him," Claire added. "I've seen what he can do, even when wounded."

"Peter has friends in the army and still scouts for them," Hubert added. "We can all make things hard on you if you make somethin' of this. Get on out of here and go do whatever the hell you're supposed to be doin'."

Craig drew in his breath and spit tobacco juice near the front wagon wheel. His upper lip quivered in a sneer as he spoke, directing his words at Peter. "Something tells me you and I will meet again, Indian, and in a whole different situation... the kind where I can cut your *guts* out if I want!"

"I hope you are right," Peter answered boldly. "Because if it should be so, it is not *I* who will be under the knife! That I can *assure* you."

Craig adjusted his leather hat and backed his horse more. "You keep something in mind, mister," he warned. "Scout or no scout, you're going to get involved with your Cheyenne relatives before things are over. Nothing got settled at Camp Weld when the Cheyenne met with Governor Evans, and there are plenty of your people out there still making trouble. We're doing all we can to keep the peace, but because the Cheyenne won't settle on anything, we still have orders from Evans himself to kill all the Indians we come across, and we'll do just that until they stop their raiding! If you're an army scout, then you're sure to get mixed up in their dirty work, and when you do, you'll be just as open to being shot down as the rest of them. I hope it's one of my bullets that does it, because I don't believe for one minute you won't help them if worse comes to worse!" He turned his gaze to Claire. "If this man promised to live like a white man for you and Indian attacks heat up, you're going to be left behind because his Indian side will always come first. Mark my words, you'll be a widow soon enough!"

He turned then and ordered his men to follow him as he headed southeast. Most of them gave Peter and Claire threatening looks as they rode away.

Claire groaned. "Oh, my God, Peter, I was so scared for you." She bent over, putting her head in her hands.

Peter nodded to Hubert Huff and Klas Albertsson. "I thank you for trying to help, but be careful doing so. The militia hates Indian lovers as much as they hate the Indians themselves."

"And I've seen what men like that can do," Hubert grumbled. "It's them kind that killed my wife, just to lie about it and get people riled against the Cheyenne."

"I stand up for what is right and fair," Klas declared. He held up his fists. "And I am good with these."

Peter couldn't help a grin in spite of the gravity of what had just happened. "That I do not doubt," he answered.

Klas fascinated him. He was the palest white man he'd ever seen, and also the biggest and strongest. He found the big Swede amusing and liked him a great deal. He was honest and unbiased. He'd come to America only a few months before and had headed west just to see what it was like. He went to work for Claire just to earn some money.

Peter turned and climbed back into the seat beside Claire, who quickly embraced him. He gently rubbed her back. "If this happens again, do not speak for me. It is insulting to a warrior to have a woman speak up for him. I will be fine and can do my own talking... and my own fighting. You know that."

"I couldn't help it. I hated the ugly things he said." Claire felt the tears coming. "It's all so unfair."

Peter kept an arm around her. "You know that I have heard all those things before. It matters little to me what they say about me, but my heart is sad over what he called you." He kissed her hair. "This is our last trip. What just happened tells me we have made the right decision to open a store at Fort Collins and settle there. Bad things are going to happen and being out here in the middle of it all is not a place for a woman carrying a child." He turned to the other men. "We will camp here." He looked at Hubert, who still stood nearby, rifle in hand. "Thank you for speaking up, but do not go too far in my defense. I understand men like that, and they will kill their own kind as easily as they will kill an Indian."

"After what happened in Denver City, and what happened to me and my wife and my farm, I *need* to speak up. It don't bother me, Peter. I'm right sorry for what that man called your wife."

"We knew when we married such things could happen, even though it was a Christian wedding. There are men who do not want to see the good in anyone, men who enjoy an excuse to kill. It makes them feel important."

Hubert turned away, shaking his head.

Peter grasped Claire's hand. "You will rest tonight. The men can do their own cooking."

Claire studied his dark eyes. "If not for the rest of us to witness, I think that man would have killed you just for the pleasure of it." She watched the bitter hatred move into his eyes.

"And now you know how the Cheyenne feel and why they fight. Every promise has been broken. Black Kettle continues to opt for peace. He wears a peace medal given him by your president and flies a flag of America in his camp, as well as a white flag to symbolize peace. Men like Sergeant Craig care nothing about any of that." He kissed a tear on her cheek, then wiped the rest of it away with his thumb. "Do not fear, *Maeveksea*. You are always safe with me. We will get through this."

"But you're going back out there, aren't you? When we're done with this load and get settled at Fort Collins, you will scout for Major Ansley again, which will put you in great danger."

"I will do what needs to be done until my people are safe. But I will be with you as much as I can be. You know that, and you know that I love you and will always come back to you. This I promise."

Claire glanced past him at the riders in the distance as they slowly melted into the horizon. "They're hunting Cheyenne, aren't they?"

Peter rested his forehead against hers. "*Aye, Maeveksea*. They are hunting Cheyenne."

Chapter Three

"You are rested?" Peter turned to tie the tent flaps together then moved into the tent beside Claire.

She sat up, keeping her feet under the blankets. "Yes. Thank you for the food you brought earlier. But I really don't need to be pampered like this. I am perfectly strong and healthy. You know that."

"You were very sick every day for the first month, and this is your first child. I want to protect my son who grows inside you."

"You don't know that it's a boy," Claire reminded him with a smile.

"I *do* know." He set his weapons aside and removed his boots, pants, and shirt, then took the tie from his hair so that it hung long and loose. Although his mother was white, this man she loved bore little proof of that.

Claire still could not get over his physique and power. This man who climbed under the blankets with her now had saved her from a fate worse than death. Not only that, but he'd saved her life from a bad arrow wound, and he'd risked hanging to help her prove the raid on her wagon train was conducted by white men posing as Indians.

Now he hovered over her, leaning down to kiss her neck.

"Peter, there are men sleeping not far away outside," she whispered.

"I wish to be inside you," he whispered in reply. "We can be quiet."

"It is not always easy to be quiet when you're moving inside me."

In the darkness Claire could feel his smile. She'd learned that Indian men loved to be praised for their manliness, whether in sex or in battle.

"Then you will have to try very hard," he told her as he pushed up the flannel gown she wore. "Your husband needs you." He slipped his fingers inside her underwear, toying with private places that belonged only to him.

Never able to say no to this man who'd first made a woman of her, Claire ran her hands over the hard muscle of his arms, forcing back a groan when he magically broke down all objections. Finally, she could not hold back a soft whimper as he moved fingers inside her to draw out more moisture, then stroked her in little circles that always took her to places beyond the present.

Before Peter came along, she hadn't even been interested in men. Other men thought her strange because she wore boy's pants and was bossy and independent – everything a woman was not supposed to be. Somehow Peter saw right through all that and had fallen in love with the young virgin behind all the bravado. He'd sensed a young woman who wanted to be held and loved and protected because she was all alone in the world. He'd saved her life and then won her heart. Now his mouth covered hers in a sweet, warm kiss that became deeper with passion as he moved on top of her. She reached around his neck and returned his kiss hungrily.

Peter raised up just long enough to pull off her underwear and unbutton his long johns. She opened herself to him, welcoming more hungry kisses as he entered her, pushing deep and making her gasp with pleasure. She felt lost in him, his broad shoulders hovering over her, his long, dark hair shrouding her face, his manhood filling her to glorious desire. She struggled to be as quiet as possible as his lips moved from her own to nuzzle at her neck, then down to suckle at her breasts while pushing himself deeper.

Because of men camped not far away he did not let the mating go on for too long. For his part, Claire knew he would much prefer doing this when they were alone and he could drink in her nakedness. It gave her shivers and brought out her desire when he talked about her milky-white skin and pink nipples. *Your eyes are green as prairie grass,* he often told her. He didn't seem to mind the scattered freckles on her face, and the fact that her flaming red hair was always a mass of tangled curls. It fascinated him that even the hairs of her love nest were red.

Now he allowed his life to spill into her sooner than he wanted, letting out a soft groan of ecstasy. For his part, being inside this small woman who had fascinated him from the moment he'd set eyes on her in Denver City brought him deep joy. He'd never thought he would fall in love with a white woman, and he worried every day about how being the wife of a half-breed might affect her. He felt a rage inside at Sergeant Craig calling her a whore. She was the most perfect, honorable and devoted wife he could have asked for.

"*Ne-Mehotatse,*" he said softly, speaking the words "I love you" in the Cheyenne tongue. "We will get underway early in the morning and get ourselves back to Fort Collins where you will be safer." He gently pulled away from her. "I will fill the wash pan with water for you." He moved to the side of the tent and lit a lantern, washing himself first.

Claire watched him pull on his long johns. She smiled at the memory of how he'd boldly undressed right in front of her and walked to a pond to wash not long after first rescuing her. A warrior at heart and used to true Cheyenne culture, he'd thought nothing of exposing his nakedness, but at that time she had been shocked and afraid.

Now her terror was over the possibility of losing him to a bullet from a Colorado citizen or the militia. Or when he scouted for the Army, there was always the danger of a battle with his own people. Most dangerous of all was the possibility something would happen that might cause this man she loved to become more Cheyenne than white and leave her to fight with his people. He'd promised never to leave her to go back to that way of life, but the atrocities being inflicted on the Cheyenne by the militia angered him greatly. She knew he constantly fought a need to join the Cheyenne against them.

She finished washing, and Peter climbed into their bedding beside her. He pulled her into his arms, her back against him. "I am sorry about what happened today," he told her. "If I had not been along there would have been no trouble."

"Don't ever be sorry for something like that." Claire fought an urge to cry. "It's those prejudiced, hateful men who should be sorry," she added bitterly. "I'm so scared for you, Peter."

He squeezed her closer. "Have you not seen that I can take care of myself? Words do not hurt me. I only worry how they might hurt you." He kissed her hair again. "You are the strongest woman I know, but that strength will be tested as my wife. We love each other enough to fight our way through it, and life will be a little easier now that we live at Fort Collins and away from Denver City and will stop traveling. I am glad we will live where you will always be able to find help whenever I am gone. I want you to feel safe, and I want you to have things easier while you carry our child."

Claire grasped his firm forearm. "It isn't over, is it, Peter? With men like those we ran into today running around the countryside causing trouble with the Cheyenne, I sometimes feel like the warring and unrest will never end. And I know where your heart lies. That's what frightens me."

"My heart lies with you. I promised I would live your way, and I will. But if I can do anything to help keep the peace with my people, I will do it. I will not war with them, and I will never leave you for them. A warrior's promise is steadfast."

But I know you heart, my husband. And I know how you love your people.

Chapter Four

The weather was cool but bearable on the return trip from Colorado Springs. Claire smelled snow in the air and looked up at an overcast sky. "I think we're going to hit snow before we reach Fort Collins," she told Peter.

"Here on the plains it snows one day and melts the next," he answered, glancing at the mountains. It was then he noticed them, a small party of Cheyenne warriors headed their way from the foothills. Riding fast. Peter reined in the team and turned to signal the other two drivers to stop.

"What is it?" Claire asked.

"Get into the back of the wagon and lie down flat," he told her.

It was then Claire saw the approaching band of Indians. "A war party?"

"Just do as I say."

One thing Peter knew was war and fighting...and the Southern Cheyenne. Claire obeyed, her heart racing with dread. Peter was one of them, yet he was also an Army scout and half white. The mood of the Cheyenne lately was not one of conciliation or reason. Too many had died at the hands of whites and the Colorado Militia for no good reason other than they were Indians.

"Hand me a white flour sack," Peter told her.

Claire scrambled to find one amid the remnants of unloaded supplies in the back of the wagon, which was mostly empty other than an empty cracker barrel and a couple of flour sacks that had broken. She grabbed one and shook the remaining flour out onto the ground, then handed the sack to Peter. Now she could hear *yips* and war whoops as the small war party galloped closer.

Peter quickly tied the flour sack onto the end of his rifle, then turned to the other two drivers. "Get down from your wagons and leave your weapons! Do not show any sign of fighting! I will take care of this." He waved his rifle in the air, showing the white flour sack in a sign of peace while Hubert and Klas climbed down from their wagons. Claire peeked at them and sensed their grave uneasiness.

Now the horses thundered closer, and she prayed for her husband's safety. She did not doubt his ability to reason with most of these people, whose blood ran in his veins. Still, it depended on what had driven the approaching warriors to be angry and want to kill. As they drew closer, she could see that was exactly what they had on their minds. She thought about First Sergeant Millard Craig and the Colorado Militia they had run into on their way to Colorado Springs. Had they committed some kind of atrocity against innocent Cheyenne? The painted faces and hateful fury in the dark eyes of the men who were very obviously bent on attacking them now told her something had happened to set them off.

Peter continued to wave the flour sack, and the Indians slowed their horses. Claire counted twelve men. Peter could take on any of them one-on-one, but twelve warriors were too much, even for all three men. Hubert and Klas held out their arms to show they had no weapons.

Peter shouted something to them in the Cheyenne tongue, and the apparent leader of the war party held up his hand to the others, signaling them to stay where they were as he rode up close to Peter.

"Two Wolves, brother to our people," the Indian called out in English, using Peter's Cheyenne name. "It is good for the whites here that you are with them, or they would already be dead!"

"Those two white men work for me and are peacemakers," Peter replied. "They have nothing against the Cheyenne. They are my good friends, and one of them saved my life once. The woman in the wagon is my wife."

The leader of the band of warriors shifted dark eyes to Claire, who sat up slightly and nodded to him.

"She is with child, Whistling Buffalo," Peter told him.

Claire felt relieved that Peter apparently knew the man.

"I heard that Two Wolves married a white woman," Whistling Buffalo answered. He actually grinned a little. "Her hair is as red as the setting sun."

Peter slowly lowered his rifle, then leaned over and set it down at his feet. "There is nothing here for you to take, Whistling Buffalo, and no reason to kill. We have no food and supplies with us." He scanned the warriors behind him, all of them looking thirsty for some kind of vengeance. "What has happened? Why were you thinking to attack us? We are peacefully headed back to Fort Collins."

Whistling Buffalo rode even closer, his rifle still in hand. "So you can scout for the army again and ride against us?"

Peter shook his head. "I have never betrayed the Cheyenne or fought against them," he replied. "You know this is so. I only scout for the army in an effort to keep the peace."

"You did fight us, two winters back, when you protected the Army leader called Major Ansley."

"It was my job to do so. Major Ansley was coming to talk peace, but the Cheyenne would not listen. I was along as a peacemaker. Those Cheyenne forced the fight. Not long ago I fought white ranchers while protecting Cheyenne members of my own family. Major Ansley came along and saved us all and drove the men away. He is a good man who wants only peace, as do I. With all that is happening here with the Colorado Volunteers, it would be wise if the rest of the Southern Cheyenne and the Arapaho headed north. Combined with the Oglala and Lakota, you would be stronger, and they need your help in ridding their promised Indian lands of the whites who go there to seek gold."

"Many whites have invaded the Black Hills, land that by treaty is forbidden to them!" Whistling Buffalo answered. "I would enjoy fighting beside the Sioux, but this land here is *ours*, and first we will fight to keep it! The Black Hills are not our home. *Colorado* is home!"

"And Colorado is also filling fast with whites," Peter told the man. "I have been in the land to the east, where there are more whites than you can count. Though the Cheyenne are great warriors, they cannot win against so many. Protect your women and children and offer peace. Stop the fighting, Whistling Buffalo."

A sneer moved over Whistling Buffalo's lips, lips that were painted red against cheeks painted black and red streaks painted under the man's eyes. "Peace? You were at Camp Weld when the white leader Evans pretended he wanted peace. You heard Evans and the Indian Commissioner Dole say that as long as the Cheyenne continue to attack white settlers and supply trains, the militia will continue coming after us. We have already tried peace, over and over, but the whites see us as warriors, and they despise the Cheyenne. When they accuse us of things we have not done and continue to attack peaceful Cheyenne camps and kill innocent women and children, we will never stop killing whites in return!"

Peter unbuckled his gun belt and dropped it to the floor of the wagon beside his rifle, then slowly took a knife from its sheath at his side and dropped that also. He climbed down from the wagon, and Whistling Buffalo dismounted and walked closer.

"I ask you, face to face, Whistling Buffalo, what has happened? You have always been one leader who tried for peace. I remember you at Camp Weld in the meeting with Governor Evans."

"The peace Evans claimed he wanted did not last. We try and we try, but the white volunteers under the bearded leader called Chivington continue coming after us, even when we are causing no trouble. Just three days ago at least forty Colorado Volunteers attacked a Cheyenne camp not far from Valley Station. Forty!" The words were growled. "There were two lodges at that camp. Two. And only six warriors, three women, and one boy, only fifteen. Those forty men killed all of them! They were peacefully camped, and anyone could see they had no chance. But they were all killed anyway. Even the women – by men thirsty only for Cheyenne blood. Big Wolf was one of those killed."

Peter sighed and turned away, glancing at Claire. She saw it then, that hint of a warrior bent on revenge. There was always that part of his Cheyenne heart that ached when he heard such news...a part of his Cheyenne heart that wanted to join those who vowed revenge.

He looked back at Whistling Buffalo. "So, now you and others are on the war path again," he answered, defeat in his voice.

"*Aye*! There is much raiding on the Platte road, and just two days ago, near Plum Creek, I and some of White Antelope's warriors attacked a party of Volunteers and killed two of them. We wounded others and killed all their horses. White Antelope was not with us. He is camped with Black Kettle at Sand Creek. The rest of us have split up to make raids against settlers and small supply trains and the white man's stage coaches. We will not stop until the whites are so afraid that they leave this land and never come back!"

Peter faced the man squarely. "And I am telling you that will never happen. You only put your women and children at greater risk. The attacks have to stop, Whistling Buffalo."

Whistling Buffalo stepped closer, practically nose to nose with Peter. "*Never*! I will let you go and spare your woman and the other two with you because I still consider you a friend. But we will not stop raiding and killing as long as the Colorado Volunteers continue murdering women and children. You tell your Major Ansley that! Tell him to bring out white leaders from the Great Father in the East who do not speak in lies. We will not speak with Governor Evans or any of the Colorado Volunteers. They do not want to hear us. They do not care. They want all of us dead and buried!" The man marched to his horse and in one leap was mounted again. He rode closer to Peter. "*Tell* the major!" he shouted. He raised his rifle and let out a chilling war whoop, then rode off, followed by the other eleven warriors.

Peter stood there a moment, watching them slowly disappear. Claire knew what he was thinking, knew his heart was heavy. Finally, he turned and told Hubert and Klas to get back into their wagons.

"Let's get ourselves to Fort Collins," he told them. "My wife needs rest, and I need to talk to Major Ansley." He climbed back into the wagon seat and helped Claire step over the seat and join him.

Peter picked up his knife and angrily shoved it back into its sheath. He then grabbed his gun belt and stood up to strap it back on, and all the while Claire could tell part of him wanted to ride off with Whistling Buffalo and join him in retaliation for the Volunteers murdering women at the small camp near Valley Station.

"Forty men against six warriors and three women," he growled.

He picked up his rifle and shoved it into place at the side of the wagon seat, then sat down beside Claire and unwrapped the reins from the post where he'd tied them. He kicked off the brake and snapped the horses into motion again.

"Things are only getting worse," he grumbled. "The damn Militia forces these things. How can the Cheyenne talk peace when the governor turns around and throws it in their faces? At Camp Weld, Commissioner Dole told Evans that if the Colorado Militia showed that they, too, want peace, it could be had. I saw Chivington's face, and I saw the look he and Evans shared at the remark. They have no intention of showing any sign of wanting peace. They want the Indians dead or run completely out of Colorado, and they don't care if they murder women and children to make that happen. The only white men I trust to truly care are Major Ansley and Major Wynkoop down at Fort Lyon. Ansley will retire next year, and I have a feeling the government will replace Wynkoop with someone not so sympathetic toward the Cheyenne. And with a civil war going on in the East, the government isn't going to give a damn what's happening out here with the Indians. The volunteers and whites in general will have free reign to handle things as they see fit, and to them the Cheyenne are no more important than coyotes and snakes – something to be eradicated like a plague."

Claire put a hand on his arm and felt tense, hard muscles. "I pray you don't get involved too deeply. You promised me you wouldn't."

Peter looked at her, and Claire could see tears in his eyes. They were not just tears of sorrow. They were tears of anger. His dark eyes were shockingly filled with bitter hatred, but quickly they softened a little as he studied her.

"I know what I promised," he told her. He put a hand over hers. "Let's get ourselves to Fort Collins and our new home. The soldiers Ansley sent to Denver City for the rest of our supplies should be back by now, and our house should be finished and ready to move into. For now, I wish only to get you home where you can rest."

Peter snapped the reins again and urged the horses to move a little faster.

Claire pulled her wool coat closer around her neck. She felt extra cold, but she did not shiver from that. She shivered from her unknown future with the warrior called Two Wolves.

Chapter Five

Late October...

Claire straightened the lace runner over a round oak dining table, then stood back to admire the table and chairs. The furniture had arrived from Omaha while she and Peter were gone, and to her delight, Major Ansley had ordered soldiers to finish building the small cabin next to the supply store before she and Peter arrived back home. It was one large room with a loft for their bed and a side room for storage and for washing.

It was small, but it was home. Claire was amazed how quickly it had been built. She had a stone fireplace with two cranes, and a brick oven built into the side of it. The fireplace area included cupboards and a countertop with a porcelain kitchen sink. Klas and Hubert, as well as Peter, carried water in for her from a nearby community well.

Life could be perfect if not for the fact that she'd sensed a restlessness in Peter ever since he'd talked to Whistling Buffalo about the incident near Valley Station. He'd been more distant, saying little as he helped stock the shelves at the store. Claire knew his Cheyenne blood had been stirred by what Whistling Buffalo told him.

Major Ansley had left on patrol with several men just two days before Peter and Claire returned. Claire prayed he would come back soon. The Major cared for Peter almost like a son, and Claire considered him a close friend. He'd played a big role in helping her and Peter prove their suspicions about white men posing as Indians attacking their own kind, and had helped get the right man hanged for it.

She turned when the cabin door opened to see Peter come inside with an armload of wood. He carried it to the fireplace and stacked it there.

"Among the Cheyenne, this would be woman's work," he teased. He turned and removed his jacket, walking to the door and hanging it on a wall hook. "The shelves are all stocked at the store," he told her.

He removed a knife from its sheath at his side and laid it on top of the ice box, which held a huge block of ice brought in earlier in the day by a man who made his living cutting ice from higher in the mountains and packing it in straw for sale to nearby settlers.

His was just another of the several new businesses in the growing area around Fort Collins. Claire thought how starting a supply store here would be far more profitable than the one she had in Denver City, where she'd had competition from several other suppliers.

"Thank you," she told Peter. "If you would have allowed me to climb a ladder and help, it would have been finished sooner. It's past supper time, but I kept a stew warm for you."

Peter walked over and slid over a bolt that locked the door. He stood there a moment then, studying her. "Promise me that when I am not around you will not climb ladders and lift heavy boxes."

Claire folded her arms. "I promise. But I don't like those words – *when I am not around.* You sound too sure about that."

He looked away with a sigh. "I will know more when Major Ansley is back. He might have learned something important." He sat down in a large wooden rocker and removed his boots. "I will take that stew."

Claire wished she could get rid of the heaviness in her heart. She walked to the fireplace and stirred the stew, thinking how out of place Peter looked inside the cabin. He should be standing in a *tipi*, his arms and chest bare, an array of weapons worn around his belt, his pants fringed deerskin, moccasins on his feet instead of boots.

"We will open up tomorrow," he told her. "You will do well."

We *will do well*, not you *will do well*, Claire thought. "I'm just glad to be out of Denver City and away from those haughty society women who used to look down on me just because I didn't dress and act like them," she said aloud. "As though it's a sin for a woman to own and run her own business. The women here are new settlers, and most of them understand the struggle it takes to make a living out here. So far, they have been kind and accepting."

Peter rose and walked to the table. "Accepting of your Indian husband?" he asked.

Claire faced him. "Accepting the fact that I have a business of my own."

He smiled rather sadly. "Claire, I know some seem uncomfortable around you, curious, judgmental, shocked, confused."

"Of course, some are that way. But as we all get to know each other, it will be fine."

He walked over to her and pulled her into his arms. "You talk about how hard this is for me, but it is hard for you, too. I want you to always be happy, Claire, and I want my son to be happy, too. I saw the suffering in my mother's eyes, and have lived with the confusion as to where I belong in this world. Our son will be raised white, because I know what lies in the future for the Cheyenne."

Claire reached up and touched his face. "Peter, I *am* happy, and our son will know so much love that he can't help being happy, too." She leaned back and looked into his dark eyes. "But his father has to be here with him, not off riding into a war that cannot be won."

Peter leaned down and kissed her, lightly at first, then more deeply, a rather desperate kiss. He released her mouth and pressed her close.

"I am not doing anything until Major Ansley returns. But when I come across men like Millard Craig and the Colorado Militia and then hear what Whistling Buffalo told me, a war goes on inside me over where my responsibilities lie."

Claire wrapped her arms around his middle and rested her head against his chest. "Two Wolves, your responsibilities lie right here with me and the child you planted inside me. I agree he should be raised white." She looked up at him again. "But you must teach him about the Cheyenne way and make sure he is proud of that part of his blood. Not only are *you* proud of it, but so am I."

He smiled slightly. "You agree he should be raised white, and you wish to live as other white women, which is only right and fair, yet you often still call me Two Wolves. If our son is going to be raised white, then you should call his father Peter. I am Peter James Matthews, remember?"

Claire smiled. "I didn't even realize I just called you Two Wolves. It just slips out naturally. When we met, you were all Indian, even to the point of doing battle with Comanche warriors. You dressed and behaved fully Indian, and you are a grand warrior, my husband. I have seen it. And that is how I always see *you*, as the Cheyenne scout who saved my life. I fell in love with Two Wolves, and though I love Peter James Matthews, for me you will always be that man."

He kissed her hair. "If we are to raise our son white, we must start living white in every way, including calling me Peter."

Claire sighed. "I usually do, but in the night...when it's just you and me...you will always be Two Wolves."

He smiled and suddenly whisked her up into his arms. "Then it is Two Wolves who will take you up to his bed. We have this night to be alone, and I worry after your opening day tomorrow that you will be too tired to be a woman for me tomorrow night. I think we should make up for it tonight, even before we eat that stew."

"Peter, someone might come calling!"

"It is much colder now, and already dark. No one will come. And the door is locked. If someone comes, we simply will not answer their knock." He carried her up the narrow stairway to the loft and laid her onto the feather mattress, then began undressing.

Claire loved watching him. He was all hard muscle, with scars from battles he'd won to protect her as well as from the Cheyenne ritual of the Sun Dance. His long, black hair hung nearly to his waist, his dark eyes were exotic. He had the kind of good looks those of mixed blood seemed to carry.

He pulled her up from the feather mattress and began unbuttoning the front of her dress, commenting again that he found it ridiculous the way white women dressed, so many stays and laced-up undergarments and petticoats and constricting clothing.

Indian women dress comfortably, in practical clothes that allow them to do their chores without things poking at them and taking their breath away. They are cool in summer and warm in winter, and usually they wear nothing underneath their tunics. White women make it so hard for a man to get to what pleases him most.

Claire smiled inwardly as she let him strip off every piece of her clothing, a ritual he seemed to enjoy. She ached at the thought of what his mother had gone through, rescued from the Pawnee when just a little girl after they'd killed her whole family. It was Peter's father who'd led the Cheyenne in the attack on the Pawnee, Peter's father who'd taken the woman in and raised her, only to fall in love with her and make her his wife. She'd loved him in return, and Peter was the result of their union.

Oh, but the sorrow his mother must have suffered when soldiers came and destroyed the camp where they lived, killed Peter's father and dragged his mother and her young son away!

She shook away the sad thought as Peter laid her naked body back into the feather mattress. She let him do with her as he wished, and she enjoyed ever touch, every kiss, every gentle exploration of her body. He softly licked and kissed his way down to private places that had never belonged to any other man. He'd been her first, and she'd learned in the most beautiful ways that lovemaking was the most erotic and pleasing act a man and woman could enjoy.

It was not that ago when she never dreamed she'd allow a man to know her so intimately. She floated upward in ecstasy as her desire built beyond measure when he tasted magic places while moving fingers inside her, making her cry out his name—"Two Wolves," not "Peter." A glorious climax came more quickly than normal, and in the next moment her husband was pushing himself inside her while devouring her mouth in his own groans of pleasure. She tasted herself on his lips as she arched upward, wanting every inch of every thrust. He filled her to the point of near pain, a pain that was sweet and wonderful and all a woman could ask for. She wanted nothing more than to please him, and she didn't mind feeling as though she was his captive, a woman being claimed by a magnificent warrior, for he was all of that. And she *was* his captive, for he owned not just her body but her heart. Nothing would ever change that.

She cried out when he seemed to grow even bigger for a moment just before his life surged into her. He grasped her bottom and thrust into her several more times before all the life was out of him and he was spent. He kissed her wildly a few more times, nuzzled her neck, then settled on top of her.

"Stay this way," he told her. "I want to have you again." He hovered over her, his hair falling around her face. He rested on his elbows, grasping her red curls in his hand and studying her green eyes by the dim light of a lantern. "You are beautiful. Tell me you will never leave me."

"Why would I leave you? I love you, Two Wolves."

"And what if I go away?"

Her heart froze. "Don't say that."

"Only for a while. When Major Ansley returns—"

"Two Wolves, I don't want to talk about that!"

"I made you a promise that I would love you forever, and that I will be father to the life in your belly. But something might happen that takes me away against my will. Know that I will always come back to you, *Maeveksea. Always.*"

Claire felt a lump forming in her throat. Peter kissed her again, wildly, like a warrior bent on taking a woman. She felt him grow inside her once more, stroking all the right places, bringing on another climax that made her take him just as wildly, fear in her heart at knowing she could lose him to another world she knew so little about. He took her as though they might never do this again, and she was determined to please him in every way, determined to make him remember where he belonged now – with his wife and the child she would give him and not riding free with the Cheyenne.

Chapter Six

Major John Ansley watched Two Wolves hammer the last nail into the sign over his and Claire's new supply store.

MATTHEWS SUPPLIES, it read.

And how long will you last as Peter James Matthews, my good friend? The major mused. *"I know how Indian you really are."* He removed his hat and scratched at his balding head as he spoke. "Peter, this place is going to do well, what with how fast a community is growing around the fort."

Peter looked down at the major and smiled. "So, you are finally back!" He made his way down the ladder. "I hope you are right about good business, for Claire's sake and for the sake of our child," he stated. "So far we are doing well." He jumped to the ground from a lower rung of the ladder and walked up to the major, putting out his hand.

Major Ansley shook his hand vigorously, feeling the man's strength in the handshake. As always, Ansley felt self-conscious of his heavy waistline and ageing, softening body when he was around Peter, whom he still saw as only Two Wolves, the young warrior who'd become like a son to him.

"And how is Claire doing?" he asked.

"She is doing well, but she works too hard. I try to stop her from climbing up and down to stock shelves, but she is a bad wife when it comes to listening to her husband and obeying."

The major laughed. "You are learning there are some big differences between Native women and white women."

Peter shook his head. "You do not know Cheyenne women so well, my friend. They are just as bossy as white women. When it comes to inside the *tipi*, the women rule the men." He shared another laugh with Ansley as he stood back to observe the sign he'd just hung. Big flakes of snow were falling, and he shook snow from his hair. "Does it look straight to you?"

"Looks fine."

"Everything left from Denver City is here now. I thank you for ordering soldiers to help us."

Peter brushed sawdust and snow from his clothes. Though the air was cold, he wore no jacket. A busy morning of carpenter work and climbing up and down a ladder had warmed him up.

"You're very welcome, my friend. After saving me and several of them a few months ago from an almost sure slaughter by Cheyenne warriors, they have all come to like you. I know there are still some who don't trust you, but you have a lot of friends among us, Two Wolves. I do miss your scouting, though. We have much to discuss."

Peter lost his smile. "That we do. I need to know what you found out on patrol, and I have a few things to tell you myself from the trip to Colorado Springs."

Major Ansley caught it...that look of a man torn between two worlds. With all he knew that was happening, keeping Peter here, living and working like a white man, was not going to be easy, especially since he needed him for more scouting.

"Come inside and see the store," Peter told him. "Claire will be glad to see you. At least I think she will. She might not like the things you have to tell me."

Ansley smiled a bit sadly as he nodded. "Lead the way, my friend."

Peter led him up the steps. "Claire keeps hot coffee on the plate of the heating stove and serves it to customers who need to warm up," the Indian told him. "She is excited about the store. Last night she studied catalogues from Chicago and New York, trying to learn what the latest fashions are there, so she orders the right underclothes and shoes and hats and material and such for the women."

Ansley grinned. "And I'm sure you consider that pretty funny."

Peter cast the major a sly grin as he opened the door. "I did not mind looking at the pictures, but I find it humorous to see all the uncomfortable things white women wear to try to pull in their waist and enhance their breasts. Cheyenne women would find it extremely funny. I can see them giggling over such things."

Ansley nodded. "I'm sure they would."

They walked inside, and Claire turned from hanging ribbon on hooks. She brightened at the sight of the major. Ansley thought her more beautiful than ever as she hurried to greet him. She'd gained a little weight, which she needed. She was such a tiny thing, he wondered how she would actually carry a child. The freckles across her nose still made her appear younger than she was, but she had a more mature look about her. She wore her torrent of red curls pulled back and piled into combs. He thought how far she'd come from the frightened, lonely young woman who'd struggled to keep her dead father's supply business going, the pitiful little thing who'd suffered an attack out in the middle of nowhere and then had been saved by Peter. And how could any woman not fall in love with the grand, handsome warrior who saved her life?

"Major Ansley!" Claire walked up and give him a big hug. "I'm so glad you're back and all in one piece. We were worried because we know things are bad and the Cheyenne are so angry over the Colorado Volunteers."

Ansley kissed her forehead. "Well, let's not talk about that just yet." He stepped back and looked her over in the way a father might, for that was how he felt toward both Claire and Peter. "You look wonderful. Healthy. How are you doing?"

"I'm fine now. That first month was awful, but I feel really good now, and I can eat without losing my meal five minutes later."

They both laughed as Peter hung up his coat. Ansley noticed he was dressed completely as a white man. "And where is that hot coffee Two Wolves tells me you serve in here?" he asked, turning back to Claire.

"Oh, I'll get you some, but I think we should go over to the cabin first. I have more there, and we all need to talk, I'm certain of that. People will be coming in and out of the store interrupting us. Hubert and Klas can watch things for us. They're out back. Klas is cutting wood."

Ansley grinned. "And I'll bet he can split a log with one whack," he joked. "Other than Peter, I've never seen quite such a strong man. I'm glad he has stayed on to help out."

"*Aye*, he and Hubert are good friends and much help," Peter told him. "I myself will be doing the ordering and bookwork. I want Claire to do as little as possible until the baby comes and even after that. She should give her full attention to our child." He touched Claire's shoulder. "Take the major to the cabin. I will get Hubert to come into the store."

He gave her a quick kiss, and Ansley saw the look of concern in Claire's eyes before she turned and led him through an enclosed walkway to their living quarters. She offered him a chair at the oak table, urging him to remove his outer coat while she walked to the stove to pour coffee into a porcelain cup.

"I've had too much coffee today, so I'll not have any," she told him as she set his coffee on the table and sat down. "I'm glad you're back, but I fear your news is not good."

Ansley hung his blue wool coat on a hook near the door, then took a chair, rubbing his hands together before picking up the coffee and taking a sip. "It's getting really cold," he commented.

"And you just avoided my comment about why you are really here, Major," Claire reminded him.

Ansley sobered. "You were right," he answered, "about the news not being good. I'm sorry, Claire." He saw the disappointment in her eyes as he removed his fur cap and hung it over the corner of his chair. He looked around the cabin, wanting to momentarily change the subject. "This is a nice little place you have here. The men did a good job."

Claire smiled. "Yes, they did. I love my cozy little house. But after the baby comes and begins to grow, we will have to add on and build a couple of extra rooms. I'm sure we will have more than this one child."

Their gazes held.

"And the more children, the less likely it is that Peter will run off and join the Cheyenne in the building tensions. Is that what you're thinking? I see it in your eyes, Claire."

She looked down at her blue paisley dress. "Something like that. Whatever your bad news is, I can add to it. There was trouble on our way to Colorado Springs, the kind of trouble that stirs the warrior in my husband."

"And you knew that was possible when you married him, Claire."

"Yes, but he made promises, and I believe him. Still, I also know how torn he is."

Peter came inside then, wearing denim pants and a red flannel checkered shirt. Ansley was always fascinated by how white the man could be when he wanted to be, but the little cabin seemed to overflow with Peter's size and power... and the odd sensation that the "Indian" didn't belong confined in these four walls. Ansley thought how Two Wolves, the Indian scout, would sometimes appear at his office out of nowhere and disappear just as quickly. He belonged to the wind and the sky and the mountains, not living and working as a white man. But his love for a white woman had changed him.

"I left my coat at the store," Peter told Claire. "The sign looks good. Later you should put on your coat and go look at it."

"I will. I'm so glad Sol Kliger finally finished painting it. He's so good at making signs."

"That he is." Peter poured himself a cup of coffee and walked over to sit down at the table. They all sat there silently for a moment, all lost in their own thoughts and concerns, all knowing the friendly conversation couldn't help moving into what was happening beyond the safety of Fort Collins and the small settlement around it.

Ansley sighed. "Peter, Claire says you had trouble on your trip to Colorado Springs."

Peter's smile faded. He took a drink of coffee, then folded his arms and faced his friend. "We had trouble both going and on our return. Neither problem was something soldiers could have done anything about. The presence of soldiers would only have made things worse on both counts. Out here the Colorado Militia overrules the Army, and most Cheyenne are currently not so fond of Bluecoats."

"The Militia! Your trouble was with them?"

"On our way to Colorado Springs they stopped our supply train," Claire spoke up. "They saw Peter, and I think the man in charge wanted to find a reason to shoot him just for being Indian."

Peter shook his long hair behind his back. "They questioned us, and their leader tried to show off his authority by threatening me. He demanded to know my Indian name, and I told him it was none of his business—nor was it his business to stop our supply train. He said he could shoot me if he wished, and I told him to go ahead, but that before I went down I would have him off his horse and break his neck!"

There it was again. The Indian. Ansley could just picture how threatening Peter must have looked at the time. When he let that deep anger show in his dark, Cheyenne eyes, it was enough to make any man back off.

"I think he believed me," Peter added. "He looked afraid, which I thoroughly enjoyed."

In spite of the seriousness of the situation, Ansley couldn't help a light chuckle. "I can just see it," he answered. "I know how you can be, Peter, and I would have backed down, too. I personally have no doubt you would have been able to do exactly what you said you would do."

"I can read a man's eyes, and this man wanted to look brave in spite of backing down. He told me he hoped we would see each other again. He bragged that if that happens, I am a dead man."

"And your reply?"

"What do you think?" Now it was Peter who grinned.

"I think you told him you look forward to meeting up with him again."

Ansley thought how white and even the man's teeth looked against his dark skin. He had a handsome smile. More than once Ansley had heard other white women comment on Peter's looks, saying it was "too bad" he was Indian, which made him off limits, in their minds, to even be friendly with. But not Claire. She saw through the danger and wildness of the man and loved him exactly for what he was. Ansley feared she was in for hurt and sorrow by doing so.

"You are right," Peter was saying. "I hope we *do* meet again. I would enjoy sinking my knife into that mans' heart! He insulted Claire, and he insulted my mother. He is lucky I kept my temper under control. If you heard what he said, you would have been proud of me for not reacting with violence."

Ansley nodded. "Probably. In the meantime, you have one year of service left with the Army, and though I hate to take you away from Claire, I need your help." He glanced at Claire and saw the fear and alarm in her eyes. "It's just for a while," he added. "I promise."

"It is because of more trouble with the Cheyenne," Two Wolves declared. "I already know this. I told you that we also had trouble on our way back here. We ran into a small war party led by Whistling Buffalo. If I had not been along, I think my wife and the two men with us would be dead. They were in a killing mood, and I don't blame them. A party of nearly forty Volunteers attacked a peaceful camp not far from Valley Station. There were only six men there, plus three women and a boy. They killed all of them, for no reason. This is not the way to make peace with the Cheyenne!"

Ansley felt his anger. "I heard about that. Word is Governor Evans and the powers that be in Washington think it's too soon to settle with the Indians. They actually believe the only way to keep the peace is to punish the hostiles for the attacks they have committed up to now."

Peter rose, his hands going into fists. "It will only make them more warlike, and in turn they will commit more attacks and kill more whites, giving Evans and the government an excuse to keep going after them and killing those who only want peace." He began to pace.

"Settle down, Peter," Ansley asked calmly. It felt so strange to call him Peter, but maybe it would help remind the man of his white side and that he could not react the way other Cheyenne would react.

Peter walked to the fireplace, putting out a hand and bracing himself against the mantle. "What are your plans, and what is it you want from me?"

Ansley glanced at Claire, who looked ready to cry. "Claire, maybe you should go lie down."

"No. I want to know what's going on."

The Major ran a hand across his balding head, pushing thin hairs behind his ears. "They are going to replace Wynkoop at Fort Lyon."

Peter remained turned away. "Of course they will. Wynkoop was a friend to the Cheyenne. He always let them go there for protection, and he provided them with food and supplies. I recently told Claire that I suspected they would replace him."

"You were right. Evans and Chivington and the government think he is too soft on the Indians."

Peter finally faced him. "Who will replace him?"

"Rumor is it will be a Major Scott Anthony. He's supposed to investigate rumors that certain officers have issued supplies to hostile Indians, against the orders of Major General Curtis, who has said he wants no peace talks or provisions handed out without his knowledge and approval. Chivington, in the meantime, is on the move and hoping to get in on the action of punishing the hostiles. We both know what that means. He'll attack any camp he comes across. He won't need a reason."

Peter glanced at Claire with sad apology in his eyes before turning again to Ansley. "And what do you want of me?"

"I want you to go back south with me, to Sand Creek. Maybe you can talk to Black Kettle and White Antelope about opting for peace at all costs. I think Major Anthony will show mercy to the Arapahos if they give up their arms, but it won't be that way for the Cheyenne. Anthony and Chivington and Evans and the whole bunch of them are bent on making them suffer to ensure they'll never make war again, and that means killing their women and children right along with the warriors. In Chivington's mind, the women and children should also die, so that the Nation as a whole ultimately dies out. I don't know if either one of us can stop any of it, but I'd like to try. I want to take some troops down to Sand Creek and parlay with Black Kettle and White Antelope. If we're lucky, Whistling Buffalo will also be there, and we can convince them to move even farther south and out of Colorado, or maybe head farther east and then north to join up with the Sioux and Northern Cheyenne."

Peter began pacing again.

"It will be difficult because deep snows will be setting in," Ansley added. "I don't know why these things always seem to happen in the winter. Of course, there probably isn't that much snow down by Sand Creek, but avoiding the snow could cost a lot of lives because they might have to stay there after all rather than trying to head east. Chivington's men are everywhere. Traveling in winter is bad for the old ones. I'd like to get them away from Sand Creek if possible, but I'm sure they believe they are safe there. If I don't get a wire giving me permission to help, I'll do it anyway, if Black Kettle and the rest of them will go with me. I could get a dishonorable discharge for helping them escape, but I don't care. I'm close to retirement anyway. By next spring I'll be back in

Pennsylvania with my wife and done with this mess. I'm tired of it all, Peter. I know this is hard on you, but I thought you might feel better at least doing what you can to stop the slaughter I see coming."

Peter leaned back his head and closed his eyes. The room hung quiet, Ansley and Claire both finding it difficult to know what more to say. Peter suddenly got up and walked over to where his heavier wolf-skin coat hung on a hook. He pulled it on and turned to Claire. "I am going off to be alone for a while. Lock the door after Major Ansley leaves. I will not be back for a few days."

Claire looked at him with tear-filled eyes. "Where will you go? What are you going to do?"

Their gazes held. "I am sorry, *Maeveksea*. I made promises, and somehow I will find a way to *keep* those promises, but for now I need to be alone." Peter turned to Ansley. "I will come to the fort in a few days with whatever information you need for the trip. In the meantime, send a wire to Washington and try to get permission to help Black Kettle." He turned and walked out.

Ansley rubbed at his eyes. "Your husband was always good at abruptly leaving and disappearing for days at a time," he told Claire. "But he's a man of his word, so if he says he'll be back, then he'll be back."

Claire forced back tears. "I knew something might happen to tear him apart and make it difficult for him to live like this. I'd just hoped it wouldn't happen so soon..." She couldn't stop a tear from slipping down her cheek then. "What if he never sees his son?"

Ansley reached over and touched her arm. "He loves you very much, or he would not have made the decision to marry a white woman. He knows you are not like his mother as far as being able to live the Cheyenne way, but he married you anyway. There is much meaning in that, Claire."

Claire nodded. "I hope you're right."

"I know I'm right. I'm sorry to take him away from you, but I think he would never be able to live with the fact that he didn't try one last time to help his people. It will be better for him to know he did his best to help than to watch them be slaughtered without being part of protecting."

Claire put a shaking hand to her hair. "I could still lose him, couldn't I? His Cheyenne spirit has more power over him than I do. I can feel it."

"I think you're wrong. I wish there were another way around this, but he has a year left in his commitment as a scout, and he would want to be a part of this. You know I'm right." He sighed and leaned back. "Do you want me to stay a while?"

She shook her head. "No. Just go next door and tell Hubert what has happened. Have him run the store for today. I might go back over there later just to stay busy, but right now I'm going to lie down."

"Please don't let this upset you to the point of affecting your condition."

"I'll be fine."

Ansley rose with a weary grunt. He took his hat from where he'd hung it on the chair and put it on. "Lock the door like Peter said to do."

Claire nodded. "I will." She looked up at him. "I know you're torn also. You've been a good friend, Major. You risked your life for both of us in Denver City when that mob wanted to hang Two Wolves."

He smiled sadly. "And that's what you still call him, in spite of the fact that you are trying to steer him to life as a white man."

"That's how I still see him—as the warrior who saved my life. I will always see him that way, which is why I have a hard time remembering to call him Peter."

"Then understand that he *is* still a warrior."

Claire rose and picked up Ansley's coffee cup. "I understand that all too well. When I married him, I thought perhaps the worst was over for the Cheyenne and some kind of peace could be made. That's why I thought he would be fine living as a white man."

"Then pray for that peace. And for your husband's soul." Ansley turned to the door. "Are you sure you'll be all right alone?"

"I will be." Claire walked to the door as the major opened it. Just as he did so, Peter rode past on his favorite horse, a paint he'd caught wild and tamed himself. He called the horse *Itatane*. He kept it in a shed and fenced area behind the cabin. He also kept Indian clothing, an extra uniform, supplies and weapons in the shed, so that he could leave at any moment if necessary. Claire noticed he used no saddle, just as a

Cheyenne warrior would not use one. He did not turn to look at either one of them as he passed. He simply rode away.

Claire knew that the rest of the day and into the night, perhaps even longer, he would not be Peter James Matthews, the name on the sign above their supply store. He would be Two Wolves. And if things did not go well on this mission, he might always be Two Wolves.

"He didn't even let me pack him some food first," she told the Major absently, staring after Peter.

"He didn't need to. The man is a survivor. He'll hunt for his own food. All he needs are his weapons and a horse."

His weapons. Claire had seen him use them, and any man who went up against the warrior Two Wolves usually regretted it.

"Moments ago, he was so happy, helping put up that sign and stocking shelves, promising to do my bookwork," she told Ansley.

"What just happened is the side of him you'll have to learn to live with, Claire. I'm sorry that my visit led to this, but he'll be back because he's just looking for news out there among the Cheyenne, so he can advise me what we should do next. I promise to make this his last scouting mission. Once this is over you'll have him all to yourself again."

"Will I?" Claire looked up at him. "I hope you're right, Major."

"I know I'm right. He loves you, and above all else he loves that baby you're carrying. He just needs some time to get used to living as a white man *all* the time. Your patience will help." Ansley grabbed his coat and pulled it on before going out the door. He stopped to lean down and give Claire a kiss on the forehead. "Stay out of the cold and be patient."

Claire nodded, hiding her tears until she closed the door. It was then she covered her face and cried, asking God to help her understand her husband.

Chapter Seven

Flames leapt from the crackling, snapping pine and aspen wood, sending glowing cinders high into the black night sky. The heat from the fire could not quite keep up with the cold early-November air that already engulfed the foothills of the Rockies, where Peter sat meditating. He wore nothing but a breechcloth and an apron, ignoring the cold at his back. This was a time to be still and pray, for there was much that weighed on his mind and heart. While he meditated, he was Two Wolves.

He raised a peace pipe given to him by a cousin, *Okohm*, whose name meant Coyote. His cousin had been killed not so long ago by white ranchers. His death still hurt Two Wolves' heart, and he'd taken his cousin's wife, Sits-In-The-Night, north to join with the Sioux, one of the few tribes remaining who continued to fight white settlement. Part of Two Wolves wished he could join them in that fight, but he knew that even if the Sioux and Northern Cheyenne prevailed for a while, the future held nothing for them but eventual submission.

"*Maheo*, guide me," he prayed, as he offered the lit pipe to the heavens in honor of the Great One above. He brought it down and smoked it, then slowly blew smoke from his lungs as he lowered the pipe, offering it to Mother Earth. He smoked it again, offering the pipe to the four directions of the earth. He carefully laid the pipe aside then and placed his hands on his bent knees, singing his prayer song.

Maheo, guide me.
Maheo, guide me.
Show me the way to go.
My heart is heavy with two worlds.

My heart is heavy with two worlds.

Maheo, guide me.

He opened his eyes and watched the flames dance before him. In them he saw his father, long dead, killed by soldiers when he was only a boy. He saw his mother weeping as soldiers took her away, letting Two Wolves go with her. Far away, to the white man's city. Always, always, his father was in his heart, whispering to him, his Cheyenne spirit calling him back home to the vast prairies and wild, purple mountains.

Here was where his heart lay. Here. Here, with the spirits of the Cheyenne, those long dead and those still living. Constantly they beckoned him.

But now there was a new face in the flames, her hair as red as the flames themselves, her eyes as green as the prairie grass, her smile as bright as a white sky, her heart as true as any Cheyenne woman's. She carried his child, his seed, planted into her in the beauty of worshipful union. She had risked much to be with him, and he had made promises to her—that he would love her forever and he would live in her world.

How long could he keep that promise? Their union was only three months old, and already his Cheyenne spirit pulled at him, asking him to return to that part of his blood, to practice the old customs, to join them in their struggle against the awful attacks by whites.

"Guide me, *Maheo*," he asked again. "Show me the way to go." With that, he pulled his hunting knife from the sheath at his side and deftly cut his left forearm, then held it out to drip blood into the flames. A blood sacrifice to *Maheo* was always sure to bring the answer he needed.

He saw Claire again in the flames, but suddenly several skeletons danced before him, grinning and screaming, *"Vehoe! Vehoe!"*

"Siyuhk!" Two Wolves shouted, actually startled by what he saw. The word meant "skeleton," and the skeletons shouted "White Man! White Man!" It was a definite warning, something to take very seriously. The white man had something awful in mind for the Cheyenne.

He rose, raising his arms and letting blood from the cut run down and over his underarm and onward, flowing down his side. He knew what he must do.

Chapter Eight

"He hasn't come back." Claire stirred cream into her tea, the clinking of her spoon the only sound in her small cabin. "It's been five days, Major." She struggled against tears as Major Ansley sighed with concern. He took a sip of the tea she'd had just served him.

"You have to give him time," he told her. "He said he'd be gone several days. I've known him for two years now, Claire, and I am aware of how Indian he can be, but he always keeps his word."

Claire nodded, quickly wiping at a tear that had escaped down her cheek. "I know. I just...I guess I didn't think something like this would happen this soon, especially since I'm carrying his child."

"He made you promises, and Two Wolves is not a man to break those promises. Something deep inside is pulling at him, and things like this will happen until he fully adjusts to this life. He loves his people, feels obligated to do something to help them while he still can, which is why I referred to him as Two Wolves instead of Peter. I know him, and right now his heart and soul are fully Cheyenne."

"He still mourns his cousin, Coyote. He's haunted by what those ranchers did to him." Claire drank some of her tea, staring absently at a sugar bowl. "That incident with the Colorado Militia on our way to Colorado Springs didn't help. I could tell he wanted to leap off the wagon and plant a tomahawk in the man's head." She smiled faintly through tears. "I've seen him in battle. It's quite something to witness."

"It most certainly is." Major Ansley leaned forward, resting his elbows on his knees. It was Sunday, and quiet. MATTHEWS SUPPLIES was closed, and many of the settlers around Fort Collins had gone to the one-room building that served both as a school and a church. Claire had stayed home...waiting...hoping.

"I've seen him in battle, too," Ansley told her. "Remember, he saved my life once, so take hope. There is that part of him that will fight his own people to protect someone he cares about, just like he fought those ranchers who killed Coyote and the Comanche scout who tried to kill you. Those he loves, whether Cheyenne or white, will come first in the end. I don't think he will ever choose the Cheyenne way for life." He reached over and patted her arm. "And once that baby is born, Claire, he will never abandon you or the child. His heart will be too full of love for both of you. Above all else, he is a man of honor, and he takes his responsibilities seriously. That's why he's been gone so long. He will find a way to do right by both you *and* the Cheyenne, just as he has done right in his job as a scout."

Claire nodded. "I believe you."

The hymn "Rock of Ages" drifted on the air from the small church not far away.

Claire met Ansley's blue eyes, eyes that were surrounded by age lines made more distinct by too many hours with the sun burning against his fair skin, too many hours in the saddle, riding the wide-open plains of Eastern Colorado.

"You are retiring in less than a year. I know it's a lot to ask, but please promise me you will stay here for a while after that if things aren't completely peaceful. I know the settlement here is growing, and there is always the safety of the fort, but without Peter I still feel safer when you're around. You've become such a good friend."

Ansley smiled kindly. "I'll stay a while, but by then you will have made some good friends right here. Peter will be back, and you'll both be raising a new baby. I know there are those who still shun you for being married to an Indian, Claire, but many of those who come here are new to Colorado and don't carry the same hatred for the Cheyenne that Coloradans and the militia do. They haven't seen true Indian atrocities. All they care about is starting a new life here, farming, opening their own businesses, starting over for whatever reason they need to. They will shop at your store and get to know you, and you'll make friends because you're a lovely woman. And you have Hubert and Klas. Those two will do anything for you."

Claire grinned and sniffed back her tears, letting out a light laugh. "I think they would. They are such good men. But Klas only stopped here to work for a while and earn money to go on to California. He might not be here next summer."

"I think he's growing to like it here, and I noticed that lately he's been talking to the lovely young daughter of one of the settlers. There is nothing like a woman to change a man's mind and make him settle where he never planned on settling."

"Oh, I hope so!" Claire took another drink of her tea. "Thank you, Major. Who would think an ornery, retiring Army Major I never even knew four months ago could become such a good friend so fast? And thank you for caring about Peter."

Ansley studied the tired lines under her eyes and noticed she wore the same blue calico dress she'd worn yesterday. Had she been up all night worrying about Two Wolves and never gone to bed?

"You take care of yourself and get some rest," he told her. "One thing you have that will rope and tie Peter right here with you is that baby, so stop fretting and keep yourself rested and healthy. You need to carry that child all the way to when he or she should be born. That baby is your insurance, but I really don't think Peter needs even that. He needs *you*. He's crazy about you, and I don't blame him. You're beautiful and resourceful and brave and strong – all the things both Indian and white men admire in a woman. He knows what you have risked for him, and he won't let you down. You believe in that. And he has to come back here because he promised me he'd scout for me the next few weeks. He won't let me down, so whatever he's deciding, he'll come back here first. He won't do anything without first talking to you about it."

Ansley rose, and Claire rose with him. She gave the major a hug. "Thank you for the visit."

Ansley patted her back. "Thank *you* for the tea and the talk. I get lonely, too, you know. I'm surrounded by a bunch of questionable rabble who need a kick in the rear every day to obey orders. Half of them probably joined the army to escape the law back East, and the other half volunteered for service in the West in order to stay out of the ugly war going on there. The only one who is educated and pleasant to talk to is Captain Tower, our doctor."

Claire stepped back. "Yes, he's a fine man."

Their gazes held. "And he was truly interested in seeing more of you before he realized you were in love with Peter. If something happens to Peter, you remember that man. He's a good man, one who'd likely accept your child and take care of you."

Claire turned away. When she and Peter first arrived at Fort Collins, Captain Tower had taken great interest in her, thinking she was just someone Peter had rescued out on the plains and had brought to the fort for help. Tower was handsome, educated and sincere in his concern for her, but by then her heart fully belonged to Peter. She had no interest in anyone else. "I'm sure he's a good man, Major, but even if... if Peter never returned I wouldn't be interested. I would take my baby and go back East." She faced him again. "But he *will* be back, and soon."

"Of course, he will."

Thunder rolled in the distance, as though to give some kind of ominous warning. "Sounds like a storm coming," Ansley commented.

The rolling boom sounded again, issuing from somewhere high in the mountains.

"Yes," Claire answered. "I fear a storm *is* coming, and not just the kind that brings wind and rain."

Ansley reached out and patted her shoulder. "Get some rest. Peter would want that."

"I will. And I have the store to keep me busy and keep my mind off things. We get busier as more people come here to settle."

She led Ansley to the door and he put on his hat.

"Good night, Claire."

"Good night, Major."

The man looked reluctant to leave.

"I'm fine. Truly," she assured him.

"I'll check on you tomorrow."

"Thank you."

Ansley left, and Claire stepped out onto the porch she'd insisted be added to her little house. She rubbed the backs of her arms against a damp chill. The weather had momentarily warmed, but she knew the rain coming toward them could turn to snow again in the blink of an eye, especially as it rolled over the mountains.

Thunder boomed again. She watched lightning flash in the distance. It all seemed to match the storm in her heart. "Peter, where are you?" she said softly. "Where are you?"

Chapter Nine

Major Scott Anthony looked up from the report he was writing, suddenly aware that someone had come into his office. Startled to see an Indian stood right in front of him, he jerked back and dropped his ink pen. "Who are you, and how in hell did you get in here?"

Two Wolves did not reply right away. He studied the man a moment, watching his eyes. Anthony was of average height, his hair a mixture of black and gray, his eyes a pale blue and showing a look of contempt.

"Private Miller!" Anthony shouted.

A young soldier appeared at the door to his office, his eyes widening when he saw an Indian facing the major. "Sir?"

"How did this man get in here?"

"I...I don't know, Sir. I left my post to – well – I had to use the privy."

"You left without telling me? I should have you horse-whipped!"

"Sir, I – I'm sorry, Sir. I was only gone about five minutes."

Anthony turned his attention back to the Indian before him. In spite of wearing an Army jacket, he looked dangerous, fully armed and standing tall. His physique alone was intimidating.

"Long enough for this sneaking thief to come in here without a sound," he growled. "He could have slit my throat before I even knew he'd come in!"

Two Wolves spoke up. "I mean you no harm."

"That doesn't erase the fact that the private there should never have left his post!" Anthony turned back to Miller. "Go find someone else to take your place. And you will not report for supper this night. You can go hungry. I'll decide on what other punishment you should suffer after I find out what this renegade wants."

"I am no renegade!" Two Wolves barked. "Do you not see the crossed arrows on my sleeve? I am a scout, stationed at Fort Collins."

Anthony looked him over. "I see an Indian standing before me, his hair long and loose and decorated with beads, beaded buckskin pants, knee-high moccasins, a hoop earring in his ear, a white stripe on each cheekbone, his body adorned with enough weapons for a war, who snuck in here without a sound."

"I am half Cheyenne, and my Indian name is Two Wolves. My white name is Peter James Matthews, and my wife and I own a supply store at Fort Collins. I was educated in Chicago, and I am just as much white as Indian. I came here to learn your plans for Black Kettle and his people camped at Sand Creek. I am to report back to Major John Ansley at Fort Collins. I see outside Fort Lyon there are Arapaho getting supplies and protection, but you do not allow the Cheyenne to come here for protection and food. What happened to Major Wynkoop? He was a good friend to Black Kettle."

"He was *too* good a friend! He's been relieved of his duties here. I am Major Scott Anthony." Anthony folded his arms. "If you're here on a mission from Fort Collins, why didn't Major Ansley come with you?"

"He is preparing for an expedition to find protection for the peaceful Cheyenne for the winter."

"And you haven't explained why you just showed up in here unannounced."

Two Wolves shrugged. He didn't care for this Major Anthony. He could already tell the man was on the side of Governor Evans and the hated Colonel Chivington. "No one was around, and the door was open, so I walked in."

"You know a man of lower rank is supposed to announce himself."

"You were busy writing something. Perhaps they are orders to attack the Cheyenne at Sand Creek, even though they are only camped peacefully and wanting food and protection."

"My orders are none of your business. Your business is to help find the hostiles who still hide out and want to make war."

"Perhaps, but I can tell you that those camped at Sand Creek are not wanting war. I already visited with them on my way here. Currently John Chivington is camped at Bent's Fort. I was told he is heading here next, and that the orders from Governor Evans are to refuse help for the Cheyenne because some of them still make war and have blocked some of the trading routes. But Black Kettle and those with him at Sand Creed are innocent of this."

"Orders are to go after *all* hostiles. Major Wynkoop was relieved of duty here because he disobeyed those orders. In intend to keep them."

"Black Kettle and his followers are not hostiles. They are peaceful! You say the Arapaho camped close by are unarmed prisoners. Black Kettle offered the same, to surrender their arms so they can winter near the fort."

"*All* Cheyenne are considered to be warlike, and Evans wants them punished – enough that they will learn their lesson and will surrender and never make war again. They have not suffered enough."

"Suffered *enough*? There are many women and children among those at Sand Creek!"

Anthony studied Two Wolves quietly a moment, his eyes narrowing. "And as Chivington says, nits make lice. Women are the only way to keep a tribe growing and strong. Eliminate the women, and you greatly reduce the future growth of the entire Indian nation."

Two Wolves struggled greatly with a desire to sink a knife into the man. His heart raged at the man's remarks. "So … Chivington will attack them?"

"I have no idea what Chivington means to do. The orders are to unarm them and march them north."

"If you do that they will escape and join Red Cloud and the Sioux. But if it is Chivington who goes after them, there will be few left to bring back and send north. He is a *killer*! He does not care about peace. He only cares about killing all Cheyenne. You can *stop* him!"

Anthony studied the scout's dark, menacing eyes. "You look like you prefer war to peace."

"I prefer *peace*, but when it comes to John Chivington, I would *welcome* war with him. His heart would soon be on the end of my lance."

A Warrior's Promise

The major nodded. "And that doesn't sound like the talk of an Army scout. It sounds like the talk of a warrior who just might decide to turn on the troops he rides with and fight them. You shouldn't be riding as a scout."

"I ride as a scout to help protect the Cheyenne and urge them to surrender. I ride as a scout for Major Ansley because he is a good friend. And I interpret for the Cheyenne and plead with them to accept peace because *they* are good friends! My heart lies in both worlds, but when this is over, I will return to my wife at Fort Collins. I do not intend to do something that would keep me from doing so."

"And if you own a supply store, there must be white blood involved. Indians can't own property and businesses. Is your wife white?"

Two Wolves stiffened. "She is."

Major Anthony frowned. "So I thought." He shook his head. "You're a strange man, Two Wolves, and I'm still not sure why you are here."

Two Wolves stepped a little closer to the man's desk, resting a hand on the pistol at his side. "I am here to find out your certain plans for Black Kettle and his band. Major Ansley will want to know."

"Black Kettle knows that if he moves to within twenty-five miles of Fort Lyon, I am forbidden to give him food and supplies, or even protection. But as long as he remains peaceful and chooses to stay at Sand Creek, he should be fine. It's those Cheyenne warriors who continue to attack supply wagons and out-lying settlements who will be the target of a final campaign to end the warring and get the Cheyenne onto reservations. Ansley needn't come all the way down here to help us keep the peace. This is *my* territory, and I have my orders. And the Third Colorado Cavalry isn't at Bent's Fort. They will be coming here from Bijou Basin. Once Chivington arrives, we will decide how to conduct the campaign against the remaining savages."

"Savages?" Two Wolves sneered the word. "They are *people*, and they are starving and afraid. And if Chivington is involved, he will not try to determine which Cheyenne make war and which do not. That matters little to him. He will show no mercy. And the remark you made about nits and lice tells me you are no better!"

Major Anthony's eyes turned to hard slits. "I suggest you leave before I decide to have you arrested for insubordination! Go back to Fort Collins and tell your Major Ansley anything you want. Just stay out of my territory and my campaign. What I do is simply the result of following orders from Major Henning and Major General Curtis, who have told me I am not to give any quarter to the Southern Cheyenne who still ride free and refuse to go to a reservation. They must first be properly punished and made to understand that they have no other choice but to give up their arms and surrender in a final peace. You've heard what you need to hear, so be on your way."

Two Wolves slowly nodded, thinking how pleasurable it would be to face this man in battle...as a Cheyenne warrior. His promises to Claire were becoming harder and harder to keep. "I will go. But I will be back."

Anthony held his gaze. "As an Army scout? As a white man? Or as a Cheyenne warrior?"

Two Wolves couldn't help a slight grin. "That I cannot answer." He turned and left, knowing in his soul that he truly *couldn't* answer the question. It depended on what he found when he came back here with Major Ansley.

Chapter Ten

Claire straightened bolts of cloth, arranging them mostly by type of material, from silk to linen to cotton to wool. She struggled to keep from thinking the worst – that somehow, for whatever reason, Two Wolves wasn't coming back. What was taking him so long?

The bell above the door to her supply store jingled, and she looked up to see Captain Edward Tower, the physician at Fort Collins, step inside.

"Hello, Captain," she greeted him. "I haven't seen you for weeks."

Captain Tower smiled, and Claire thought what a handsome smile it was. The man had dark hair and blue eyes and was giggled about by other women who thought him the most eligible bachelor in the area. Before Claire married Peter, and while she waited at Fort Collins for Peter to return from taking some of his relatives to the north, Captain Tower had tried to woo her.

Tower nodded to her, tipping his hat. "And you are looking beautiful, as always. There is nothing prettier than a happily married woman who is carrying." He looked her over. "You *are* happy, right?"

Claire knew good and well that the man had never approved of her marrying Peter, who in the captain's mind was simply the Indian scout named Two Wolves and the kind of man white women didn't marry.

"Of course, I'm happy," she told the captain with a smile. "My business is actually more successful here than it was in Denver City. Of course, part of that was due to Vince Huebner and his bunch, but thank God the man is dead and all that is over with."

"Yes, that's a terrible thing you and Two Wolves had to go through in Denver City," the captain told her.

"It's Peter, Captain. He goes by his white name now, remember?"

Captain Tower walked over to study various brands of cigars. "Yes, but I've only known him as Two Wolves the whole time he's been scouting for us. I have trouble remembering to call him Peter."

Claire did not miss the hint in his words. *Once an Indian, always an Indian.* She finished straightening the bolts of cloth and walked around behind the glass counter where the captain stood. "Actually, I sometimes have trouble remembering to call him Peter myself." She waited while Tower continued to study the contents of her display cabinet. "What can I help you with, Captain?"

He raised his eyes to meet her gaze. "Two things. Just to see your smile, and to buy some cigars." He straightened then and stood back a little, folding his arms. "It worries me that the smile you greeted me with didn't quite look genuine."

Another hint. He suspected she wasn't happy because Peter had been gone too long. She wanted to dislike the captain, mainly because her womanly instincts told her he still felt she shouldn't be with Peter. Still, she couldn't quite dislike him because of that. She knew deep inside that the man truly did care about her well being, even if he wasn't interested in her romantically.

Claire deliberately gave him her best smile. "And you have been talking to Major Ansley about me and my husband," she answered. "You don't fool me, Captain Tower. I appreciate your concern, but I am just fine, and this is a genuine smile."

His own smile blossomed into one that would win any woman's heart. No matter how hard she tried, she couldn't dislike the man.

"Good," he answered. "I will never stop being concerned for you, Claire Matthews, and I wish you would call me Edward."

Claire shook her head. "It's just not in me to call someone in uniform by his first name."

He removed his hat and bowed. "Then I shall have to come back in the garb of a plain citizen. Would that help?"

Claire couldn't help a light laugh. "Not really. I call most men who come in here by their surname. It's just the way I am. Now, what about the second thing you came in here for?"

The captain sighed and leaned closer to the counter. "I need some *Old Chum* tobacco. Do you have any?"

"I have that, and I have *Amphora*, but that's a bit more expensive."

"Oh, I know that. That's why I buy *Old Chum*. Besides, I like it. Do you have cigarette papers?"

"I do. But I thought you said something about cigars."

The captain nodded. "That, too. What would you recommend?"

"*Me*? For goodness sake, I don't smoke cigars!"

That brought a laugh for both of them. "I should hope not," he answered. "I just thought you might know the most popular cigar men come in here to buy."

Claire leaned in a little to look through the glass. "Well, the *Monterrey Le Hoya de San Juan* are popular, but so are the *Anthony y Cleopatra*. I've heard men comment that those are milder. I also have *TAF's*. They are the cheapest. Or you might want to consider a pipe. I have a beautiful Peterson. It's a new brand, and I'm lucky to have even one. I ordered it from Chicago. Of course, it's more expensive than the others. I also have Meerschaum and Iwan Ries." She looked at him then, and he'd leaned in a little too close. Claire drew back and put her hands on her hips.

"I don't know if I've helped or just made your choice more confusing."

The captain just stood there a moment, studying her. "How are you, Claire? Really?"

Damn him. "Why do you keep asking me that?"

"Because, as you said, I've been talking with the major and I know Two Wolves – er, Peter – has been gone much longer than he should have been."

Claire folded her arms. "Well, Captain, my health is just fine, and I know my husband well enough to know he'll be back soon."

The captain straightened a little but kept his hands on the counter. "Don't be so defensive, Claire. I'm truly concerned about you."

"And I think you should pick out whatever it is you intend to buy and get back to your duties at the fort, Captain."

Their gazes held for several seconds. Tower let out another long sigh. "Yes, I suppose I should."

Claire fought tears, and he could tell. That made her angry with herself, which in turn made it even harder not to cry.

"Claire, I didn't come here to upset you."

"Didn't you?"

"No. I truly didn't. I came here to remind you that if you have any problems with your pregnancy, I *am*, after all, a doctor. My specialties are gunshot wounds, arrow wounds, cuts and broken bones. But I've delivered babies, and although I'm no expert, I understand that things can go wrong, especially with a first child. I have enough experience to know how to help if that happens. Your husband is living in a dangerous world, whether as a scout, or if for some reason he takes the side of the Cheyenne. Men like Peter risk their lives practically every day. I just want you to know the major and I, and very likely a lot of others, including Sergeant Becker's wife, are all here for you if you need any one of us. Gertie Becker looks on you like a daughter, and I'm sure the major does, also. You're beautiful and sweet and likeable and, regardless of how much Peter Matthews loves you, you have that aura of a scared young woman when he's not around. The man saved your life more than once, and you only feel safe when he's by your side. Do you think none of us see that?"

Claire swallowed and quickly wiped at a tear. "You are completely out of order talking to me this way."

"Yes, I am, and I'm sorry. All I want is for you to know there are a lot of people around here who care about you and will always be ready to help. I'm glad you have Klas and Hubert, but I'm talking about people who truly care in more ways than shooting someone who might threaten you. There is more than bodily harm that matters. The *heart* also matters. I care too much about you to see yours broken."

Claire took a deep breath. "I might remind you that you are talking to a married woman."

"You needn't remind me of that. And I didn't come here to upset you, but I see that I have, and I apologize. Single men get pretty lonely out here. I've over-stepped my bounds, but it's only because I think about you and care about you a lot. I just wanted to get that off my chest and remind you I'm here to help if you have any problems health-wise."

"Or *heart* wise?"

The captain smiled again. "That, too. Please accept my apologies, and understand that I respect your marriage and have nothing but good intentions."

Claire softened. "Captain, I was with Peter day in and day out after he rescued me from that attack on my wagon train a few months ago. We went through a lot together. Things that showed me very vividly what a brave and honest and good man Peter is. I am perfectly aware of the battle that rages in his soul, but he knows the future holds nothing but sorrow for the Cheyenne. He is only out there in an effort to help them. I'm sure he'll be back any day. In the meantime, I know I have friends like you and the major and Gertie to help me, and I appreciate that. Just know that Peter is one of the finest men I've ever known, let alone the bravest, and I trust him implicitly. I can't begin to measure how much I love him."

The captain nodded. "And you are the strongest young lady I've ever met. No fainting flower, that's for sure."

"I should hope not. I was raised most of my life by just my father and worked right along-side him, loading freight wagons, hitching horses and even oxen, driving those freight wagons, working with nothing but men, dressing like a boy and giving no thought to knitting and quilting clubs and teas and dances. I may not be very big, but I'm damn tough, Captain, and I'll manage this marriage just fine."

The captain shook his head. "I'm sure you will. I'd like to think, though, that we can be good friends."

"I already think of us that way."

He smiled. "Good. Now, I'll take a tin of *Old Chum* and a box of cigarette papers. I can't afford a pipe, but I might consider some of those cigars after our next campaign."

"And that would be?"

"Heading south. There is trouble brewing down there with Black Kettle and the Cheyenne. The new man in charge down at Fort Lyon is refusing, by orders from the governor, to distribute food and supplies to them. The powers that be felt Major Wynkoop was too good to the Cheyenne – that they need to be punished for attacks on ranches and supply trains."

"You can't blame *all* of them for what a *few* of them do."

"Governor Evans does, and so do a lot of others. And then there is Colonel Chivington. At least he *calls* himself Colonel. He's an Indian hater of the highest order, and word is he's headed south, where the Cheyenne are peacefully camped and waiting to hear what they should do next. They've been chased away from Fort Lyon and offered no protection."

Claire put a hand to her forehead. "My God, I'm sure Peter knows all of this. He's probably down there trying to keep the peace."

"That's not going to happen. And he knows Ansley is waiting for him to get back here and report on all of that and go with us to Fort Lyon."

Claire pushed at some wild strands of hair that had escaped the bun she'd wound her hair into that morning. She always had trouble getting a brush through the tangled mass of curls that refused to obey any kind of pinning or setting combs. But her wild red hair was part of what Two Wolves loved about her. *Maeveksea.* Red Bird Woman. She smiled at the memory of the first time he'd called her that.

"Then I'm sure he'll be here any day now," she told the captain.

She stooped to open the sliding glass door to the shelf where the tobacco and cigarette papers were. She took out a tin of the tobacco and a box of papers and set them on top of the cabinet.

"Do you want these wrapped?"

"No, Ma'am. I'll just take them out and pack them in my supplies. We're all keeping ready for when Peter gets back. But when he leaves with us he'll be Two Wolves to me and the others." He reached into his pocket to get the money to pay her.

"Which means that almost as soon as he gets here he'll leave again," Claire said absently.

"I'm afraid so."

Claire took his money and pushed the key to open her register.

"You keep Klas and Hubert close while we're gone, understand? You could even let them run this place and go stay with Gertie. It might be good for you to have some woman company for a while."

"I'll think about it." Claire met his gaze. "Thank you for caring. I believe at times it's a little too much, but I know you are sincere."

The captain nodded. "That I am, Mrs. Matthews." He accented her name as though to tell her he knew his place...and hers. He took his supplies and walked to the door, nodding to Claire once more before opening it to walk out. It was then he saw Peter riding up to the store. He wore Army pants, but a fringed buckskin shirt, his black hair long and loose, a bandana tied around his hair and forehead. In spite of the cold, he wore no coat. Peter glanced at him, and the captain saw white stripes painted on his cheeks.

He was not Peter. He was Two Wolves.

Two Wolves drew up his horse in front of the store, holding the captain's gaze as he did so. The captain felt a chill at the warning look in Two

Wolves' dark eyes. The man knew of his interest in Claire, and no one wanted to be on Two Wolves' bad side, not when he was all Indian, which he was at this moment.

The captain stepped outside. "Welcome back, Two Wolves. It's about time. Major Ansley has been waiting for you. I'll tell him you're finally home."

Two Wolves still sat his horse. "Tell him I will report to him in the morning," he answered.

The captain adjusted his hat. "I'll do that." He turned around and shouted through the doorway. "Claire, your *husband* is finally home." He walked off the stoop and mounted his horse, nodding once again to Two Wolves before riding off.

Chapter Eleven

"Peter!" Claire didn't even close the cash register before running around the end of the counter and hurrying outside. Peter slid off his saddleless mount and quickly enfolded his wife into a strong embrace, crushing her close, her feet off the ground.

"I was so scared something bad had happened to you!" Claire exclaimed, feeling lost and warm in the folds of his strong arms.

Peter kissed her hair as he lowered her, but she continued to hug him tightly, her face against his chest. He kept his arms around her for warmth. "Something *did* happen," he told her, "but it was not physical, and it will never keep me from you, *Maeveksea*. Never."

Claire looked up at him, and instantly his lips met hers. He was back! He'd kept his promise...for now. His beautiful, gentle, deep kiss gave her all the reassurance she needed. Klas Albertson appeared at the doorway then.

"Peter!" he yelled, a broad smile on a face that always looked sunburned against his blonde hair. "Sure it is good to see you!"

He came down the steps, and Peter kept an arm around Claire as he shook Klas's hand.

"And you," Peter answered. "Watch the store, if you will. I'm taking Claire to the house. We have much to talk about."

"Ya, it is no problem. I will tell Hubert you are back. Business has been good, but your wife, she has been very worried. Will you stay now?"

Peter shook his head. "I can't. Maybe a couple of days, but no more. I have to talk to Major Ansley tomorrow. I know he wants me to head out with a company of men soon. There is a lot of trouble in the South."

"Ya, I understand. You be careful." Klas looked him over. "You look more like Two Wolves today, my friend. You have been among your people."

"I have." Peter gave Claire a reassuring squeeze at the remark, knowing when his Indian side emerged it worried her. "Take care of my horse and gear, will you?" He let go of Claire long enough to take his rifle from the beaded leather sheath that held it tied to the side of his horse.

"Sure," Klas told him.

Peter held is rifle in one hand and kept his other arm around Claire as he walked with her to their house next door.

"You were gone longer than you said you would be, Peter," Claire told him. "I was scared you'd decided to stay with the Cheyenne and not come back."

"I told you that would never happen. I made vows to you, *Maeveksea*, and you carry my child."

Two women walked past them, staring. One of them let out a small gasp and put fingers to her lips, as though frightened of the "Indian" she saw.

They hurried on together, both of them whispering.

Claire knew what they were talking about. How could she be the wife of an Indian? She smiled inwardly at being pretty sure they were likely a bit jealous of her virile, handsome husband. Protocol said they should be shocked and disapproving, but they were also women, and few women could miss all that was man about Peter James Matthews. She walked inside the cabin with her husband, and instantly she was in his arms again, his lips melting into her own. It was a long, delicious kiss that told her nothing had changed.

"I have missed you so!" Peter told her when he left her mouth to let his lips drift across her neck. He turned to bolt the door, then lifted her and carried her up the stairs to the loft and laid her on the bed. "I do not want to talk yet. I just want to touch you and make love to you."

Claire had no objections. Other than Army pants and boots, he was all Two Wolves at the moment, a silver earring shaped like a feather in one ear and an array of weapons on his belt, and wearing a buckskin shirt and deerskin coat. She watched as he removed his weapons, wondering if he'd had to use them, wondering what he had learned while he was gone.

He removed his coat and buckskin shirt, revealing his hard-muscled torso, then sat down and pulled off his Army boots and socks. He stood up to remove his gun belt, then unhooked his Army pants and pulled them off. Through it all his gaze never left hers. They needed this. It was understood.

Here was the man who'd taken her virginity in a *tipi* somewhere out on the Colorado plains. Here was the man torn between two worlds, but his love for a white woman kept bringing him back to that side of himself.

"I hate that you have to leave again," she told him.

"As do I," he answered. He climbed onto the bed and straddled her, still wearing his long johns. He began unbuttoning the front of her dress. "You still carry my child?"

"I do. He is a happy baby."

"He?"

"You're the one who said it was a boy," she told him with a smile.

"*Aye*, I did. And how do you know he is happy?"

"Because I've begun feeling him move around and kick, even though I still don't show much. I just know he is laughing and anxious to get out of me and run to his father."

Peter grinned broadly. "I can't wait to hold him."

Claire sobered. "Peter, where have you been?"

"We will talk about that later."

He pulled off her dress, her shoes, her stockings. He began unlacing her camisole, and Claire closed her eyes as he felt her breasts with strong hands.

"You are so beautiful," he told her. "I have missed your sweet mouth and your full breasts and your wild, red hair." He pulled off her ruffled panties and leaned down to kiss the hairs between her legs, then kissed his way up to her belly, kissing her extra there as though to kiss the baby inside it. He gently ran a hand over her stomach. "You are swollen with my child. It is not so noticeable when you are dressed, but now I can see it. Promise me that even when I am gone you will be careful." He kissed his way up to her breasts, lingering at her nipples, pushing up on one breast with his hand and gently sucking it. "Soon my son will suckle here. I might be jealous."

Claire laughed lightly. "In a few months when you do this, you will taste your son's milk."

Peter grinned and moved to her neck. "*Ne-mehotatse, Maeveksea.*"

I love you, Red Bird Woman. Claire knew the meaning of the words. "And I love you, Two Wolves. I always feel safer and happier when you are with me."

"I will always be with you, even if just in spirit. But first there is something I must do. I will need you to be patient and to believe me when I tell you I will never leave you for long. You must trust me."

Before she could answer he smothered her mouth with a deep, delicious kiss. Opening her legs to let him settle between them was as natural as breathing. He continued the deep kiss while he reached down to stroke her secret places in the magical way he had of making her feel wanton. She felt his hardness against her thigh, ached to feel it inside her.

His passion took over then. He hungrily moved back over her throat, her breasts, her belly... until his lips were searching and tasting and arousing that most private place that only this man had ever touched and tasted and invaded, making her cry out his name... but that name was not Peter. It was Two Wolves, for that was always how she thought of him in these moments. It was Two Wolves who'd made her a woman, Two Wolves who'd planted his life into her. His long hair brushed at her thighs as he brought her to a long-needed and erotic climax.

Quickly he moved his lips back over her body once again, and in the next moment she finally felt the invasion she craved. His hardness filled her to ecstasy, almost painful in its size, a lovely, exotic pain that made her arch upward to greet his thrusts... beautiful, fulfilling, hard, needful thrusts that branded her as Two Wolves' woman and no one else's, ever. His own groans of pleasure increased her joy and fulfillment that she was pleasing him.

Their lovemaking continued for several minutes. He rose to his knees and grasped her bottom and pushed into her depths until she wondered how her small self could take in so much. She met his gaze and saw the look of a conquering warrior. She grasped the rungs of the brass headboard of their bed and gave back as much as he took, until finally she felt his life pulsing into her.

She couldn't imagine anything more pleasurable than letting this man take her any way he chose, and she wondered if other women had any idea how beautiful and exotic this could be...if their men took them this way, in full nakedness and light. She'd heard one woman giggle once with another while shopping for a camisole, whispering that "he gets under my nightgown under the quilts at night and does the naughtiest things to me."

"I don't much like it," the other young woman answered. "John is too quick about it."

Neither woman knew Claire had been kneeling behind the counter straightening some ribbons in a drawer. She smiled now at the conversation. She couldn't imagine "not liking this much." Two Wolves made her feel wanton and alive and loved and wanting more.

And more she did get.

"I wish to stay inside you," Two Wolves told her.

He kept hold of her bottom and began the thrusts again, until she felt him grow harder again, until soon his thrusts took over. He moved in a way that his penis stroked that magic spot. A second, even deeper climax made her groan with pure need and wantonness.

Claire forced away the worry over the fact he would leave again. For now, there was only this—making love as only Two Wolves could make love to a woman—glorying in the man's perfectly muscled body, his handsome face, his moving smile, the long hair that enshrouded her when he leaned close again, meeting her mouth in delicious kisses. His chest pressed against hers while strong hands grasped at her bottom and pushed in order to bury himself as deeply as possible all over again.

They would make love yet again, she was sure, and probably yet again before the day was out. No one would bother them, for they knew that after so long apart, Mr. and Mrs. Peter James Matthews would want to be alone. No, Two Wolves and Red Bird Woman would want to be alone. She wasn't lying in their log home. She was lying in a *tipi*, and this man was bringing out the woman in her that she once never even knew existed.

Chapter Twelve

Claire moved the coffee pot to a trivet in a corner of the hearth fire, away from the hotter coals. She turned a piece of ham cooking in an iron fry pan, then added two eggs. She enjoyed the new pan, which had four legs so she could use it over the fire without needing yet another trivet to keep it off the hot coals.

"The good smells woke me up."

Claire turned to see Two Wolves standing at the foot of the loft stairs. This morning he looked more like Peter again. He wore cotton pants and a black flannel shirt. No paint. No weapons. His hair was drawn back and tied at the nape of his neck.

She turned away and took hold of the long handle of the fry pan and moved it a little farther from the fire before she looked back at Peter. "So, today you are Peter Matthews," she said, folding her arms.

He smiled rather sadly and nodded. "Today I am your white husband. And a very hungry husband also. I am sorry I slept longer than you. I seldom do that."

"You apparently had a long, hard ride getting back here."

He winked. "And a long, very active night after I arrived."

Claire couldn't help blushing. She turned back to the ham and eggs. "As did I."

Peter laughed lightly. "I enjoyed your welcome embrace, Mrs. Matthews," he told her teasingly.

"And I enjoyed welcoming you," she answered. "You fell asleep pretty quickly after all the, uh, lovemaking. We haven't had a chance to really talk, Peter."

She turned back to the fire, and Peter walked up to wrap his arms around her from behind to give her a squeeze. "The talking will come today." He kissed the back of her neck and left her to sit down at the table. "Why was Captain Tower here yesterday?"

Claire caught the hint of jealousy in the question, and it struck her then why her husband had been a bit commanding in his lovemaking when he first came home. He'd seen Captain Tower leaving the store. She leaned close to the fry pan and scooped the ham and eggs onto a plate, then set the food on the table in front of him. She picked up a knife to slice off a piece of homemade bread already on the table.

"He wanted cigars and some tobacco," she answered.

"They sell those things at the fort commissary."

Claire met his gaze. "Not the kind of cigars I sell."

"And no one as beautiful as you works at the commissary." Peter turned his attention to cutting a piece of ham. Claire got the distinct impression he was thinking how nice it would be to sink that same knife into Captain Tower. "The captain has an eye for you. He always has."

"Peter – "

"How many other men from the fort have come here for supplies?"

Claire was surprised at the tone in his words. "None."

"And there is my point. Only Captain Tower. He is a very handsome white man, and he has good standing."

"As do you, Peter James Matthews," Claire answered, feeling a bit of anger at her husband, something she'd never once felt before. "And you, my husband, are a very handsome, actually far *more* handsome than most Indian *or* white men, I might add—or have you forgotten your white blood?"

He stopped cutting and stared at his plate. "There are times when I wish I *could* forget."

Claire closed her eyes and sat down across from him. "Peter, what happened out there? Why are you acting like this? There were times last night when I felt like you were trying to prove something to yourself when you made love to me. That's not my Peter, or I should say Two Wolves, the man I fell in love with and whose baby I'm carrying. And I carry his child with great pride and anticipation and pleasure, because it was Two Wolves who planted his life inside me, life I very gladly accepted. I can't help who stops into the store on the pretense of buying tobacco. It's not as though I invited the man. He was every bit a gentleman and was only there a few minutes. If the man has an interest, I can't help that, other than to be very adamant in reminding him I am married. Are you calling me a wanton woman who would easily fall for some other man just because he says nice things to me? I hope you aren't going to be like this every time you return from one of your scouting excursions."

Peter set down the knife and leaned back in his chair, meeting her gaze. He sighed before speaking, and a rather apologetic smile crossed his lips. "Of course not. I know you better."

"Then don't talk the way you are talking. I'm upset enough over how long you were gone. It frightened me, and the way you just behaved frightens me because I feel like you're deliberately steering me toward some other man so I'll be taken care of in case the next time you leave you really don't come back. That's always my worst fear."

He looked her over lovingly. "Unlike most white men, a Cheyenne man does not break his promises."

"And plenty of white men don't break theirs either. You know I don't see you as just Cheyenne or just white. I see you as my *husband*, and I love you to the deepest parts of my heart. You are my hero. I've seen you fight and risk your life to protect me and save my life. You carry the scars that prove it. I will never look at another man the way I look at you. Surely you know that."

Their gazes held. "I know that you are beautiful. And I know that Captain Tower has an eye for you. But I also know him personally from having ridden at his side in battle. I think part of me wants to know that if something happens to me—"

"Don't talk that way. Nothing is going to happen to you. I don't even want to entertain the idea." Tears sprang into her eyes. "I only have you for a couple of days, I'm sure. And once your time of service is up, I hope you stop all of this and will do no more scouting.'"

"I have told you I will. That has not changed."

"Then stop picking out other men for me. The only man I love and want is you, whether you are Two Wolves or Peter James Matthews."

Peter suddenly grinned. "You are very cute when you are angry."

"And you are very mean to even suggest I would have an interest in any other man." She rose, pouting, and took another china plate from a cupboard, making ready to put some food on it for herself. Two Wolves grasped her arm then, and she momentarily thought how quiet he could be in sneaking up on someone. She'd never even heard him scoot his chair back. That was the Indian in him.

He turned her, and she looked up at him, the plate still in her hand. "Do not be angry, *Maeveksea*. I would not be a man if I did not have feelings of jealousy and possessiveness for my beautiful wife."

Claire sighed as he pulled her into his arms. "Neither feeling is necessary." She still held the plate as she moved her arms around him. "I love you to the ends of the earth." She looked up at him, and he leaned down to kiss her deeply, then kissed her eyes, her forehead.

"Then we will not speak of this again," he told her. "It is only that I have been away from you longer than I had planned."

"And I think I proved to you last night who I love and who I belong to," she answered. She met his gaze again. "I am your woman and always will be, just as I'm sure your mother, though she finally remarried after your father's death, always belonged to your father in her heart."

He kissed her once more. "Let's eat before the food is cold."

"I'm for that. All that activity last night has left me hungry."

Peter laughed lightly. "And you will need more food for the same energy tonight, let alone the fact that you are eating for two now." He left her to sit down again, and Claire put some ham and eggs onto her plate and sat down across from him. She cut into a piece of ham herself, but before she could put it into her mouth someone knocked at the door.

"I'll get it," she told Peter.

She walked to the door and unbolted and opened it to see Major Ansley standing there. He removed his hat and bowed slightly.

"Claire Matthews, you are absolutely glowing," he told her with a wink. "I can't imagine why, unless it's because your husband is finally back."

Claire grinned and stepped back to let him inside. "He most certainly is. And you are just in time for breakfast and coffee, Major. I have a feeling you timed your visit in hopes of just that."

Ansley laughed and leaned down to kiss her cheek, then turned to hang his hat and coat on a hook near the door.

Peter rose, and Ansley walked over to shake his hand in greeting.

Claire felt a hint of dread. She loved Major Ansley like a father and always enjoyed his company, but his presence reminded her that Peter would soon leave again.

Chapter Thirteen

"Take a chair, Major," Peter told Ansley. "Claire will fix you a plate and some coffee. I am glad you are here. It saves me a trip to the fort today. I'd rather spend the day here with Claire, since I am sure we will be leaving soon."

Ansley sighed and took a chair. "I'm sure your wife isn't happy about that, but I planned on heading out tomorrow. First I need to know why you were gone for so long."

"I have not even told my wife yet. I wanted just to greet her and enjoy her company for a while first."

Claire brought food and coffee to the Major.

"Thank you," Ansley told her.

Claire cut off a piece of bread for him. "I think you should both eat first. If all you do is talk, your food will be cold," she told both of them.

She picked at her own food, then rose to set it aside and move the cooking pan off the fire. She walked over to a rocker and sat down, picking up a lovely blue knit jacket one of the settler women had made for her baby. She held it up. "Look what Louise Bonner made," she told Peter.

He glanced at the jacket and smiled. "Very nice of her."

"Gertie Becker is crocheting a baby blanket for you," the Major told Claire. "And I think she wants to hold a party a month or so before the baby is born, so the other women at the fort can bring gifts for the child."

"Oh, that's so nice!" Claire exclaimed. There had been a time when she wanted nothing to do with all these "womanly" things, but Peter had changed all of that for her.

"That is good of her," Peter added. He shoveled food into his mouth as though in a hurry to get to the real reason for Ansley's visit.

Ansley did the same, and both men slugged down their coffee. Peter rose and went to a cupboard, coming back with a box of pre-rolled cigarettes and offering one to Ansley. Both men took one and walked over to the fireplace to light them with a long match. Peter inhaled deeply before moving his chair away from the table and sitting down again, his long legs sprawling out before him. Ansley took a chair nearby, grunting a little as he again lowered his hefty body into a chair.

"I'm not sure how well I'll do on a long campaign," he told Peter, "what with this bum knee and being a little too fat."

Peter grinned. "A long campaign will help you lose weight."

Ansley chuckled. "Spoken by a man who is much younger and in perfect shape. Your day is coming, Peter."

"I suppose."

Ansley drew on his own cigarette before letting out another long sigh as he sobered. "So, tell me what you learned." He cleared his throat. "I have a feeling I don't want to know." He glanced at Claire. "You realize I'll be taking your husband away again, I suppose."

Claire felt her stomach tighten. "I have no doubt, Major. I don't like the idea of him leaving again, especially on a long campaign." She dropped her gaze, studying the little knitted baby jacket. "Does he really have to go?"

Ansley rubbed at his eyes. "I'm afraid so. He's too good a negotiator with the Cheyenne, and I have a feeling that will be really important."

"Very important," Peter added. He smoked again for a moment. "I do not like the new man at Fort Lyon. He is little better than John Chivington himself. I can tell he is an Indian hater and he is a yes-man. He will do whatever the governor and those above him tell him to do, and right now they are telling him not to help the Cheyenne in any way–that they are warriors who must be punished however the government can punish them. The Arapaho receive help and protection at Fort Lyon, but the Cheyenne do not. They are not allowed any closer than twenty-five miles from the fort, per orders from Governor

Evans and Major Henning, who is in charge of the Upper Arkansas River area."

"So, it's true that Wynkoop is gone?"

Peter nodded. "They felt he was too kind to the Cheyenne, too sympathetic. Wynkoop was good at handling the Cheyenne, but these new men want nothing to do with helping them in any way. They seem bent on creating circumstances that are bound to lead to war. They *want* war—an excuse to kill Indians."

"I take it you searched out the Cheyenne at Sand Creek."

"I did. The relatives I have left are in the north now. You know that I took them there. But I have one other cousin among the Southern Cheyenne—a woman named *Skiomah*. It means Little Robe. She has a new baby, and she is very afraid for her little girl's future. The camp at Sand Creek is led by Black Kettle. They are not sure what to do because Anthony has refused to give them any help for the winter. That is why they are camped so far south, where the weather will be a little milder, but the hunting there is not as good, and every time a hunting party goes out they risk their lives. White settlers shoot at them for no reason. The whole camp would like to move north and join the Sioux and their relatives in the Dakotas, but they know Chivington and his Colorado Volunteers are out there waiting for an excuse to attack them. Black Kettle thinks that perhaps if they make no trouble over the winter, they will be allowed to stay closer to Fort Lyon and will be able to safely hunt. Perhaps they can make a new treaty."

"And what do you think?"

"I agree Black Kettle should try, but I do not trust Chivington or Major Anthony. I think nothing the Cheyenne do will matter. I am hoping if we go down there, you and I together can convince Anthony to make no move against Black Kettle—perhaps even convince him to let them come closer to Fort Lyon for better protection from the Colorado Volunteers. That would be even farther south and warmer. Anthony told me that Chivington and the Third Colorado are at Bijou Basin and preparing to move northeast. That is a bad sign. Sand Creek lies in that direction from Fort Lyon."

Ansley shook his head and leaned forward, resting his elbows on his knees. "I agree. If there is any way we can stop him, we have to do it."

"The problem is that his orders come from the governor himself," Peter reminded him. "Evans would prefer that the Cheyenne were wiped off the Colorado map. Now they are trapped at Sand Creek and have no way of reaching their relatives in the north without risking being attacked by Chivington. I am not sure what you can do legally, but we have to try."

Ansley nodded. "I still want to escort Black Kettle's camp east to Kansas. I telegraphed Washington for permission. That will take a few more days, so I asked that the answer be sent to Fort Lyon, so we don't waste time sitting around here waiting for an answer. Washington overrules Chivington and Governor Evans, so if we could get permission, we can get Black Kettle out of there. I'm hoping I'll have that telegram when we get to Fort Lyon. That will help stop Chivington from making a move against Sand Creek."

Peter put out his cigarette. "You are a good man, Major. I appreciate your efforts. I knew you would want to help. You will always be my good friend."

Ansley leaned back in his chair. "And you will always be like a son to me." He glanced at Claire. "Remember what I told you a few weeks ago. If things go bad here, you and Peter can always come to Pennsylvania after I retire. You would be most welcome there, by my wife and me both."

Claire smiled in appreciation. "Thank you, Major, but right now I can't imagine living anywhere but in Colorado. Peter's roots are here, and after what we've been through to save my business and now build it up around Fort Collins, it just doesn't seem right to leave it all." She looked at Peter. "But this thing with Chivington and the Southern Cheyenne has to be settled first. I understand that." She looked back at Ansley. "Just keep my husband safe."

Ansley laughed lightly. "It usually ends up the other way around. Two Wolves has saved me and my troops more than once. He generally needs no help in times of danger, but I'll keep my eye on him."

"Thank you." Claire smiled, looking at Peter again. "I know this man can very well take care of himself, but the hatred out there is so great now that I can't help worrying."

Ansley rose with a heavy sigh. "I fully understand." He reached out to shake Peter's hand. "Can you be ready by tomorrow morning?"

"Much as I hate leaving Claire again, I will be ready." Peter shook the major's hand firmly. "Thank you for listening."

Ansley nodded and walked to the door, putting his hat and coat back on. "Thanks for breakfast, Claire. You take care of yourself while we are gone. I know Two Wolves is looking forward to a fine, healthy baby. Once this thing is over, you can finally settle in as a family." He met her gaze. "I'm sure you understand that we could be gone several weeks if we're able to escort Black Kettle and his band into Kansas."

Claire glanced at her husband. "I know." How she hated the thought! They would be headed into danger, having to go up against Chivington and his Volunteers. Whether riding alone or with the Army, Two Wolves was risking his life. "Just bring my husband safely back to me."

"I'll do my best." Ansley nodded to Peter and left.

Claire met Peter's gaze. "I can't forget how that sergeant with the Colorado Militia threatened you when we were taking those supplies to Colorado Springs. Too many people are eager to shoot down any Indian they see, Peter, and half white or not, you look all Indian, especially when you ride as a scout."

He folded his arms. "Did you not see how I handled Sergeant Craig when he stopped us on our trip to Colorado Springs? And have you not seen me in battle?"

"I most certainly have, and I have no doubts about your abilities in war, Peter Matthews, but there is such a thing as people who would not hesitate to shoot an Indian in the back."

He smiled and shook his head. "I will be fine, and I will come home to you sooner than you think. You will see."

Claire turned to clean off the table. "I hope you're right, my dear husband. Just remember you have a child on the way. I intend for this baby to be held in his father's arms."

Peter walked closer and pulled her into his arms. "You must trust me, *Maeveksea.*" He leaned down and kissed her cheek. "I have made promises to you, and I will keep them."

She rested her head against his solid chest. "Those promises are all I will have while you are gone. That and prayer."

He pulled her even closer, and she cherished the feel of his embrace, for it was here she felt safe and loved. *God, be with this man and protect him,* she prayed.

Chapter Fourteen

Claire crawled into bed, her back to Peter, who always slept naked. She wore her flannel gown, and he pulled her against him as she snuggled under two quilts and into the feather mattress. She relished the feel of his strong arm around her, his knees bent into the back of hers.

"It's so cold tonight," she said softly. "I'll worry about you out there in the cold winds and snow. Both are sure to get worse."

He buried his face into her mass of red curls. "You worry too much about too many things. I have lived that way for years. My people know how to stay warm in winter. They line their *tipis* with heavy buffalo robes, and always there is a central fire. They wear fur clothing and deerskin or buffalo-skin moccasins up to their knees. I will dress the same tomorrow when we head out."

My people. That's what worried Claire. He still thought of the Cheyenne as his people, as though that's where he belonged.

What about me? Claire wanted to ask. *I am also your people.*

She said nothing, preferring no arguments or hard feelings tonight, which deep inside she felt could be their last night together.

"The hard part for them now is finding enough food," Peter told her. "The buffalo are fast disappearing."

Claire felt him tensing up.

"It is the white man's way of making sure no Indian thrives, a way to force them onto reservations. Kill off the buffalo, and you kill off the Indian." His embrace tightened. "Soon Black Kettle, and in the north Red Cloud and Crazy Horse and Sitting Bull, all will become *hakadah*...the pitiful last."

Claire caught the deep sadness in his words. "I'm so sorry, Peter. I wish I could change things. But I have a feeling the Cheyenne and the Sioux and others will find a way to preserve their ways, their language and customs and beliefs. Even if on reservations, they need to cling to that. The elders have to continue to teach the young ones."

Peter sighed deeply. "It is good to hear you talk that way. The sad part is many other tribes are completely gone now. Wiped out by white hatred and slaughter. They are no more. I am only trying to keep that from happening to the Cheyenne."

"I know. But the way you talk sometimes, like tonight, scares me. I'm not even sure I want to make love tonight before you leave. It's too sad, because I'm so afraid it will be the last time you hold me."

He kissed her hair and moved over her, forcing her onto her back. He hovered over her then, his hair falling around her face and shoulders. "It will not be the last time. This I promise."

Her eyes teared. "When you call them your people, it makes me feel left out. I wasn't going to say anything, but –"

He cut off her words with a deep kiss, as he reached down with one hand to pull one side of her gown up over her hip.

"Do not speak this way," he told her. "*You* are also my people, because you care about the Cheyenne and you love a Cheyenne man. You carry his child. Just remember that Cheyenne women are proud of their husbands when they ride off to war. They fear for them as any woman fears for her man in times like these." He kissed her gently then, reaching down to pull up the other side of her gown. "Even the white wives at the fort will fear for their men, knowing there could be fighting. But it is these moments, being inside the women he loves, that gives a man strength and courage, and the determination to live so that he can come back to this." He pressed his hardness against her thigh.

Claire closed her eyes and opened herself to him, hating the thought of his leaving, yet loving the power and strength that emanated from every part of him, including that which he then pushed inside her in a commanding way, as though to assure her he was a man who knew how to survive so he could come back to her.

Silent tears trickled down the sides of her face as she arched to greet his thrusts, wanting him to fill her, wanting to remember what this was like with this man of men. Their lovemaking was different from the night before. That lovemaking was a form of greeting, a fulfillment of being together again after too long apart. This time things were slower, gentler, more determined, more of a farewell instead of a greeting.

Most of the day he had been Peter, but tonight...tonight he was Two Wolves again, showing his captive that lying with a Cheyenne man was beautiful and fulfilling. She truly was his captive, for he owned her heart and soul in a way that no other man would ever own her. He was the Cheyenne man who first took her not all that long ago, somewhere on the open plains...the Cheyenne man who had so gently made a woman of her when she was so sure she did not even want a man that way...the Cheyenne man who took her from a scared, defensive young girl who always dressed like a boy and struggled to save her father's freighting business, to a blossoming young woman who wanted nothing more than to be beautiful for him—a young woman who proudly carried his baby.

He moved in a slow rhythm that gradually built her need to a wild, passionate climax, which in turn only increased her need to feel him inside her. She cried out his name as he buried himself deep, and the name she cried out was Two Wolves, not Peter.

Two Wolves, her warrior.

Two Wolves, her protector.

Two Wolves, her conqueror.

Two Wolves, who owned her.

Twice she'd seen him in vicious one-on-one battle with fierce Comanche warriors. She'd seen him face several white men on his own to protect Cheyenne women and children. She'd seen him face down a grizzly bear, refusing to kill the beast because she was the mother of two small cubs. Only an Indian would want to preserve a mother bear's life because of her babies. And she knew that when he faced the Colorado Militia men on their trip to Colorado Springs, he truly would have been able to break Sergeant Millard Craig's neck before the man got off a shot. Craig had known it, too. That was why he'd backed down.

She ran her hands over her husband's muscled arms and chest as he took her, returning his deep kisses with passion and deep desire. His life spilled into her, but he kept up his rhythmic movements until she felt his full hardness again. He rubbed against her in a way that brought a second climax. They kept up the passionate lovemaking until both were spent.

"*Nemehotatse, Maeveksea*," he groaned softly. He moved off her and ran a hand over her belly. "Take care of *nahahan*, our son. While I am gone, think of the white name we should call him. I am thinking his Indian name should be *Okohm*, after my cousin who was killed by the ranchers when you and I traveled with him and his family."

"That is thoughtful of you. I think you said the name meant Coyote."

Peter stretched out on his back. "It does, and coyotes are clever and good hunters. It is a good name."

"And what will we call him in everyday life? *Okohm*? Coyote? Or the name I give him, which I think should be John, my father's name?"

He turned to his side, resting his head in his hand as he studied her in the dim light of an oil lamp. He smiled softly. "I promised you we would live the white man's way, so we will call him John. But I will teach him all I know about the Cheyenne ways, the language, the respect for nature. I will teach him to hunt, and I will teach him to be proud of his Cheyenne name and his Cheyenne blood."

Claire traced a finger over his eyebrows, down his nose. "And what if your son is born with red curly hair and freckles?"

Peter laughed. "I did not think of that!" He kissed her. "It will not matter. He carries Cheyenne blood, no matter if it shows."

"And I will be as proud of that as you will be. And *he* will be."

Their gazes held, both wanting to avoid what was to come, both wishing morning would never arrive.

"I love you so, Two Wolves," Claire said softly, the tears wanting to come again.

He smoothed some of the curls away from her face. "As I love you, Red Bird Woman."

"Come back to me."

"You know that I will. I just cannot promise how soon."

"Come back before your son is born."

"That is many months away. I am sure to be back by then. And you must promise me to stay close to Klas and Hubert and to let them do the heavy work."

"I promise."

"Visit with Gertie at the fort. She is a good woman and a good friend. She, too, will be worried while her husband is gone. The company of other women will help you feel better."

"A little, I suppose. But we will all worry. I know your main objective is to go to Sand Creek and help Black Kettle, but there are still warring Cheyenne out there who will not like seeing more soldiers come."

Peter kept stroking her hair as he leaned closer and kissed her again. "Stop inventing things to worry about. Do you forget that most of those Cheyenne know me and we are friends? I even have a cousin among those at Sand Creek and she has a baby, a second cousin to me. How many times do I need to remind you I will be fine?"

"Constantly," she answered, smiling sadly.

"Then I tell you again. I will be fine, and I will be here when our son is born."

Claire snuggled against him, kissing his chest. She ran her hands over his arms again, over his chest, his hips and thighs. She stroked that which was most manly about him, wanting to remember.

"You are making me want you again," he told her with a grin.

"As I want *you* again," she answered softly.

Peter moved a hand under her gown to feel her breasts, then helped her pull it all the way off. He ran his hand down to her private place and toyed with her, bringing on yet another need to feel him inside her.

They made love again, desperately, wantonly, in a heated farewell they wished could last forever.

Chapter Fifteen

Mid-November...

Claire leaned back into Peter's wolf-skin jacket, then wrapped her own wool coat tighter around her neck. She wore a stretchy wool hat over her head and ears against a cold wind that blew against her face, tiny flakes of snow mixed in the wind. Peter kept his left arm around her as he guided his horse with his right hand.

Claire sat astride Peter's calico gelding, *Itatane,* which he claimed "runs like the wind and reads my mind." The horse's name meant "Brother," and for this mission he'd painted the symbol of hope in yellow on the horse's shoulder. On its rump he'd painted an eagle in red, a symbol for courage, wisdom and strength. He would need all those things for a successful mission. Today he used an Army saddle and all its strappings, bedroll and supplies.

Claire's heart ached as she saw Fort Collins ahead. Soon Peter would leave her. She'd insisted on coming with him in order to see him and touch him as long as possible before he would ride off with the soldiers. Behind them Hubert drove a buggy that he'd take Claire home in once Peter left.

As though to read her thoughts, Peter pressed her closer. "It will be all right, *Maeveksea.*"

"I hate it when you're gone," she answered, looking up at him.

He gave her a quick kiss. "And I hate being away from you. Remember what I told you. Go nowhere alone. Stay close to Hubert and Klas. Join with some of the women in quilting–something besides the store to keep you busy. And if you want to visit Gertie Becker, it would be good for both of you. Gertie worries, too. But do not ride to the fort alone. Have Hubert or Klas take you."

"I will." Claire studied his face, two white stripes painted horizontally across each cheek. His hair hung long and straight from beneath a wide fur headband that covered his ears, and a silver earring dangled from one ear. He wore woolen Army pants and knee-high black boots, but under his coat he wore a fringed deerskin shirt, and over that a bone hair-pipe breastplate. On the gun belt about his waist hung not only a holster and Army Colt .45, but a large hunting knife and a tomahawk were secured by the belt. Two rifles rested in their boots at *Itatane's sides*, as did a bow. A deerskin sheath decorated with fringes and feathers and holding arrows was slung over his shoulder and hung at his back.

He would be Two Wolves until he returned home. The man who held her now was the man she'd fallen in love with, the man she'd been together with for weeks after they first met, with no separation. Now, since she'd become his wife, he'd already left her for nearly two weeks, and now he was leaving again, returning to the world of scouting for the army as well as the world of his people. Today he was Cheyenne. For all the talk of "captured" white women, she truly was one, for he'd captured her heart, and it would never be just hers again.

Claire felt proud to ride into the fort astride *Itatane*, proud to be the wife of Two Wolves. If they lived among the Cheyenne she would be the honored wife of a warrior. She smiled at remembering him telling her once that among the Cheyenne, the wives "ruled" inside the *tipi*, where the warrior had to obey her wishes. She closed her eyes for a moment, listening to the gentle, rhythmic tinkling of the tiny pieces of tin tied by rawhide strips to *Itatane's* strappings. Two Wolves had explained to her once that rhythmic drumming, or the rhythmic shaking of turtle rattles and the rhythmic jingle of bells and pieces of tin shaken together represented a connection to the spirit world and awakened souls from the past to guide the person who owned the drums or rattles. They were considered sacred and a form of protection. To Claire, the sound brought a feeling of peace and strength. The more she learned about the

Cheyenne culture, the more she loved it, and the more she realized that their beliefs and religion were not so different from Christian beliefs and prayers for guidance and strength.

Now she saw Major Ansley ordering a Company of what looked like at least fifty men to get into line. All kinds of activity abounded on fort grounds—wives gathered to bid their husbands farewell, a few children standing with them. Claire recognized those women she'd befriended when Two Wolves first brought her here, Emily Sternaman, married to First Lieutenant Robert Sternaman. The couple had a year-old baby boy. She spotted Sarah Flower, married to Captain Stephen Flower. Their three-year-old son stood clinging to his mother's skirt. Gertie Becker smiled and waved at Claire, but Claire could see the worry in her eyes. Her husband, Sergeant First Class Harry Becker, was a robust man who always had a jolly outlook on life. She spotted Private Thomas Lake and Privates Billy Carver and Stanley Cooper, who both nodded to her and smiled, then called out greetings to Two Wolves.

"You gonna' make sure we keep our scalps?" Billy joked.

"If you lose your scalp, I will be the one to take it," Two Wolves teased in return. "I will not let some other warrior out-do me."

Billy and some of the other men laughed, and Claire felt proud that most of these men held a great respect for her husband, as well as trusting him to keep them from danger.

She spotted Captain Tower then. He nodded to her, then to Two Wolves. Claire could feel the hint of tension and rivalry as the two men studied each other, and Two Wolves held her a bit closer. Claire knew he was enjoying the pride of calling her his wife and parading her in front of Captain Tower. He drew his horse up beside Major Ansley.

"It is going to be a cold journey," he told Ansley. "And I smell snow in the air."

"I'm afraid so," Ansley answered. "November sure as hell isn't the best time to be doing this."

"Did you send the wire to Washington?"

"I did. Now we have to hightail it to Fort Lyon and try to beat Chivington to Sand Creek."

"I am ready," Two Wolves told him.

Hubert pulled the wagon near the troops and waited while Two Wolves dismounted and lifted Claire down. He walked her around the other side of the wagon.

"Remember all that I have told you," he said, holding her arms in a firm grip.

"I will," Claire told him, unable to quell the tears in her eyes. "Two Wolves, I don't feel good about this. Between the Cheyenne who are still at war, and Chivington and the Colorado Volunteers, I'm scared for you."

Two Wolves gently put his hands to the sides of her face. "Look at me, *Maeveksea*. It is I, Two Wolves, and I have been on many missions like this one. And I will be riding with at least fifty men. I will be fine."

Claire grasped his wrists and turned her face to kiss his right palm. "I know. I love you, Two Wolves. I need you to come back to me and be here when your son is born."

He smiled the devastatingly handsome smile that completely melted her heart. "There is nothing I want more. I will be here. This I promise. And you know how much I love you and the life you carry." He leaned down to meet her lips, kissing her gently. "It is the Moon when the Wolves Run Together," he told her then. "I will be back by the Moon of Strong Cold. That is January. We will sit by the fire together, and I will place my hands on your belly and feel my son moving and kicking. He will be strong because *you* are strong, the strongest and bravest white woman I have ever known besides my own mother. It will be good, *Maeveksea*. You will see." He kissed her once more, then moved his hands to grasp hers and squeeze them for reassurance. "I must go now. The sooner I leave, the sooner I will return."

Reluctantly, Claire let him lift her into the wagon. She took a seat beside Hubert, who reached behind her and grabbed a blanket he'd brought along. He opened it and spread it over her lap.

"There you go, Ma'am," he told her. "I'll get you back to your warm cabin fast as I can. Things will be okay. You just take care of yourself for Peter so's you're nice and healthy when he gets back."

"Thank you, Hubert." Claire smiled for the rather homely but kind man who always wore overalls and looked like he was ready to go out and plow the fields.

Claire turned once more to watch Two Wolves mount his horse again, looking tall and intimidating in the saddle.

"*Nemehotatse, Maeveksea,*" he told her.

"And I love you, Two Wolves."

Finally, he tore his gaze from her and kicked *Itatane* into motion, riding up beside Major Ansley, who shouted the company of men into motion, giving the hand sign to head out of the fort. Captain Tower nodded to Claire as he rode past.

"Take care of yourself," he told her, tipping his hat slightly.

"I will. And you take care of *your*self and watch out for my husband."

Tower smiled and shook his head. "I highly doubt I'll need to do that." He studied her a moment longer before turning his horse and heading out.

Claire watched after the soldiers for a good ten minutes as they paraded into the distance, swords clanking, horses snorting, saddles squeaking. And above it all she heard the tinkling of the tin bells on her husband's horse.

"I'm scared for him, Hubert. There is a lot of trouble brewing in the south."

"Somethin' tells me your husband is used to trouble, and I expect he handles himself real well no matter what. You shouldn't worry so, Ma'am."

Claire watched Two Wolves finally disappear over the horizon. "I'll never stop worrying." She couldn't hear the bells any longer. There was nothing now but the sound of the wind on the plains and the feel of wet snowflakes against her face.

Chapter Sixteen

Two Wolves quickly urged *Itatane* around behind a high slope, away from the wide, flat plains of eastern Colorado. He'd spotted movement far in the distance to the east, as well as to the west. He quickly dismounted and took a telescope from his gear and worked his way to the highest point of the hill. He looked around the western foothills through the telescope, patiently turning things into focus.

"Colorado Militia," he said softly.

He turned the telescope to the east, watching carefully. The movement there was so far away it was difficult to tell even with a telescope who it was. After a few minutes of squinting and concentrating he realized it was Indians, and in Colorado that meant Cheyenne. The militia were headed straight for Major Ansley and his men. Once they made it that far east, they might spot the Cheyenne.

From what he could tell, the band of Cheyenne was peaceful. He could see that women and children were along. Were they trying to head northeast out of Colorado to relatives in Kansas, or would they head straight north into Wyoming or Montana? If the Militia spotted them, it would mean deep trouble for the Cheyenne.

He rose and leapt onto *Itatane's* back, turning the horse and heading the nearly half-mile back to Major Ansley and his men. He always rode well ahead of them to scout the way and watch for danger. *Itatane's* hooves spewed snow and mud as Two Wolves charged at a gallop to reach the troops quickly. When he came in sight of them he saw Major Ansley raise his hand to halt the procession. As he came closer he realized Captain Tower rode alongside Ansley. When he finally reached the major he reined in.

"What's wrong?" Ansley asked.

"Colorado Militia west of us and headed this way," Two Wolves told him. "And a party of Cheyenne is east of us. I believe they are peaceful. There are women and children along. It is likely they are trying to get out of Colorado, perhaps into Kansas. I could not tell if they were among Black Kettle's people. They were too far away for me to recognize faces."

Itatane shuddered, his overheated breath coming out in steamy clouds against the cold air.

Two Wolves patted his neck. "I will let you rest now, my brother," he said soothingly.

"What do you advise we do?" the major asked him then.

"It is not my decision, Sir. But since you ask my opinion, I would keep heading south, but veer a little west to intercept the Militia. They are likely headed for Fort Lyon, as we are. If we can keep them busy and steer them straight south, we can keep them from coming across the Cheyenne."

"You sure it's not a war party?" The question came from Captain Tower.

Two Wolves bristled. Was the captain suggesting Two Wolves would protect the Cheyenne even if they were out to attack whites? "I know a war party when I see one, and never would there be women and children with them. And if it was a war party, I would advise the major to intercept them. And I would try to reason with them to leave Colorado for the winter. Perhaps wait for us to bring Black Kettle and his camp to join them. You know me well enough, Captain, to realize I would not deliberately avoid warring Cheyenne who might attack innocent people. I am trying to show that those Cheyenne left in Colorado are not out to make war."

Captain Tower's horse whinnied and shook its mane as Tower and Two Wolves' gazes locked. "I was just asking because you said they were far away. I thought maybe you could have misread what you saw."

"Not so far away that I could not recognize several *travois* carrying supplies, and women walking behind the men. I only said I could not see their faces well." Two Wolves yanked *Itatane's* reins and backed the horse a little, turning his attention back to Major Ansley. "What will you do?"

Ansley sighed, removing his beaver hat and shaking snow from it before putting it back on. "I am going to take your advice and try to intercept the Volunteers. Do you think we can catch up to them before nightfall?"

"If we head a little more west. I know it is off our course, but it might save lives. I will need a fresh horse. I rode *Itatane* hard to get here."

Ansley looked back at the men. "We've been going at a pretty good pace already. Some of the men are complaining, but they're spoiled. It's been a while since we went out on patrol. They probably think we're going to stop here and make camp."

Two Wolves pulled off the wool band he wore around his ears and shook his hair behind him. "There is too much daylight left. We have to try to catch up to the Volunteers. If we are lucky, they will make camp early. If we catch up to them we can camp nearby and keep an eye on them—make sure they keep going south. Perhaps we can ride with them all the way to Fort Lyon."

Ansley nodded. "And if John Chivington is with them, can you keep your temper and not make trouble? I know how much you hate the man."

Two Wolves rested a hand on the handle of the knife he wore at his side. "I will do my best, but I would find great enjoyment in taking the man's scalp."

Ansley grinned and shook his head. "You just remember you have a wife waiting for you back at Fort Collins."

Two Wolves glanced at Captain Tower, whose own concern for Claire showed in his eyes. The look he saw there seemed more of a warning that if Two Wolves deceived Claire and turned to his warrior ways, Tower was ready to take his place in Claire's life.

"That pretty little red-head back home should help you think reasonably," Ansley added. "I helped keep you from a hanging not all that long ago, Two Wolves. I don't care to have to do that again. Besides that, you'll soon have a son or daughter who needs you."

Two Wolves dismounted. "I do not need to be reminded, Major. Have someone bring up a horse for me."

Ansley turned his mount and shouted to Sergeant Becker to bring up a fresh horse. Becker left the lineup and rode back to the two men who herded a small remuda of spare horses at the back of the line.

Two Wolves began unloading *Itatane*, aware that all the while Captain Tower watched him. He unloaded weapons, supplies and his Army saddle, then patted *Itatane*'s rump before looking at Tower, who'd also dismounted to give his horse a moment of relief.

Two Wolves faced the man squarely then, holding himself in the proud and challenging way a Cheyenne warrior often presented himself. "You have something to say, so say it," he told the captain.

Tower held his gaze. "I was just thinking that if we should get into some kind of conflict, it would be easy for one of us to accidentally harm the other, and it would look like part of the battle."

Two Wolves stepped closer. "You mean you could shoot me, and no one would know it wasn't the enemy who did it."

Captain Tower grinned a little. "Or visa-versa."

"Yes. If it was a fight with Indians, I could land a hatchet or an arrow into you, and others would think the Cheyenne did it."

"It *would* be a Cheyenne who did it. I'm *looking* at him."

Two Wolves slowly shook his head. "Surely you know me better, Captain. How long have you ridden with me on missions like this?"

"That was all before you took a white wife."

Two Wolves studied him closely. "A woman you took an interest in the moment you set eyes on her. I am not blind, Captain. Just remember that Claire Matthews is *my* wife and she carries *my* child. But I will tell you something that will surprise you. I have thought that if for some reason I should be killed, I can think of no white man whom I would trust more than you to see that my wife is taken care of. But as long as I am alive, she is Mrs. Peter James Matthews."

Tower frowned in surprise at the remark. "Are you saying –"

"You know what I am saying."

Tower slowly nodded. "I have never been able to figure you out, Two Wolves. You are two different men in one body. And I'll admit it. I had a strong interest in Claire when you first brought her to the fort and then left for those two or three weeks. She was still single, and she was scared and alone. I respect you as a Cheyenne warrior, but it was difficult for me to realize that woman really does love you and that she intended to marry you. I didn't agree with that, but she made her decision. And it's because of the dangerous life you lead that I was worried."

"You know full well I can take care of myself in battle. And I have too much honor to kill a man who does not deserve killing, even if that man has an eye for my woman. And once this mission is over, we will winter at Fort Collins and by spring I will be a father and will no longer scout for the army. I will be a white man in the fullest sense. Do not worry about Claire. I have made promises to her that I intend to keep. In the meantime, you need not fear showing me your back, as I hope I need not fear the same from you."

Tower slowly nodded. "You needn't fear, but it's not because I wouldn't like to see you out of the picture. It's because I know what losing you would do to Claire. She adores you. Anyone can see it in her eyes. So, you be sure to keep your promises, Two Wolves. It's this Indian side of you that worries me."

Sergeant Becker rode up to Two Wolves then, leading a roan mare. "Here you go, Two Wolves! What the heck did you see up there, anyway?"

Two Wolves tore his gaze from Captain Tower. "Colorado Militia. We are going to pay them a visit and keep them busy and away from a band of Cheyenne farther east. I do not want the militia to know they are there."

"Good idea." The sergeant turned his horse and headed back to his place in line while Two Wolves packed the fresh horse and mounted up, taking the reins to *Itatane* to lead the horse beside him. By then Captain Tower was also mounted again.

Two Wolves turned his horse to face the captain. "We are *both* warriors, Captain. You a white warrior, me a Cheyenne. But we fight on the same side, I assure you."

Tower nodded and smiled rather sadly. He put out his hand. "I think we should shake on that."

Two Wolves glanced at the out-stretched hand, then took hold of the man's wrist, squeezing hard. Tower in return grasped Two Wolves' wrist in a firm grip. "Let's just agree to look out for each other. If worse comes to worse, *one* of us has to return to Fort Collins to take care of those left behind."

Those left behind ... like my wife, Two Wolves thought. "*Aye,*" he agreed. "One of us does have to return. It would be better, though, if we *both* returned. Just remember that the new settlement around the fort is growing every day with new settlers, and with them come young women who are looking to marry. Perhaps you will find a wife among them."

Tower couldn't help a light laugh then. "Perhaps. Do you intend to seek one out for me?"

"I would be very happy to find you a wife."

"I'll just bet you would." Tower laughed again and re-joined Major Ansley at the head of the company. Soon he heard the soft, rhythmic jangle of the tiny twists of tin Two Wolves had re-tied to his fresh mount. *Spirits talking,* Two Wolves had told him when they first rode out of Fort Collins. The captain thought how the sound did have a kind of calming effect. Two Wolves rode past them, leading them southwest.

"Two Wolves!" Ansley shouted to him.

Two Wolves slowed his horse and let the major and the captain catch up.

"Stay close this time," Ansley told him. "I don't want you riding into that camp of no-good Militia alone. You look too Indian, and you're liable to get shot down before you get a chance to explain yourself."

"But then I could shoot back and kill some of them," Two Wolves answered with a grin. "I would not mind that."

"Well, we need you with us, so just do like I say. Right now, you're one of us, and I'm ordering you to stay with me and the captain when we approach their camp."

Tower noticed a rather sly, amused look in Two Wolves' eyes when he answered the major with, "As you wish."

Captain Tower knew that obeying orders was not something Two Wolves cared about, but he respected the Ansley, so he obeyed. Two Wolves turned his horse and rode just slightly ahead of them, and Tower watched him, admiring the proud way he sat a horse.

Tower couldn't help wondering how different things might have been if he'd met Claire before she met Two Wolves. He knew he didn't have a chance at winning her away from a man like that, but he damn well wouldn't mind watching out for the woman if something should happen to her husband.

Chapter Seventeen

Claire handed Gertrude Becker a cup of coffee, then took a seat opposite the woman in a rocking chair near the hearth. "I'm so glad you came to visit, Gertie."

"Well, I'm here as much for me as for you. Harry has ridden out on more missions like this than I can keep track of, but the worry is always the same."

Claire put a hand on her belly when she felt a flutter of movement. "This is all new for me, and I don't like it at all, especially since I'm pregnant. Even so, for the short time I've known Peter, I don't know what I'd do without him."

Gertie pushed a strand of gray hair behind her ear. "Then you can imagine what it's like after forty years together. The worry is the same."

Claire sighed. "Of course, it is. And you've been going through this for years. I guess that, young or old, it helps to share the worry."

She sipped some of her coffee, watching the sadness in Gertie's eyes. She suspected the woman's hair had turned gray sooner than it should have just because of the hard life she'd led. She'd known Gertie only a couple of months, but she'd become like a mother to Claire, whose own mother had died when Claire was very young. Being around Gertie was comforting.

"Yes, it does help," Gertie answered with a rather sad smile. "But in your case, you are at least young enough to go on and find another man. Me...I'm old and fat and gray. I'd just be left a homeless old woman."

"Goodness, that's just silly," Claire answered. "You are a lovely woman, a wonderful homemaker and cook and a caring person. And you told me when we first met that you have a son and a daughter back East, even a couple of grandchildren. Surely you could live with your son or daughter."

"Oh, I suppose, and I would love to be with my grandchildren." Her blue eyes showed a longing that made Claire feel sorry for her. "But I wouldn't' want to be a burden on either of my children."

"I'm sure neither of them would think of it that way. If my mother was still alive and needed help, I would be there for her. Your children are lucky they still have their mother." Claire set her coffee cup on a small table near her chair and rose to check on bread baking in the brick oven built into the side of the fireplace. "Tell me about your children, Gertie. Talking like this helps keep me from worrying about Peter." She used her apron to grasp the handle to the oven door, then opened it to see the bread had risen over the top of the bread pans but still wasn't browned enough.

"That bread smells really good," Gertie commented. "Of course, by the looks of me you can tell I eat far too *much* bread."

Both women laughed lightly as Claire sat back down. Gertie's heavy bosom rose and fell as she sighed deeply before speaking again. "My son, Harry Junior, works as an accountant for the railroad. In his last letter he told me the government is actually thinking about building a railroad that would connect New York with California. Can you believe that?"

Claire studied the fire crackling in the hearth. "Oh, my goodness, that doesn't seem possible!"

"After all the growth and change I've seen over the years, I don't consider anything impossible anymore," Gertie answered.

Claire thought about Peter...and the Cheyenne...how they were losing so much of what was once their land. "I can't imagine how that will affect the Indians," she said on a sad note.

"Oh, my, yes, it will just be another reason to chase them onto reservations. A railroad means more settlement, more towns, more growth, and more reasons to rid this land of its Indians. It's very sad for them." Gertie took another deep breath. "But enough of that. I was telling you about my son. He and his wife Lorraine have a ten-year-old daughter they named Gertrude, after me. Isn't that nice?"

Claire smiled. "It is. If I have a daughter, I'd like to name her after Peter's mother, in her memory. Her name was Ella Lynn. She must have been so heart-broken to see her husband killed before her eyes. And she must have been very strong, insisting on taking her Indian son with her to a place where she surely was treated with disrespect. She made sure Peter got an education, and she loved him so dearly." She drank more coffee. "Tell me about your daughter."

Gertie's blue eyes shone with love. "My Sarah is married to a farmer. Most people think of farmers as poor, but Grayson has quite a big farm, with hired help, and of course the kids are approaching the age where they can help with a lot of the chores, at least the two older ones. Johnny is eight, Susan six and Billy three. I've never even seen Billy yet. I haven't had the chance to go back to New York to see them. I know how busy Sarah is, so I would hate to add to the household burden."

"*Burden*? For goodness sakes, Gertie, you could relieve her of a lot of work! You could help watch the youngest child, and you could help with cleaning and cooking and some of the farm chores. I'm sure Grandma Gertie would be more than welcome by the family. And with all your son-in-law's farmer friends around, you might even find another man. There could be a widower or two among them."

Gertie burst out laughing. "Don't be silly!"

Claire smiled and finished her coffee. "You just never know." She rose to check the bread again then took some knitted hot pads from the fireplace mantle and removed the bread pans.

"As I said, young lady, you do at least have the advantage of youth and beauty."

Claire set the last bread pan on the table and straightened, pain suddenly piercing her heart. "I would never want another man. Never."

Both women sobered. Gertie rose and walked to stand behind Claire. "And there you go, child. Do you think it's any different for a woman my age? That first true love is a memory that never goes away. And I'm sure it would be pretty hard to replace a man like Peter. He's so handsome and so skilled and brave. I feel better knowing he's out there with Harry. And you should remember he knows Cheyenne ways, so he knows better than anyone what to look for."

Claire took a deep breath against a sudden urge to cry. "I know. It's his knowledge of the Cheyenne ways and being Cheyenne himself that scares me. There are times when it seems like he has no white blood at all."

"But he has *you*, and you are carrying his child. That's your insurance that he will do anything he has to do to get back to you."

Claire turned and embraced the woman. "Thank you for coming."

Gertie patted her back. "I'm just glad you're here. I enjoy your company." She pulled back. "Emily Sternaman and Sarah Flower and two new women at the fort want to form a little club for knitting and quilt making and such—something to keep all of us busy while our husbands are away. You should come one or two days a week, so we can all meet at each other's quarters. Getting together like this really helps."

"I think I'd like that," Claire told her, her mood brightening. "I have the store to look after, which also helps, and I've gotten to know some of the women here at the new settlement, so I'm finding ways to stay busy. But I can take a day or two a week to come into the fort. Hubert and Klas can look after the store when I'm not here."

"Good." Gertie grasped her hands and squeezed them. "Now—are you going to fatten me up even more with some of that bread?"

Claire laughed through her tears and quickly wiped at her eyes. "Don't forget that I will soon be getting fat myself. I feel the baby moving all the time." She turned to cut one loaf of bread, smearing a piece with freshly churned butter. "Sit down, Gertie, and I'll get us more coffee."

"This is a lovely little cabin," Gertie told her. The men did a fine job, which shows you how much they like and respect Peter. Of course, they all call him Two Wolves because that's just about the only way they have seen and known him. And by the way, Sarah Flower is also expecting again, at almost the same time you are, so next spring we can have a double celebration. And what a perfect time—when trees and flowers are coming back into bloom and birds are nesting and the grizzlies are waking up."

Claire sat down to butter her own piece of bread. "Yes, it *is* perfect timing, isn't it?" She sighed. "I just hope Peter is here when the time comes."

"He will be, dear. He will be."

Claire shivered. Outside the wind howled in a sudden snowstorm. She hated the thought of Two Wolves out there camping in the cold and snow. How nice it would be if he could be here and they could snuggle under the quilts together to stay warm. "I'd better add some wood to the fire."

She got up and walked over to the wood pile next to the fireplace, taking three logs and adding them to the coals and partially-burned wood already in the hearth.

Stay warm, Two Wolves, she thought. *I'll be with you tonight.* The life in her belly rippled in movement again. To her it was a sign that Two Wolves was with her, inside her very being.

Chapter Eighteen

The sun settled behind the Rockies as Two Wolves and the soldiers approached the camp of Colorado Volunteers. By what little daylight was left, Two Wolves counted fifteen tents already set up, and several men sat around a large campfire trying to keep warm. Everyone's breath, as well as that of the horses, came out of noses and mouths with visible steam, and Two Wolves guessed the night would be one of the coldest yet this season. A million stars already sparkled in the fast-darkening sky, which meant no clouds to hold in the heat.

"Who goes there?" someone shouted.

Major Ansley put up his hand to signal the rest of the men to halt. "Major John Ansley, United States Army!" he shouted, his words clearly heard through the crisp, silent air.

"We don't need any help from the Federals!" the other man yelled in reply. "Here in Colorado we *are* the Army! Go camp someplace else!"

"Too dark!" Ansley shouted. "We will camp right here. We can share a few rations if need be."

"Bullshit!" came the reply. "We don't need no fuckin' rations!"

Two Wolves bristled. Not only did he hate anyone who rode with the Colorado Militia, but just by the way they talked now, he could tell they were out for a kill and didn't want the regular army around.

"Don't give them one damn thing, Major," he told Ansley. "They deserve nothing."

What bothered him more was that the voice yelling to them sounded familiar.

"I'm just trying to keep the peace and hope they'll let us ride with them tomorrow," Ansley answered. "Especially if they are headed for Fort Lyon. And don't forget we want to turn their attention from those Cheyenne to the west of us."

"I'm coming out to talk," came the voice again.

"You watch yourself, Two Wolves," the major warned. "They're going to get spicy when they see you."

"I do not fear any of them.". As though sensing trouble, Two Wolves' horse shuddered and skittered sideways. Two Wolves patted its neck. "Settle down, girl." He heard a horse from the remuda behind them whinny, and he grinned. He knew *Itatane*'s particular whinny. *Aye, we are one soul*, he thought inwardly. *You sense trouble, too, my friend.*

In minutes two men rode out to them, one of them carrying a lantern. It was just dark enough that it would be difficult to see faces unless Ansley and his men came closer to the fire. The Militia apparently did not intend to let that happen. The militia man with the lantern held it up, lighting up first Major Ansley's face, then moving the lantern to see Two Wolves better.

"Well, well, well, who do we have here?"

It was the familiar voice.

"I am Two Wolves, Army scout. Hold that damn lantern to your own face."

The soldier with the lantern moved closer, and Two Wolves stiffened. "So, it is you! Sergeant Craig," he said with a sneer.

Craig spat tobacco juice to the ground beside Two Wolves' horse before adding, "I remember you, too. You're that fuckin' Indian we came across a few weeks ago. You were haulin' some supplies to Colorado Springs, and your white whore of a wife was along."

Two Wolves moved his horse closer.

"That's enough!" Major Ansley shouted at both of them. "Two Wolves, who is this?"

Two Wolves moved his hand to his hunting knife, staring coldly at Sergeant Craig the whole time he spoke. "He is the man I told you about when I first returned with Claire after our trip to Colorado Springs. He calls himself Sergeant Millard Craig, and he is scum. He insulted Claire and threatened all of us."

"Any woman who lays with an Indian *deserves* to be insulted!"

"*Heyoka!*" Two Wolves snarled, heading straight for Craig.

Ansley charged his horse between the two men. "That's enough!" he ordered. "Captain Tower, take hold of Two Wolves' bridle. Pull him back!"

The captain obeyed, glancing at Two Wolves and knowing damn well that if he didn't want to be held back, no man would be able to stop him.

Two Wolves jerked the horse backward with a quick yank on the reins, pulling the bridle right out of the captain's hand.

"I do not need you to hold my horse!" he told Tower.

Ansley kept his horse between Sergeant Craig and Two Wolves. "I am Major John Ansley from Fort Collins," he told Craig. "We're headed for Fort Lyon. If that's where you are going, we intend to accompany you."

"Not with that damned Indian along, Major!" Craig answered. "You have a pretty uppity scout there. I can smell a troublemaker a mile off. I'll not have any Cheyenne warrior riding with us when it's Cheyenne we're *hunting*."

"You are not out to hunt," Two Wolves barked. "You are out to *kill!*"

"Stay out of this," Ansley ordered, keeping his eyes on Craig. "We aren't here to make trouble, Sergeant. We're only here because we have business at Fort Lyon. We came upon your party by accident. Where are you headed?"

"We aim to catch up to Colonel Chivington down at Fort Lyon. Got word he's on a campaign against the warrin', thievin' hostiles."

Two Wolves felt great alarm. "He is already at Fort Lyon?"

"I wasn't talkin' to you, Indian!"

"Where is Chivington headed?" Ansley asked.

"I don't much know. That's what I intend to find out when I get to Fort Lyon and talk to Major Anthony," Craig replied. He backed his horse. "Follow us if you want. I can't stop you. But you stay *behind* us. And I don't want to see that scout anywhere in my gun sites!"

Ansley rode straight up to him again. "You shoot my scout, and I'll chase you down and make sure the federal government *hangs* you. That young man is like a son to me, and if the government doesn't have your head, I'll risk my future and shoot your ass myself! I don't care if I get cour*t*-martialed for it. Understand?"

Craig frowned. "Why in hell are you stickin' up for a damn Indian? You've likely battled the Cheyenne yourself. You know what sneaky, murdering bastards they can be! You've probably lost men fighting them."

"Only the few who are fighting to stay in a place they have called home for a hundred years are the ones still fighting. I fight back because it's my job, but if anything can be done for peace, that's what we have to try to do. Now, get the hell back to your camp, Sergeant, and we'll by-God *not* follow you in the morning. We'll ride right *alongside* you, and Two Wolves will ride with us. I have twice as many men as you do, so I suggest you get back to yours and let them know they will have company in the morning."

Craig backed his horse again. "Just know that your precious scout threatened me the last time we met. He all but dared me to pull my gun on him so he could break my neck! That doesn't sound like a peaceful Cheyenne to me."

"Do you wonder how it feels as a knife slides across your neck?" Two Wolves asked him. "If I were you, I would not sleep too deeply from now on."

"Two Wolves!" Ansley growled.

"You hear that, Major?" Craig sneered. "He'd slit your throat just as easily if he felt like it. You get into it with the Cheyenne and he'll *join* them against you!"

"I've already been in a fight with the Cheyenne when he was along, and he saved my life and the lives of others. Get back to your men."

Craig turned his horse. "Let's go," he told the soldier with him. "I don't want to hang around these fucking Indian lovers."

Both militia men rode off. Ansley breathed a deep sigh. "Jesus, Two Wolves, you sure don't make my job easy."

"Someday I will *kill* that man," Two Wolves answered. "That is a promise!"

"And you'd *hang* for it. Remember that! I did my best to save you from a hanging only three months ago, remember? And I couldn't stop that mob in Denver. If it weren't for Hubert Huff, you'd no longer be with us."

"I am grateful for what you did, but I will not forget that man's insults to Claire."

Ansley rode up closer to him. "And Claire is the whole *point*. You think about *her* before you go around challenging the Colorado Militia! She needs you to get back to her."

Two Wolves glanced at Captain Tower, who gave him an "I told you so" look. Then he turned his attention to Ansley again. "Do not worry about me, Major. I am very aware of what I need to do. And if that man dies, he will not see it coming. In the meantime, I want him to spend his nights wakeful and worried. Let him wonder if and when I will show up in the darkness and make sure he never insults my wife again."

Ansley shook his head. "You remember what I told you. And I'm damn glad you consider me a friend and not an enemy."

"You will always be my friend. I am grateful for your words in my defense."

"Don't make me regret them, Two Wolves."

Their gazes held in mutual respect and friendship. "You won't. For now, I am worried about the fact that Chivington is out there somewhere on a campaign to kill Indians. I hope we reach Fort Lyon in time for the orders you requested."

Ansley nodded. "So do I. I know you'd like to ride straight to Sand Creek first, but I need those orders before I can do anything." He left Two Wolves and rode back to the men, ordering them to make camp for the night.

Captain Tower faced Two Wolves. "I suggest you remember you're half *white*. Claire's last name is *Matthews*, as is yours."

"I do not need to be reminded. Nor should I need to remind you that she is, as you said, my *wife!*" Two Wolves turned his horse and rode off into the darkness.

Chapter Nineteen

Three men entered MATTHEW'S SUPPLIES at the same time, appearing to Claire to all be together. One wore a long wool coat over a wool suit with a vest. He glanced around the store, then set eyes on Claire and looked her over strangely. He turned to the other two then and nodded.

Claire felt a strange, unnamed threat. She reached under the counter for her .44 Colt pistol and laid it near her cash register.

"Can I help you?" she asked.

"Oh, we're new here," the man in the suit answered while the other two browsed the store.

Claire got the distinct impression they were only pretending to shop.

"We've lived mostly in Kansas, workin' ranches here and there," the man in the suit continued. "Decided we'd head to California and look for work there. California's a lot warmer than here."

Claire watched the other two, whose "shopping" seemed to keep bringing them closer to the counter. She guessed the man in the suit to be in his late forties. The other two were much younger, perhaps no more than her own age of twenty.

"Well, gentlemen, I have plenty of supplies here. But this most certainly isn't the time to head for California, what with winter upon us and two mountain ranges to cross to get where you're going." Claire watched them carefully.

"We've been to the saloon," one of the younger ones spoke up, saying the words in a bragging fashion, as though he was proud he'd been to a drinking establishment.

The young man who'd made the comment wore knee-high boots and cotton pants. A shaggy, wolf-skin coat hid whatever he wore under it.

Claire moved closer to the cash register again, placing her hand on the six-gun. "And why do you think I care where you've been?"

The young man shrugged. "Just to let you know there's rumors over there at the saloon."

Claire glanced at the third man. He wore a stained, floppy hat typical for cowboys. A shock of unkempt, shoulder-length blond hair stuck out from under it, and he needed a shave. Spurs on his boots jangled when he walked, and his walk was more of a strut. He stepped hard so the spurs made a noise, as though to accent he was some kind of rough and rugged horseman. She could see that under his wool jacket, which was lined with sheep's skin, he wore a plaid shirt.

She turned her gaze to the older man. "What kind of rumors?"

He grinned through teeth brown from chewing tobacco. "Oh, things like some real pretty woman runs this store all by herself," he told her. "I always figured that was a man's job. Just thought we'd see if the rumors were true." He looked her over hungrily. "The part about her bein' pretty was true. We ain't seen a woman pretty as you in a while."

Claire bristled. "Plenty of women help their husbands run supply stores. I've run one since I was a young girl. My father started this business, and I took it over when he died. And if you gentlemen aren't really here to buy anything, you can leave," she added. She wrapped her hand around the handle of the gun.

The young man in the wolf skin coat chuckled. "Don't get your dander up, ma'am. We were just curious on account of, in this case, they say your husband is a Cheyenne Indian and owns this store right along with you. Everybody knows Indians can't own nothin'."

"My husband is also half white. His name is Peter James Matthews, and he has every right to own whatever he chooses to own. But he is also a skilled warrior, and he's right out back getting some wood," she lied. "So I suggest all three of you leave before he comes in here and finds you threatening me."

All three men ambled even closer, and all reeked of whiskey.

"Ma'am, we already checked," the other young man told her. "Ain't nobody out back, and folks at the saloon say your husband is an Army scout and he's on his way south with soldiers from the fort. But there ain't no reason for you to lie. We're just here to see if the rumors was true and to get a look at a real pretty gal."

"This is our pa," the one in the shaggy coat told Claire eagerly as he walked closer to the older man. "His name is Cal Sweet. I'm Bo, and my brother over there is Jasper. All of us, we need some money to get on to California. We thought maybe you could help us out with money instead of supplies." He grinned as he let the words sink in.

Claire realized that not only were all three of them drunk, but the young ones seemed ignorant and unschooled. She took hold of the pistol and held it up, waving it at all three men. "Get out! All of you!"

Cal glared at her. "Ain't no need for a gun, Ma'am. Just hand over what money you have in that cash register there, and we'll be on our way."

Claire fired a warning shot, shattering a stack of china behind Jasper, whose eyes widened in surprise.

"Don't think I don't know how to use this gun?!" Claire shouted at them. "I missed you on purpose, but I won't next time. Now get out!"

"Ma'am, you really ought to put down that gun," Cal told her. "I ain't about to let a woman get the better of me, so before I—"

Claire fired again, and Cal flew backward, a hole in his chest.

"Hey, you shot our pa!" Bo yelled. "You Indian lovin' bitch!"

Claire turned the gun on Bo and pulled the trigger, but the hammer jammed and nothing happened. By then Jasper had his own gun out, and he fired it. Claire felt a sting to her right arm, and the blow sent her reeling against the canned food shelves behind her. One of the cans fell and hit her on the head as she went down, and for a moment, things went black.

"Get the money!" Jasper shouted.

Claire felt someone standing near her then heard the *ding* of the cash register drawer being opened.

"Let's poke her!"

It was Jasper's voice. Claire felt a hand running over her leg. She groaned and struggled to fully wake up as he grasped at her bloomers.

"The bitch lays with Indians. She shouldn't mind a white man having at her."

"Leave her be, Jasper! Let's take the money and get out of here before someone comes running at the sound of gunshots!"

Claire suddenly felt a deep pain on her left thigh. It continued downward. "That'll teach her to shoot our father!" came a voice. She heard the jangle of Jasper's spurs.

Something made a slamming, crashing sound then. "Hey! What the hell are you doing?"

It was Hubert's voice. Claire wanted to yell at him to be careful. But then she heard the loud *boom* of a shotgun. She came around more just then to see Jasper's body fly over the counter and land near her. The sheepskin lining of his jacket showed deep red from blood that soaked it, blood that came from an ugly, huge hole in his chest.

"Don't shoot!" she heard Bo yell. "We was just after a little money!"

The shotgun *boomed* again.

Somewhere in the back of her mind Claire remembered that Hubert always carried a double-barrel Colt shotgun. He must have opened the other barrel on Bo.

Were all three men dead? She tried to move, but nothing seemed to want to work.

More voices now. More people must be coming into the store.

"Mrs. Matthews!" She recognized Klas's voice. "We will get you a doctor. My God! What did they do to your leg?"

Her leg? She'd been shot in the arm. It was only then she remembered the initial pain in her left thigh. The spurs...Had Jasper done something to her with his spurs? She felt someone pull her dress back down. She was lifted in strong arms then.

Klas. Even Two Wolves had commented more than once about the man's size. "There is a new doctor in the settlement now," she heard Klas tell her. "I will take you to him. You hang on now, Mrs. Stewart. You have to think about the baby. You do not want to lose the baby."

What doctor was he talking about? For some reason Claire actually wished it was Captain Tower. At least she knew him and knew he cared about her. She didn't want to be taken to some strange doctor.

Two Wolves! Where was Two Wolves? If he'd been here, this would not have happened. Had she killed Cal Sweet? Voices all around her. Cold air. She was sure it was Klas who held her. She could tell he was practically running.

Two Wolves, I need you. Would he even come back to her?

The baby! Hang on to the baby!

Warmth again. Then things went black.

Chapter Twenty

Sergeant Sam Goodrich shivered against the bitterly cold morning. The eastern skyline was just beginning to brighten from a sun not fully risen. The Cheyenne camp below them was amazingly quiet. Smoke curled from inside the *tipis*, and an American flag hung limply over one of them. He'd heard Black Kettle owned a flag and figured that must be his *tipi*.

There were surely families inside those *tipis*, huddled together to keep warm. This time of year, and most certainly this hour of the morning, he doubted anyone in that camp expected any kind of confrontation with soldiers, nor did it look like those below would likely even *want* to fight, which was why Goodrich could hardly believe his ears when he heard the conversation between Colonel Chivington and one of his lieutenants.

"Sir, that looks like a pretty peaceful camp," the lieutenant told Chivington.

"There is no such thing as a peaceful Cheyenne, Lieutenant, man, woman or child. Set up the howitzers while I take some of the troops down along the creek bed and surround the camp from the other side. Blowing up some of the *tipis* will rid us of whoever is inside, and when they start running, we will shoot them down from all directions."

The lieutenant was visibly hesitant. "Sir, there are likely mostly women and children in those *tipis*."

"And nits make lice," Chivington answered. "What better way to rid Colorado of all Cheyenne forever than to kill the youngest and leave no one left to procreate?"

The lieutenant sighed. "Much as most of the men here are hot to kill Cheyenne warriors, some of them will hesitate at killing women and babies."

Chivington faced him. "Ninety percent of my men will have no trouble at all, Lieutenant, including me. And if you continue this protest I will have you court-martialed and shot. Am I understood? This is *war*, Lieutenant, and it's likely a lot of those men down there have killed innocent whites. And if we let their women and children live to produce more of their filth, this war will never end. Now get the howitzers into position!"

The lieutenant did not reply. He backed his horse and obeyed.

Sergeant Goodrich felt ill. From then on, he saw only hell and damnation and wondered if just being here meant he would never make it to heaven.

Minutes later, shells from several howitzers exploded into *tipis*, blowing them and whoever was inside apart. In seconds, the camp fell into complete chaos. Women and children began screaming and running. Men emerged from other *tipis* with bows and arrows, some with rifles. They appeared to be trying to guard the women as they shouted orders in their own language. Several warriors gathered around the *tipi* that displayed the American flag, as though thinking the soldiers still might just come down to parlay. An older Indian man emerged from that *tipi*.

Black Kettle, Goodrich thought.

Troops of the First Regiment had already ridden down to the southern end of the dried-up creek to cut off the camp's herd of horses so they could not use them to flee. They had orders to shoot down every horse there.

Major Anthony's battalion from Fort Lyon was along and stationed more to the southeast. The Third Regiment began firing right over Anthony's men and all hell broke loose. Soldiers attacked on all sides, by foot and on horseback. Major Anthony's men joined them.

Indians fled in every direction, most of them women and children, some still naked, with only blankets for protection from the cold. But blankets could not protect them from bullets and shrapnel.

Goodrich held back. He couldn't quite allow himself to take part in the carnage that followed. This was not war. This was slaughter. He rode in slowly, seeing soldiers shoot down fleeing women, some ripping children and babies from their arms and either shooting them or stabbing them with bayonets. The valley at Sand Creek turned red with blood, the air filled with *yipping* and war whoops, most of them coming from the soldiers rather than the Indians. Those shouts were mixed with screams—not just normal screams of fright, but screams of horror—women begging for their lives and for their children's lives. He saw little ones with big brown eyes and innocent wonder lined up and shot—saw babies thrown about like toys. Some ended up with their heads bashed in or cut off. To his right a soldier was raping one of the women. He suddenly stood up and ejaculated into her face, then rammed his bayonet into her chest. A little boy who'd stood in terror beside the woman started running. The soldier pulled out his pistol and shot the boy in the back.

Cheyenne men, many of them old, fought bravely but were shot down or bayonetted, as they were helpless against so many armed and prepared soldiers. The carnage continued beyond what would be considered a "victory." For the next several hours soldiers hunted down those who'd managed to flee far beyond the camp. Goodrich was compelled to ride with his company in search of those who'd escaped. He only watched as several warriors who'd managed to find a hiding place deep in the overhang of one high-banked area of the creek bed were trapped there by soldiers and not even given the chance to surrender. They were shot down for no good reason other than to be used for target practice.

Goodrich, a young man who'd been made sergeant only because of a lack of qualified men, and who'd never even seen a battle between Indian and soldier, decided he would not be missed if he simply rode away from the sight. He headed back through the camp, where the shot and bludgeoned bodies of women and children lay strewn about. One child, perhaps a year old, was sitting beside his dead mother, screaming in a chilling way. When the child looked up at him, he realized the reason for the screaming. One arm was missing, and blood poured from the stub. Goodrich felt only pity for him, and he realized the child would likely die anyway. Why let him die in such horrible pain? He pulled out his sidearm and shot the child in the head.

"Now I've done my duty," he muttered. "They can't say I disobeyed any orders."

He broke into tears and turned away to vomit.

Chapter Twenty-One

Within another two days, Major Ansley and his troops made it to Fort Lyon. To Sergeant Craig's seething objection, the Federals surrounded the militia the entire way. Two Wolves rode beside Ansley, enjoying Craig's ire, as well as the fact that the militia had no idea there was a large tribe of southern Cheyenne heading north several miles west of them. Two Wolves could only pray they would make it to their relatives in Kansas or the Dakotas without trouble from any other militia that might be out there roaming the foothills. Not only was that a worry, but Colorado citizens in general were apt to shoot at any Indian who came anywhere near them. That was Claire's biggest worry as far as his own safety was concerned.

I love you, Maeveksea. I will make it back to you. Every night he'd gone off alone to pray to *Maheo* to keep his wife and the child she carried safe. He should be with her. She had grown used to depending on him for help and protection, and sometimes it seemed as though his heart was being ripped in two over this divided world he lived in.

He noticed Sergeant Craig suddenly bolt, heading into the fort.

"Craig is already heading inside to talk to Major Anthony," he told Ansley. He pointed at Craig.

"To hell with him," Ansley answered. "We'll go see Major Anthony right away ourselves. We should have received a wire from Washington by now." He turned to Captain Tower, who rode behind them. "Have the men bivouac here outside the fort until I come back for them."

"Yes, Sir." Tower glanced at Two Wolves. "You be careful around that damn militia."

Two Wolves couldn't help a faint smile. "I am honored that you care."

"It's not exactly you I care about. I don't want to have to go back to Fort Collins with bad news for your wife. She could lose that baby over it. Remember that."

"I think about her all the time. And believe it or not, I am glad for how much you and the major care about her. But right now, it is John Chivington and what he might be up to that worries me most."

Two Wolves turned his horse and headed for the fort entrance.

"You'd better follow Two Wolves before he gets himself in more trouble, Major."

Ansley frowned. "Keeping him *out* of trouble is no easy matter." The two men saluted each other, and Ansley kicked his horse into a run to catch up with Two Wolves.

I don't like any of this, Captain Tower thought. He turned and shouted orders to the rest of the men to dismount and rest their horses until further orders.

Private Kenneth Stubelt came inside Major Anthony's office and saluted Lieutenant William Lattimer.

"There is a Sergeant Millard Craig of the Colorado Militia here to see you, Sir. He says it's urgent."

Lattimer looked up from the desk. "Send him in."

The private nodded and walked out. Seconds later a rather unkempt Sergeant Craig came inside and closed the door.

"Pardon my dusty, unshaved appearance, Sir," he said, walking closer to Lattimer's desk. "But we've been ridin' hard to get here, hopin' to catch up with Colonel Chivington. The private out there says he's been here and gone, and that Major Anthony went with him. How long ago did they leave?"

Lattimer frowned with irritation. "I believe you should be saluting me, Sergeant, and properly introducing yourself, even though by your uniform I can see you're volunteer Colorado Militia and not part of the regular army."

"Oh! Yes, Sir!" Craig removed his hat, revealing stringy blond hair. He straightened and saluted. "I am Sergeant Millard Craig, Third Colorado, and I'm in charge of a small company of men trying to catch up with Colonel Chivington, as I explained. We was told he's on a campaign against the Cheyenne, and we aim to be part of it."

Lattimer frowned as he stroked one long, curled end of a mustache he'd been growing for months. "You're a little late, Sergeant Craig. Chivington headed for Sand Creek the night before last. Major Scott Anthony, who is normally in charge here, went with him. Black Kettle is camped at Sand Creek, and Chivington intends to route him out, kill however many Cheyenne he can, and take the rest prisoners."

Craig scowled. "Damn. I was hopin' to catch up and be part of the battle."

"Well, you probably passed his army on the way here. Chivington would have been well east of you, since Sand Creek is northeast of Fort Lyon. I doubt it will be much of a battle, though, Sergeant. Black Kettle is one of the more peaceful Cheyenne leaders. I suspect we will end up with more prisoners than we care to have around. I'm sure the governor will see that they are placed on reservations outside of Colorado. He wants this territory rid of its Indians by spring."

Craig grinned. "Well, Sir, the fact that Chivington has likely already ravaged Black Kettle's camp is going to be bad news for the Company of U.S. troops that followed us here. They were hoping to find a wire from Washington giving them permission to accompany Black Kettle, and any Cheyenne who wants to go along, north to relatives in the Dakotas, or east into Kansas. Me personally, I just wish I was with Chivington right now, helping spill the guts of every man, woman and child in Black Kettle's camp, right down to the little buggers still suckin' their mama's tits." Craig walked over to a spittoon that sat against the wall and spit tobacco juice into it.

Lieutenant Lattimer grimaced. "I have to say, Sergeant, that you do not behave or carry yourself as a proper soldier should. I am not a fan of the Cheyenne, but your attitude is a bit over the mark, and your personal appearance and behavior are an insult to the army. You volunteers need more discipline."

Craig smiled, his teeth brown from the tobacco juice. He looked the lieutenant over, wondering if the younger man had ever even fought the Cheyenne. Lattimer was small built, a very trim man with a waxed mustache that twirled up on each end. "Well, now, Lieutenant, I figure if I go out there and kill Indians, I've done my job. I don't need to be all prim and proper about it. And if you ever had to fight one of them Cheyenne bastards, you'd agree they all deserve to die. A Cheyenne warrior would hack you to pieces before you could fire your gun."

As though verifying Craig's opinion, Two Wolves barged into the room unannounced, not wearing a coat, and so fully decked out with weapons and looking so "Indian" that Lattimer's eyes widened and he stood up

"There's one of those murderin' bastards now," Craig told Lattimer. He followed his words with a chuckle.

"Who are you?" Two Wolves demanded of the lieutenant. "Where is Major Anthony?"

Lieutenant Lattimer stepped back. "Private Stubelt!" he yelled, as though he thought he needed help.

"He won't hurt you, Lieutenant," Craig told the man, still grinning. "That there is Two Wolves, an Army scout, but if he turns to his warrior side out there in the hills and you run into him, he'll have your scalp in no time."

Two Wolves turned a dark glare to Craig. "I think you should leave before it is *your* scalp I take!" He started for Craig to throw him out of the room.

Craig reached for his sidearm.

"Hold it!" Major Ansley walked in then.

Private Stubelt hurried in behind Ansley. "What do you want me to do, Lieutenant?"

"Just stay right there and keep your eye on the Indian," Lattimer told him. He looked Two Wolves over. "Is it true you're an Army scout?"

"I am. Do you not see the crossed arrows stitched onto the front of my vest?"

"It might behoove you to wear a uniform, Two Wolves, before some soldier or private citizen shoots you just because you're Indian."

"Oh, he's only *half* Indian," Craig sneered. "Me and Two Wolves there have already met. He claims to be half white, and his white name is Peter James Matthews. Married to a white woman even. 'Course we both know the only kind of woman who would lay with an Indian."

Two Wolves glowered at him, resting a hand on the hatchet he wore on his weapons belt. "One day you will *die* by my hands!" he threatened.

"That's enough!" Ansley ordered. He moved up beside Two Wolves, pressing his arm. "Remember where you are—in a fort full of soldiers who don't know all about you."

Two Wolves turned to Ansley, and even Ansley felt a bit threatened by the look in his eyes.

"The man I want to kill is no soldier. He only *pretends* to be one." He looked at Craig again. "But he is just a worthless excuse of a man who enjoys killing Indians. I see it in his eyes. And he *smells*. This room *reeks* of his stink!"

"And if I'm lucky, Two Wolves, the smell of me is the last thing you will remember before you die."

Two Wolves met his gaze and grinned. "The smell of you will be flowers to my nostrils as I carve out your heart for the things you said about my wife." He jerked his arm away from Ansley's grip. "Do not worry, Major. I will not kill that man here in this place." He looked back at Craig. "I will wait until he does not expect it. I prefer that he must always look over his shoulder, wondering if I am there, watching him, waiting for him." The look he gave Craig then caused the man to lose his smile. "Do not forget that I *am* half Indian," he warned Craig. "I can be watching you, and you will not even know I am there."

"What the hell is going on here?" Lattimer demanded. He faced Major Ansley and saluted. "I don't mean any disrespect, Sir, but I would like an explanation for *all* of this!"

Ansley turned to Two Wolves. "It might be best that you stepped back, Let me handle this."

"I will cause no more trouble here," Two Wolves answered. He turned his attention to Lieutenant Lattimer. "My apologies for alarming you. It is that man over there who brings out the warrior in me." He stepped back just slightly, turning to grin at Sergeant Craig, who still rested a hand on his sidearm but definitely looked afraid. Two Wolves thought how perfectly enjoyable it would be if Craig actually pulled out that gun. He would never give the slovenly bastard a chance to fire it!

"I am Major John Ansley," the major told Lattimer. "I'm here with a company from Fort Collins to the north, and we are on a peace mission, hoping to go to Sand Creek and find Black Kettle. We want to escort him and those in his camp to relatives in the north up in the Dakotas, or east into Kansas. I sent a wire to Washington and asked them to reply here to Fort Lyon, so I wouldn't lose time getting to Black Kettle. Did you get the wire?"

"I did, but it only came yesterday. By then Colonel Chivington had been here and left. You and I both know what the orders are from the powers that be here in Colorado—to seek out as many Cheyenne as possible and teach them a lesson—clean them out of Colorado, either by battle or by taking prisoners and sending them off to reservations. Even if I'd received that wire before Chivington arrived, it would have done no good. A man like that would never listen to Washington. He considers himself purely Colorado Militia and above the regular army. The Governor wants Colorado rid of the Cheyenne, and although he claims he wants it done peacefully, Chivington is not a peaceful man when it comes to the Cheyenne. He's a man who tends to do what he pleases, no matter what the orders are that come down from higher up."

Ansley didn't need to touch Two Wolves to feel his fury. It filled the room, even though at the moment he said nothing.

Craig broke into a wide grin again. "I sure wish I was with Chivington. He ought to be having a heyday right about now."

"Shut up, Craig!" Ansley ordered.

"Maybe I'll take my men and head that way anyway—pick up some of the pieces Chivington leaves behind."

Surprisingly calm at the moment, Two Wolves again faced Sergeant Craig. "One day *you* will be scattered in pieces in the foothills, and the wolves will have food for the winter!"

"I want no more of that talk in here!" Lattimer ordered. "This is not the place for it. Army scout or not, if you don't stop these threatening remarks, I'll have you thrown in the brig for insubordination! And you make one move toward Sergeant Craig inside these fort walls, I'll have you shot, which I have every right to do."

"You'll do no such thing!" Ansley stepped closer, slightly in front of Two Wolves. "This man is one of my best scouts and a peacemaker. He's here out of concern for what John Chivington might be up to. He has relatives out there among those with Black Kettle. The Cheyenne there are trapped, and you damn well know it. Major Anthony refused to afford them any kind of protection or food and supplies. Black Kettle is a peaceful man and wants no trouble. He was even awarded a peace medal at a recent council meeting, and he flies an American flag over his *tipi*! That doesn't sound to me like a man who deserves to be starved out for the winter or attacked by Chivington and his murderers."

"I should go," Two Wolves told Ansley. "If we are very lucky, Chivington has not attacked Black Kettle's camp yet. If I ride hard, I can warn Black Kettle. Alone I can move faster than a whole company." He looked at Lieutenant Lattimer. "How many men does Chivington have with him?"

Lattimer closed his eyes and sighed. "It's much more than a company," he answered. "He has at least five hundred men with him, and Major Anthony joined him when they left here. He took about two hundred more men."

Two Wolves whirled, glaring at Major Anthony. "Seven hundred men! There are perhaps two hundred Cheyenne camped at Sand Creek, many of them women and children!"

"Well now, them men will have a fine time with some of them women before they cut out their privates," Craig baited Two Wolves.

"You!" Two Wolves started for him, but Ansley moved between them. "Don't do this!" he told Two Wolves. "You know what will happen."

Craig chuckled.

Two Wolves stepped back, turned his attention to Lattimer. "Major Anthony should have *stopped* Chivington!" he roared.

"He tried to," Lattimer told him. "He warned Chivington that an attack on a peaceful Cheyenne camp would only cause more war and raiding than we could even handle. But the colonel had his mind made up, and you and Major Ansley hadn't arrived yet to interfere." Lattimer tried to explain again. "I'm sure you know as well as I the kind of man John Chivington is, and when he decides to go to war, he goes to war."

"Black Kettle is *not* at war!" Two Wolves shouted. "There are *families* with him at Sand Creek. You know that Chivington has no sympathy for any Cheyenne, whether a warrior or a newborn baby!"

"I have no say in any of this," Lattimer answered. "Major Anthony's orders were to give no more aid or protection to any Cheyenne more than twenty-five miles from here, and most remain farther away. We are already burdened here with providing safety and supplies for the Arapaho who hang around here like vagrants. What happens to those Cheyenne who have refused to leave Colorado or go onto reservations is not my concern, and a lot of them continue to make war. We've had several reports of attacks on supply trains and settlers."

"And Major Anthony and those with him will live to regret doing nothing." Two Wolves faced Ansley. "I must go to Sand Creek."

"You stay right here with us! We'll all go together."

"That will take too long. Only *Maheo* knows what Chivington has already done." Two Wolves started away, but Sergeant Craig pulled his sidearm and hurriedly stepped in front of him, thinking he was safe as long as there were others there to witness. He shoved the gun against Two Wolves' chest. "You'd best stay here, boy!"

Before anyone could react, Two Wolves knocked the gun from Craig's hand, sending it flying across the room. It fired when it landed, the bullet shattering a window. By then Two Wolves had smashed his fist into Craig's face, breaking the man's nose and causing him to fall backward onto a table, which cracked in half as man and table both went down. Two Wolves walked out.

"Two Wolves!" Ansley shouted. "Don't go there!" He ran after him. In the background he heard Lieutenant Lattimer storming behind him, ordering two guards at the door to his quarters to stop Two Wolves.

Their attempt was useless. Two Wolves landed a strong forearm against the neck of the man on his left, sending him flying, then wrestled away from the second man who'd grabbed him from the right. He slammed him up against a wall. "I do not want to kill you," he growled. "So, stay out of my way!"

The solder slid to the floor, and Two Wolves ran outside and leapt onto *Itatane*. He whirled the horse and faced Major Ansley. "I am sorry."

He charged out of the fort.

Ansley turned to see Lieutenant Lattimer beside him. Lattimer raised his sidearm and aimed it at Two Wolves. Ansley batted his arm, causing the gun to fall before Anthony could fire it.

"Let him go!" Ansley ordered.

Lattimer glared at him. "Sir, I believe you had no right doing that."

"I had *every* right. Two Wolves is *my* responsibility." Ansley turned and mounted up, heading out of the fort.

Outside fort grounds, Captain Tower saw Two Wolves riding hard toward him. "What's wrong?" he called out.

Two Wolves slowed his horse for only a moment. "Chivington has already gone to Sand Creek."

He said nothing more before charging away, his long black hair flying in the wind and mud and snow spewing from under *Itatane's* hooves.

Captain Tower stood there dumbfounded as Major Ansley rode up beside him. He looked up at Ansley. "What does Two Wolves think he's going to do?"

Ansley dismounted, removing his hat and feeling too warm despite the cold weather. "Just be with them, I guess. Just be with them. God knows what he's going to find, Captain. Chivington has a full night and day's start on us. Two Wolves will never catch Black Kettle in time to warn him."

Tower turned away. "Damn! This trip has all been for nothing."

Ansley rubbed at his eyes. "We tried, Captain. We tried."

"What do you think Two Wolves will do if he goes there and finds a massacre? You know what Chivington is capable of."

"I don't know what he will do, Captain. The mood he's in right now, I just don't know." Ansley watched Two Wolves and his horse disappear over the horizon.

Chapter Twenty-Two

Claire awoke to pain. "Two Wolves," she muttered. Where was he? How many times had he been there for her when she was hurt? That was how they'd met, how she'd fallen in love with him. He'd saved her life, doctored her himself, prayed over her, kept her warm, protected her. How she needed him now.

"Claire?"

She recognized Bertie's voice.

"Bertie." Claire opened her eyes to see the hefty woman hovering over her. She felt a cool cloth to the side of her face. "Where...am I?"

"You're right here in your own bed, dear. I'm going to stay with you. A doctor who lives in the settlement now, Doctor Harvey Lane, he took the bullet from your arm and stitched up the awful wound in your thigh. What one of those men did to you with his spur is just unforgiveable. We poured whiskey into the wound and washed it out good several times before the doctor finally stitched it up. It looks awfully red, but it's not swollen, and we're hoping there will be no infection. God knows the kind of filth spurs pick up in horse stalls and such."

"My head..."

"Not much to be done about that, love, except to let it heal. You took quite a whop on your forehead from a big old can of beans. You have a knot on your head, and it's all purple, but now that you're awake and you recognize me, it's a big relief. A good sign there's no real damage done."

"Two Wolves. I need Two Wolves. He knows how to take care of me."

"Of course, he does, but he's still gone with the major, dear. Remember? If he could, he'd be right here taking care of you instead of me."

Claire tried to think straight. She remembered shooting a man... She moaned when she also remembered the sound of Hubert's shotgun, as well as the awful pain in her thigh."

"They didn't... touch me bad... did they, Bertie?"

"No, sweetheart, they didn't get that far. Hubert and Klas went charging in before they could even run out of the store. The way I hear it, you killed the older man yourself, and Hubert shot the other two. They're all dead now, Claire. You don't have to worry about them coming after you. But from now on, you shouldn't ever work in that store alone. All these new people coming here to settle, you just can't be sure who's good and who's bad."

"I want Two Wolves." Claire couldn't fight the uncontrollable need to cry. "I need him."

"You have plenty of friends here who care about you and who will help, love," Bertie told her. "Two Wolves needs to be out doing what he's doing. He'll be back sooner than you think."

"Captain Tower. He's a good man. He should be my doctor. I don't want a strange man treating me."

"Captain Tower is with Two Wolves and the major. This doctor seems like a good man, Claire. He has already delivered two babies and fixed a young boy's broken arm. He's a widower, looks around fifty years old. He's very polite and caring—lost a son to the war and a wife to pneumonia and said he just left home back in Virginia because he couldn't live with the memories there."

Claire moved her right arm and cried out. "My arm!"

"The bullet went right through. It will be sore, but it's just a flesh wound," Bertie explained.

"The baby?"

"The baby is fine. He's still kicking and squirming. I felt your tummy myself a few times to be sure. Sweetheart, that child is definitely his father's son—strong and full of energy and ready to run off and jump on a horse and ride with the wind. I can't believe I feel that much movement when you're no more than three or four months along and still hardly showing. That's a good sign."

Claire watched as Bertie rose with a slight grunt.

"I've heated some broth," she said. "Now that you're awake you should eat something. I'll bring you a bowl with a piece of bread."

"Thank you. What would I do without you?"

Bertie stopped at the doorway. "Honey, I don't mind at all. This just helps me keep from worrying about Harry. What I do mind is the fact that those men hurt you like that. It's just a shame. I can just imagine what would have happened if Two Wolves had walked in on them hurting you like that." She shook her head. "They would have needed a shovel to pick up all the pieces."

Claire couldn't help smiling at the thought. Oh, yes, the damage her husband could do to any man who harmed those he loved was chilling. He was a true warrior. The men who'd attacked her were lucky they'd died instantly, and not at the hands of Two Wolves.

She moved a little. Everything hurt. She decided to lie still. The baby was too important. She didn't want to do anything to bring pain and stress that might cause her to lose her son. And it *was* a son. She was certain of it. She had to do everything possible to keep this baby. It meant the world to Two Wolves, and it was the one thing that would make him come home as soon as he could, even if he were wounded.

She lay listening to the ticking of the clock on the wall, watched its pendulum swing back and forth, each movement representing another second Two Wolves was gone. She knew he was good at what he did, knew his skills, knew he'd done this, many times. She chastised herself for worrying so much, but Two Wolves had been her whole life since her wagon train was attacked last summer, all her drivers killed. She remembered running...Running...She'd lost her shoes, run through the foothills in the dark of night.

And then he grabbed her. She'd been so terrified at first. She could smile now at his words when he pushed her to the ground and lay on top of her to protect her. *I will not hurt you,* he'd told her. He'd killed for her that night and rode off with her. And her life was never the same after that. Sometimes it almost seemed so much longer ago that it all happened. He'd killed for her more than once on their journey to safety, and when she suffered an arrow wound he'd brought her back from the brink of death.

Oh, how she longed to be in his arms now. Longed to hear his voice.

Bertie came into the bedroom carrying a tray. "Here you go, dear."

She set the tray aside and leaned down to help Claire into a sitting position. Claire groaned with pain, the worst of it in her left thigh. While Bertie propped some pillows behind her, she managed to lift the blankets with her left hand. She pulled up her nightgown to see heavy bandages on her leg.

"Bertie, how bad is it? Will I have an ugly scar?"

"I'm afraid you probably will, Claire, but don't you worry about it." Bertie sat on the edge of the bed and took hold of Claire's hand. "The point is, you're alive and healing." She squeezed her hand. "That's all Two Wolves will care about."

"I suppose." Claire wiped at a tear. "I just have a bad feeling about this trip. I get this sense of something being terribly wrong.

Bertie patted the back of her hand. "You've just suffered a terrible attack and you're still injured. You'll feel better as you heal, Claire, and it's possible your husband will be back by then and all will be fine."

"I hope you're right." It struck her then. "My God, I killed a man!"

Bertie scowled and rose. "He deserved it. You did the right thing, Claire Matthews. Two Wolves would be proud of you. He would call you a true warrior for fighting back the way you did.

Claire couldn't help smiling again in spite of her tears. The mention of Two Wolves' warrior pride always made her smile. "Yes, I think he would, wouldn't he?"

"You bet."

Claire touched her belly and gently rubbed it. It was Two Wolves' life she felt there, and she felt warm at the thought of what he'd done to plant his seed inside of her. *God protect him*, she prayed inwardly. She hated the fact that somewhere out there John Chivington was hunting Indians

And Two Wolves was hunting John Chivington.

Chapter Twenty-Three

Two Wolves moved carefully among boulders and thick brush, using his spyglass to see what was happening below. When he first spotted Black Kettle's camp at Sand Creek he held back, realizing that not only had Chivington already been there but that he was *still* there, with all seven hundred or so troops. Fury moved through his blood like hot coals, making it difficult not to charge into the troops and kill at least two or three before their bullets would most certainly cut him down. He had to think about Claire and the baby. Had to think about his promises.

He raised the spyglass again, hoping against hope the carnage wasn't as bad as he'd thought, but there it was. Burned *tipis*, horses lying dead in a heap, and bodies everywhere. Bloody, mangled bodies. And not just warriors but old men, many, many women. And children...even babies.

He lowered the spyglass and sat down behind a huge boulder, unable to control his tears and literally shaking with anger. Chivington's men were lolling around as though it was just another day "on the job," seemingly unaffected by what had taken place yesterday. How they could just make camp amid all the carnage and blood was beyond imagination.

He heard shouting then and caught the words "move out tomorrow." Then he heard something about souvenirs. He wiped at his tears and took a deep breath, finding it next to impossible to control his rage. He got to his knees again and looked through the spyglass.

Sergeant Craig and his men! They were riding into Chivington's camp. Two Wolves's secret vow to kill Craig was renewed in his heart.

"I will run my knife from your privates to your throat," he muttered.

He saw movement to the right of Craig, and to his horror he could tell some of Chivington's men were walking among the dead Indians. Some leaned down, and Two Wolves squinted to decipher what was happening.

One soldier rose, holding something in his hand.

A scalp! Some of Chivington's men were scalping the dead Indians. More joined them, bending over various dead bodies. One man let out a war whoop and rose, also holding something up, but it was not a scalp. It was something else—a body part. He couldn't be sure what it was, but it looked like the body he'd ravaged was a woman's.

They were cutting up bodies! For souvenirs? For some kind of sick trophy? When he looked again a man was holding up a baby by the head. He whacked the body in half with his sword, then whacked it off at its neck. He tucked the head into a burlap bag.

Shouts, war whoops and whistles abounded as the men celebrated. Two Wolves watched Craig and his men ride into the carnage and begin taking their own scalps, as though they'd been a part of the "great battle."

"*Ehaveseva! Aye*, tobacco chewer, I will kill you, and you will know by whose hand you are dying," he seethed. He wished he could kill *all* seven hundred or so of them. In this moment it would not bother him in the least to put every man down there to death. "All of you are *utatu!* Horse shit!"

Was his cousin *Skiomah* down there? Was she among the women being ravaged by the soldiers now? Was the baby's head that of her own little son? Maybe she had escaped and was now in need of his help and protection. Maybe she and her baby lay frozen somewhere out on the plains.

He bent over, holding his stomach. Never in his life had he hated anyone as much as he now hated John Chivington and Sergeant Craig and every other man down there. How could he go back to Claire now? Somewhere out there were those who'd fled this devastation, freezing, starving. Surely when word got out about this, the entire Cheyenne Nation would rise up in retaliation. This had all been so unnecessary. Chivington and his men had not "made war." They had simply pillaged and murdered innocent Cheyenne. He had no doubt these men would go back to Denver and boast about their "victory in battle." They would exaggerate the number of Cheyenne and lie about how all this had started, say they'd been attacked.

Claire. He had to think about Claire. That was the one and only thing that kept him from committing suicide by heading into that den of murderers and killing as many as possible.

He rose then and led *Itatane* into heavier cover. He tied the horse to a small tree and unloaded his gear. It was obvious Chivington would camp here one more night. When they left tomorrow, he would follow. He would stay hidden and he would wait... wait for the chance to kill Sergeant Millard Craig. That was one promise he intended to keep. He shivered into his wolf-skin jacket, realizing he could build no fire tonight for warmth. The soldiers below would see it. How nice it would be now if he could crawl under the quilts with Claire in their cozy cabin. How nice it would be if this had never happened. His quest for peace when coming along on this venture would never be realized now. Every Cheyenne left in Southern Colorado, both those for peace and those for war, would be on the warpath now. There would be no stopping it, and Two Wolves himself burned with the same desire.

"Ne-tsehese-nestse-he?"

Two Wolves paused, all senses alert. A voice had come from nearby, asking if he spoke Cheyenne. He slowly set his horse blanket and knapsack on the ground but did not turn around

"I *am* Cheyenne," he answered softly in his native tongue. "I am a scout, but not for the murderers below. I am friend to a kind man who only wants to help, as do I. I am not your enemy."

He thought about Major Ansley—what a good man he was—how he'd run out on him. What was Ansley thinking? He knew instinctively he would not and could not return right away to Fort Collins. He had to go on from here. He had to help however he could.

"Who are you?"

He heard a rustling sound a few yards behind him.

"Turn around," the voice told him.

Two Wolves turned to see a young Cheyenne man, perhaps only seventeen or eighteen years old, holding a sturdy piece of wood as though he meant to use it as a club if need be.

"I am *Nisima*. What are you called?"

Two Wolves recognized the name as meaning Young Brother. "I am called Two Wolves. I came here as quickly as I could when I heard Chivington was on his way to Sand Creek, but I am too late to warn Black Kettle. Is he alive?"

Nisima shook his head. "I am not sure." The young man looked Two Wolves over. "If you are an Army scout, how can I trust you?"

"I do not scout for volunteers like Chivington and his men. I scout for a man called Major Ansley, and he was coming here to help Black Kettle escape to the east, but we learned at Fort Lyon that Chivington was already well on his way here. I have seen what he and his men did. I am full of hate and vengeance, as you surely are." He saw the fear and sorrow in the young man's eyes.

"They killed my mother and a young sister and brother," *Nisima* answered. "They shot my mother in the back and ran a sword through my little sister. She was only four summers. They rode down on my brother and shot him in the back of the head. He was seven summers. They also killed my father. It is bad what they have done." He frowned. "Why are you not with the Army troops?"

"It is as I told you. I left my Company behind and rode hard to get here because of Chivington. Now that my commander knows Chivington went ahead of him and knows he would likely ravage Black Kettle's camp, it is not likely he will come here at all. He was supposed to escort Black Kettle and those with him to safety. It is too late for that now." He looked around, studying the trees behind *Nisima*. "Are you the only survivor?"

The young man shook his head. "No. I saw a few others escape. Most of them headed south. I am the only one who came this way and made it through the soldiers' lines." He closed his eyes. "All day I heard the screams, women begging, babies bawling, children crying. This was not a true battle between soldier and warrior. I felt my heart being torn from my body, but there was nothing I could do. Most of those here had few weapons, and I had none. The soldiers surprised us early in the morning, before the sun rose. No one expected it. Warriors lay naked beside their wives, and women and children slept. We were a peaceful camp. It is wrong what those men have done!"

He stepped a little closer to Two Wolves. "I wish to go down there when the soldiers leave and see if I can find other relatives. Perhaps I can bury some of them."

Two Wolves nodded. "The soldiers will likely leave tomorrow. I intend to follow them to see if I can give warning to others they might be hunting. And there is one man among them I promised would one day die at my hands. I am going to watch him, and when I get the chance I will cut him open like a fresh kill."

Nisima lowered the club. "Will you help me find others who escaped?"

"*Aye*, I will help you. I know all of this land well. I think I know where some might have gone—probably south to the Arkansas River, and some east into Kansas Territory if they are able. They all had to find other camps if they are to survive, and that is where many of the Cheyenne still are camped for the winter."

"My people will make war now, as often and as vicious as never before. You are an Army scout, but after what you have seen, perhaps you will join us."

Two Wolves frowned. "I have much to think about, but I will not betray you."

"Tomorrow we will look for those we love and then be on our way," Young Brother told him. "If there is to be war, I want to be part of it."

Two Wolves felt like a traitor to Claire but was unable to stop a warrior's need deep inside to seek revenge for the carnage below.

"As do I," he answered. "Tomorrow we will seek the bodies you wish to find, and then we will seek out those who escaped and join up with them. We will help them find others and take shelter. For now, I will tear the crossed arrows from my shirt and travel with the Cheyenne. I still hope for peace, Young Brother, but after what I have seen, I do not think it is possible."

Nisima held up a fist, and Two Wolves put his own fist in the air. Never had he felt more "Indian" than at that moment.

"I will ride with those who seek revenge for Sand Creek!"

Chapter Twenty-Four

HEADQUARTERS DISTRICT OF COLORADO,
In the Field, Cheyenne Country, South Bend, Big Sandy, Nov. 29.
GENTLEMEN:

In the last ten days my command has marched three hundred miles–one hundred of which the snow was two feet deep. After a march of forty miles last night I at daylight this morning attacked a Cheyenne village of one hundred and thirty lodges, from nine hundred to a thousand warriors strong. We killed chiefs Black Kettle, White Antelope and Little Robe, and between four and five hundred other Indians; captured between four and five hundred ponies and mules. Our loss is nine killed and thirty-eight wounded. All did nobly. I think I will catch some more of them about eighty miles on the Smoky Hill. We found a white man's scalp not more than three days old in a lodge.

J. M. CHIVINGTON,
Col. Commanding District of Colorado
And first Indian Expedition.

(Chivington's greatly exaggerated wire to Fort Leavenworth after the Sand Creek Massacre–taken from *The Fighting Cheyennes*, by George

Bird Grinnell, 1915, Charles Scribner's Sons. Reissued by the University of Oklahoma Press, 1955)

From the Author: Along with the many lies in the above report, it is not true that Black Kettle was killed at Sand Creek. He died four years later in a surprise attack on yet another peaceful camp on the Washita River, this one led by George Armstrong Custer.

Chapter Twenty-Five

Early December, 1864...

Claire finished stringing popcorn for the small Christmas tree Klas had cut for her. It still hurt to walk, but the ugly cut on her thigh was healing well, and she thanked God she'd suffered no infection. What she hated most was having an ugly scar. Only Peter would ever see it, but still, it was another scar on top of the one in her side from the arrow wound she'd suffered when they first met. The wound Peter had treated himself.

Her headaches were gone, and now she never worked in her store without Klas or Hubert being there with her. Her recovery was hastened when several women from the growing settlement around Fort Collins visited her with gifts and food, assuring her of their friendship and offering invites to their homes for Christmas if her husband didn't make it back by then.

The thought brought an ache to her heart. This would have been their first Christmas together, but Peter still wasn't back. She'd made so many plans, including making a big dinner for Klas and Hubert and Major Ansley. As a gift for Peter, she'd ordered very tiny bells that she intended to sew into a long piece of narrow red satin ribbon, which he could wind into his hair. He often tied feathers, or silver and leather hair pieces into his waist-length hair, which he always kept clean. She shivered at the thought of how his hair softly caressed her skin when he was making love to her.

She thought she heard the clatter of a wagon just outside the cabin, and just as she set the popcorn aside there came a knock at the door.

"Mrs. Stewart, Major Ansley and his troops are back."

It was Klas. Claire gasped with excitement as she rose and limped to the door to open it. "Is Peter with them?"

Klas removed a wool cap. "I don't know. I did not see them myself. I heard it from the blacksmith across the street. He's just returned from shoeing some horses at the fort and said the soldiers were riding in when he left."

"Hitch a wagon, Klas. I want to go there right away."

The big Swede nodded. "I knew that you would. I already have a wagon ready."

"Oh, thank you!" Claire grabbed her long woolen coat from a hook nearby and pulled it on. "Hurry, Klas."

"You do not have a hat. It is very cold, Mrs. Stewart."

"Oh, wait!" Claire hurried to the bedroom and grabbed a wool scarf. She wrapped it around her head and neck, glad she already had shoes on. She didn't want to waste one minute. Peter was back! She limped back to the door and outside, buttoning her coat along the way. Klas helped up into the wagon seat and snapped the reins to one of the big freighting horses Claire still owned. He headed through mud and snow toward the fort. Claire's heart pounded with excitement, but also with worry. Normally Peter would have come to her first before riding on into the fort. But then this had been a big mission, and maybe he had reason to go to the fort first.

Even more doubt began making its way into her heart when she realized the soldiers were back much too soon. Their original mission had been to accompany Black Kettle and his camp north, which would have taken a good two or three more weeks, maybe longer. Why were they already back?

"Klas, I'm worried."

"Ah, but we will know soon, ya? The important thing is that your husband is home."

"Yes." Claire said nothing more as she shivered against the cold air and buttoned her coat even higher. It was only ten minutes to the fort, but the ride seemed to take forever. Finally, Klas drove the wagon into the parade grounds, which were filled with horses and men and shouts.

Soldiers were dismounting and unloading gear. Some of them looked at her and nodded, but she didn't like the look in their eyes, as though they carried bad news.

"Drive up to Major Ansley's headquarters," she told Klas.

Her chest tightened as the major's facility came into sight, and she still saw no sign of Peter. He'd promised he would come back as soon as possible. Where was he? Maybe he alone had taken on the job of accompanying Black Kettle north.

In the distance she could see Gertie hugging her husband. So, Harry had made it back just fine. She was glad. She spotted the major near his quarters then. He was handing his horse off to a private.

"Major Ansley!" she shouted before Klas even halted the horses.

Ansley hurried up to the wagon. "Claire Stewart, what are you doing out in this cold?"

"Peter! Where's Peter?"

Klas finally drew the wagon to a full stop and kicked the brake lever as Claire reached out to the major. Ansley helped her down.

"I heard you were back already," Claire told him before her feet even touched the ground. "What happened? I thought you'd be gone longer. You were going to accompany Black Kettle to relatives in the north." She looked around, beginning to panic. "Where is Peter?" she asked again.

Ansley glanced at Klas with a worried look, then scowled slightly as he took Claire's arm.

"Let's get you out of this cold." He hurried Claire up the steps to his quarters. "You come in, too, Klas," he ordered.

"Ya, I will come." The big Swede followed, removing his wool cap and shaking out his shoulder-length blond hair. They all went inside, where a private had built a fire in a pot-belly stove that nicely heated the major's quarters. Ansley made Claire sit down, then walked around his desk and sat down with a heavy sigh. The room hung too quiet for a moment as Ansley removed his hat and set it on the desk. He looked over at a private who'd followed him inside. "Get Mrs. Stewart some hot tea or something."

The private saluted. "Yes, Sir." He turned and left, and Major Ansley looked at Claire.

Claire read the pain in his eyes. "Something happened to my husband!" she said, panicking.

"Calm down," Ansley told her. "Nothing has happened to him that we know of yet, but the last I saw of Peter—or I should say, Two Wolves because he was very much Cheyenne in that moment—he was headed for Sand Creek."

Claire felt suddenly weak. "The last time you saw him? Why didn't you go with him?"

Ansley rubbed at tired eyes. "Claire, when we reached Fort Lyon, Chivington had already been there and left for Sand Creek. When Two Wolves heard that, he was extremely upset, and he just took off. He thought because Chivington had a good five hundred men with him, he could ride faster than they could, giving him time to warn Black Kettle. But I know for a fact he didn't make it in time. We can only hope he wasn't there when what Chivington calls war finally broke out. Two Wolves would have been in the middle of it, and considering it was Chivington, he would have fought right alongside Black Kettle and the others. To make matters worse, we ran into those Colorado volunteers and that Sergeant Craig you and Two Wolves told me about—the one who stopped you on your trip to Colorado Springs. They were headed for Sand Creek, too. Craig and Two Wolves had an altercation before Two Wolves took off, and Craig's bunch rode in the same direction, wanting to catch up with Chivington—for an excuse to kill Indians, I'm sure. Either way, Two Wolves was riding into trouble, plus trouble was hunting him from behind."

Claire struggled not to cry. Klas took a chair beside her and touched her arm. "This is Peter we are talking about, Mrs. Stewart. I have never seen him warlike, except that day the militia stopped us. I could tell from what he was like then that he is not a man to go up against. He is smart, and he loves you and will want to get home to you. I think he will do just that. You should not worry."

"I'm sorry, Claire," Ansley added. "I tried to stop him, but you know Peter. When he makes up his mind, no one will change it. I wish he'd come back with us. I waited a few extra days, but when he didn't show, I had to get my men back here. My peace mission was finished. In fact—"

He stopped speaking, as though he'd already gone too far. "Damn!" he swore as he rose from his chair. "Claire, when we got back to Fort Lyon there was already a telegram there from Fort Leavenworth, where they'd received Chivington's report. Chivington claimed he'd attacked Black Kettle's camp and met up with at least a thousand warriors and fought a brave battle. Says they killed Black Kettle and White Antelope and Little Robe."

Ansley turned to look out the window at troops still unloading gear and putting up horses.

"I know damn well from what Two Wolves told me about Black Kettle's camp that there is no way in hell there were a thousand warriors there. He told me there were mostly women and children. And knowing Chivington, he attacked early and without warning. That statement about his men behaving nobly is a damn lie. I'm worried about what Two Wolves found when he got there, worried about how it will affect him."

"Dear God," Claire said softly. She hung her head and wept. "I've lost him."

Ansley walked around his desk and knelt beside her chair. "I don't believe that, Claire. There is no way that man won't come back to you, but he's out there right now, figuring out where he truly belongs. What he likely found will affect him deeply. He just needs time to get over it. Come hell or high water, he'll come back for you and your child. Just give him some time. He's probably still hoping to talk the Cheyenne out of turning this mess into a full-fledged war. Once word gets out about this, they are going to be fighting mad. They won't take this lightly, and they won't be in any mood to talk peace. Two Wolves probably wants to do what he can to stop more bloodshed."

Claire shook her head. "He's an Army scout. The mood the Cheyenne are in, they'll want to kill him, too."

"I don't think so. Two Wolves is too good at what he does. He's *one* of them, and they know he's done a lot to help them. He'll be all right."

"And the militia will want to do more killing. You said Craig and his men were right behind my husband."

"And Two Wolves is a cunning man." Ansley rose. "I'm not worried about the Cheyenne *or* the soldiers. I'm more worried about the fact that Two Wolves dearly wants to kill Sergeant Craig. Before this is over, he'll find a way to do it. I just hope he's smart enough not to get caught. I love that young man like my own son. You know that."

Claire looked up at him. "It wasn't that long ago that he almost got himself hanged in Denver City. If he kills Sergeant Craig and it's found out, it could happen for real next time. That awful man deserves to die, but I'd rather it was some other way. And right now, I'm worried Peter has decided to re-join the Cheyenne and die a true warrior. After what happened at Sand Creek, he could be thinking that very thing. His Cheyenne blood would be just as angry as the rest of the Cheyenne must be."

"I've wondered the same thing," Ansley told her. "When we stopped at Fort Lyon and learned Chivington was on his way to Sand Creek, I could see Peter was all Two Wolves in that moment. There was no arguing with him and no stopping him. The look in his eyes even scared me." Ansley touched her shoulder. "But one thing I know is that *nothing* is as important to him as you and that baby."

Claire seemed to wilt. Klas caught her. He looked up at Ansley.

"She was attacked in her store a couple of weeks ago," he told the major. "A man cut her leg with his spur. She shot one of them, and Hubert shot the other two with his shotgun."

"My God!" Ansley knelt beside Claire again and grasped her arm. "The baby?"

Claire straightened, determined to believe her husband would come home and even more determined that when he did, she would be strong and well and still carrying his child.

"The baby is fine," she told Ansley, "and yes, I believe he'll do all he can to come back home."

Ansley grasped her hand and squeezed. "That's the spirit. I believe it, too. Peter James Matthews is a good and honorable man. He has some personal things to wrestle with, but you and that baby will win out above everything else. He'll be back, I'm sure of it. Just tell me you won't work in that store alone ever again. I'm so sorry about happened. Peter will be livid, and so sorry he wasn't here to defend you."

"It's probably better that he wasn't," Claire said weakly. "He might have ended up in a lot of trouble killing white men. And I'm okay. Klas and Hubert already made me promise not to work alone again."

"With all these new settlers coming in, there is no telling how many are good people and how many are just men running from the law back East," Ansley grumped. "And when he finds out what happened, Peter will definitely not leave again once he's home."

But he's out there somewhere surrounded by enemies. Claire clung to Ansley's hand as she rose. "I was hoping you were all on your way north with Black Kettle and his band, hoping Peter would be back here by Christmas. I guess that might not happen now." She met the major's gaze. "I'm sure you're very tired, Major. I'll let you get things organized here. Maybe you can come by later when things calm down. And you and Captain Tower are welcome to come over for Christmas dinner, whether Peter makes it back by then or not."

Ansley nodded. "Thank you. I'll be praying he *is* back by then. But I have to tell you that Captain Tower isn't back yet either. I sent him on with several men to check out what really happened at Sand Creek. And he's going to try to find Two Wolves."

Claire closed her eyes. "I hope Captain Tower is all right. He's a good man."

"Two Wolves will look out for him."

Claire thought how Peter had told her in so many words that if anything happened to him, she should consider the fact that Captain Tower cared about her. It was as though he was warning her that he might ride off and end up fighting for the Cheyenne and never come back. She put a hand to her belly. No. He wouldn't leave this child. He simply wouldn't.

Chapter Twenty-Six

"We must join up with the Cheyenne on the Arkansas," Young Brother told Two Wolves. He'd found a horse among those the soldiers hadn't stolen or shot and had tied a rope bridle to it. Now he had something to ride, and between him and Two Wolves, they'd found a few supplies in the remains of the devastated camp. They'd packed those onto two more horses, and now they traveled together, following Chivington and his men as they headed farther south.

"First, we should keep following Chivington," Two Wolves told Young Brother. "He is likely hunting more Cheyenne. We might be able to warn them, or even fight with them against the militia. Chivington has sent at least half of his men back, probably to Fort Lyon. We saw Major Anthony among them. With fewer men backing up Chivington, the Cheyenne might have a better chance of fighting and killing some of them."

Both men had looked for loved ones left at Sand Creek after Chivington left. Young Brother found his mother and sister, but not his brother or father. Two Wolves found his cousin, Little Robe, and her baby, both dead and mutilated.

Using poles they managed to salvage from what was left of the *tipis* at Sand Creek, they had constructed two scaffolds, putting Young Brother's mother and sister together on one, and Little Robe and her baby on the other. It sickened Two Wolves to have to pick up his cousin and the baby in pieces rather than in their full bodies. He'd sung a prayer song to *Maheo* to allow his relatives to walk as whole beings to the land of grass and buffalo in the Great Beyond.

Two Wolves and Young Brother then headed out to catch up with Chivington. They followed the man and his troops for the next three days. Two Wolves still had his spyglass and watched their every move. His heart pounded with a thirst to kill when, two days before, he'd spotted Sergeant Craig's men as they finally caught up to Chivington. Chivington's troops had loitered around Sand Creek long enough that Craig had managed to find them.

Now I have you in my sights, Two Wolves thought. Killing Craig would not be easy, but he vowed to do just that before heading home. He might never get another chance. Still, now there was a new problem. Yesterday Captain Tower and about twenty-five of the troops from Fort Collins also caught up with Chivington. Two Wolves realized that if Ansley had heard about Sand Creek, he surely had gone back to Fort Collins, figuring nothing more could be done. He must have sent Captain Tower on ahead to see for himself what had happened, and Tower had probably decided to catch up to Chivington to try to reason with the man.

His heart felt heavy realizing that Major Ansley and the rest of the men had likely reached Fort Collins by now. Claire would be upset that her husband hadn't returned with Ansley. He wished he could explain why he wasn't home yet—wished he understood it himself. What happened at Sand Creek wounded him deeply. He felt compelled to follow Chivington and witness whatever other atrocities the man had planned. People needed to know the truth.

His concern now was which way to go. This morning the troops had broken up. From what he could tell, Sergeant Craig and his men, as well as a few of Chivington's soldiers, had for some reason joined Captain Tower and the soldiers from Fort Collins. A good one hundred strong, they'd all headed northeast, most likely back to Fort Lyon. At the moment the dust they stirred was still visible.

"I think perhaps Captain Tower was unable to reason with Chivington," Two Wolves told Young Brother as he again watched with his spyglass. "And it is likely Chivington wanted nothing to do with Craig and his men, so he gave him orders to leave with Tower and ordered some of his own men to go along, probably for protection. I am sure that once they reach Fort Lyon, Craig and Tower will have two very different stories to tell." He turned away from the boulder hiding him and faced Young Brother. "At least Chivington will go on with fewer men."

"I cannot wait to see where any of the troops go, Two Wolves," Young Brother answered. "I wish to go to the Arkansas River, where I am sure those who escaped have gone. I will warn them Chivington might be coming."

"Good. Since Captain Tower is leaving with Sergeant Craig, I am responsible to follow and protect the troops from Fort Collins if possible, at least until they reach Fort Lyon."

"And you will follow because you want to kill the militia man you told me about."

Two Wolves nodded. "*Aye*. This is my only chance." He put a hand on Young Brother's shoulder. "I hope you find some of your relatives still alive, Young Brother. For now, I must follow Captain Tower and his men. If I find a way to kill Sergeant Craig, I will then come to the Arkansas and find you. I must do all I can to speak for peace. After Sand Creek, that might be impossible, but for now I cannot yet go home."

"Once I have found my relatives, I will ride with those who make war." Young Brother tossed his hair behind his shoulders, his eyes showing heat from a thirst to kill. "It might be dangerous for you to join us and try for peace," he added. "The warriors will not be in a mood to think about anything but revenge."

"I still have to try," Two Wolves answered. *For Claire's sake*, he thought. There had to be some kind of peace before he and Claire could truly be happy together—some kind of peace for the betterment of the mixed-blood children they would have. For the son Claire now carried. He couldn't go back to her yet. Not after what he'd seen. Not when the Cheyenne would now be itching to fight with more vengeance than ever... and not until Sergeant Millard Craig was dead, by his own hands.

"I go now," Young Brother told him, leaping onto the back of his horse. "I must find my relatives and Black Kettle."

Two Wolves rose and walked over to untie the pack horses. He thought how eager and full of hope Young Brother was. It made him sad, because he knew that in the end the Cheyenne could never win a war against whites. He led the pack horses to Young Brother. "Take both of them with you. Those survivors you find along the Arkansas will need these supplies. I will meet you in a few days."

Young Brother nodded. "Be careful, my brother. Right now, you are surrounded by enemies. Even some Cheyenne are your enemies."

Two Wolves nodded. "Tell those you meet up with that I am their friend and will be coming to them."

"*Aye.*" Young Brother reached out and grasped Two Wolves' wrist. "And if you get a chance to ride with warriors into battle, whose side will you be on?"

It was a question Two Wolves had wrestled with ever since finding the slaughter at Sand Creek.

"My heart lies in two worlds, Young Brother, but if that time comes, I will find it difficult not to join my Cheyenne brothers in battle."

Young Brother smiled wickedly. "*Aye!* I have heard of you—heard that you are a warrior to be feared, even though white blood runs in your veins. I would be proud to fight at your side." He turned and rode off.

Two Wolves watched him disappear into the deeper shadows of the foothills. He suddenly felt very alone, and very confused. He pushed together the graduated layers of the long spy glass and shoved it into his supplies, then glanced over at the Army saddle he'd left on the ground. For the next several days he would be only Cheyenne, and a blanket on his horse's back was all a Cheyenne warrior needed. He leapt onto *Itatane*, glancing in the direction in which Young Brother had ridden. He was already out of sight.

He turned then, heading out of the foothills to follow Captain Tower's troops... and Sergeant Millard Craig. *One thing I will do before I return home, Sergeant Craig, is sink my knife into your heart. I will find a way.*

Chapter Twenty-Seven

Captain Tower headed for Fort Lyon with mixed emotions. He'd seen what was left at Sand Creek. Some of his men had vomited at the sight. Vultures were circling overhead, some already feasting on the gutted bodies of women and children. When he'd met up with Colonel Chivington and his volunteers, the story Chivington told him did not match what he'd seen. Supposedly, Major Anthony had already gone back to Fort Lyon with prisoners and dead bodies for burial.

"There were plenty of dead bodies left behind," Tower told Chivington.

"No different from the dead bodies of coyotes or prairie dogs," Chivington answered.

"They were women and children!" the captain replied.

"The only way to end this scourge is to prevent more from being born, Captain Tower."

Tower could hardly believe his ears. He'd replied that the Cheyenne were not a "scourge," like a disease that had suddenly invaded Colorado. They had been there first. If anything, the white man was a scourge to the Cheyenne. He'd pleaded with Chivington to end the slaughter. It would only cause the Cheyenne to retaliate in full force.

"We've worked hard to keep what peace we have," he reminded Chivington.

"And you, Captain, have no place among my troops. I'll not tolerate any man who has sympathy for Indians! You've been to Sand Creek, and you've been here to talk to me, which you say were your orders from Major Ansley. Your job is done, so you should leave this camp.

I am sending Sergeant Craig and his volunteers with you, as well as a few of my troops. The Cheyenne will be on the warpath now, and you have only twenty men along. The few extra I am sending will give you a stronger force if you should be attacked. And once Craig and my men refresh their supplies at Fort Lyon, they have orders to head into the foothills and root out stray Cheyenne camps."

"That's *our* job farther north!"

"And the Federal troops will only herd them onto reservations or escort them north," Chivington argued. "I know about the wire your major received to escort Black Kettle and his band to safety. Thank God I reached Black Kettle's camp first and did what *should* have been done."

"Pure slaughter is what you did. You, Colonel Chivington, are a disgrace! Eventually people will learn the truth, and you will be kicked out of Colorado Territory."

Tower scowled now at the memory of their conversation.

"Bastard!" he grumbled.

He'd left only because Chivington was right about his duties there being finished. But it irked him to have to ride with Craig and his bunch. They wouldn't "root out" any Cheyenne they found. They would burn their camps and murder every one of them. Smaller camps of families trying to escape to the north would be slaughtered.

Now he was stuck accompanying Sergeant Craig back to Fort Lyon. Still, his bigger concern was finding Peter Matthews. He did not want to go back to Fort Collins without him.

"Damn it, Peter, where in hell are you? You have pregnant wife waiting for you." He scanned the foothills to his left, the open plains ahead and to the right and behind them. That was when he spotted them, just small dots on the southwest horizon, but several riders coming, nonetheless.

He put up his hand. "Halt!"

The order echoed down the ranks, including Craig and his men.

Sergeant Craig charged up beside Tower. "What the hell is going on?"

Tower nodded toward the horizon. "I think we are about to be attacked."

Craig squinted to see. "Shit, I think you're right. They must have ridden a few miles west of Chivington. I'll bet the Colonel doesn't even know they headed right past his camp." He grinned. "No matter. I sure as hell ain't gonna' run from the chance to kill Cheyenne! Let's dismount and dig some trenches. Quick!"

"We have to make sure they are on the war path," Tower told him. "We might be able to talk to them."

"After Sand Creek? Are you crazy?"

"We have a scout out there who might have gotten those Cheyenne together and talked them into giving themselves up. If he saw our troops, he might be bringing them to us. He knows me and these men."

"You mean that sonofabitch Two Wolves?"

Captain Tower fought an urge to knock the slovenly Craig from his horse. "That's exactly who I mean."

"And you're a fool! How do you think Two Wolves felt after what he found at Sand Creek? He ain't gonna' be no Army scout no more, Captain. He's gonna' be *Cheyenne*. And if he's comin' with a bunch of warriors, he's a *part* of them, and he's aimin' to kill some soldiers just like *they* are!"

"Not me and *my* men, you idiot! If he's with those warriors, you can save a lot of lives by letting me talk to Two Wolves first."

"*Piss* on Two Wolves! I *hope* he's with them! This is my chance to kill him!"

Tower's horse whinnied and shuffled, as though realizing trouble was coming. "Or his chance to kill *you*," he answered.

Craig spit tobacco near Tower's horse. "Well, we'll just see about that, won't we? Meantime, unless you want to run like a yellow rabbit, you'd better have your men make ready to fight."

"I don't need you to tell me what to do, Sergeant. You take care of your own men. I'll take care of *mine*."

For one brief moment Tower considered riding hard in retreat, but the army had learned early on that in Indian country Army horses loaded down with saddles and heavy gear couldn't outrun the swifter Indian ponies that carried hardly more than one man on their backs. And at the moment there was absolutely nowhere for the soldiers to run for cover.

There was nothing but flat land everywhere but the western foothills, and that was exactly where the on-coming Indians had ridden from. There was no hope of retreating in that direction.

Tower turned and rode back to his men, ordering two of them to gather the horses and keep them together in the center while the rest of the men took small spades from their gear and began frantically digging holes and trenches in a wide circular formation. Indians nearly always attacked by circling the enemy. The only hope of not being attacked from behind was to form a circle.

Tower raised his spyglass, and his heart sank a little. He figured there were a good fifty warriors coming. His men combined with Craig's came to eighty. But when facing angry, warring Cheyenne, a *hundred* against forty wouldn't be enough. The Cheyenne were clever, seasoned, brave, tough and incredibly able fighters.

He turned his horse and rode in front of the men, shouting orders. "No one fires a shot until I say so!" *Damn it, Two Wolves, where are you when we need you?*

Chapter Twenty-Eight

In minutes wild war whoops filled the air. The approaching Cheyenne warriors were most certainly not wanting to talk peace.

"Damn Chivington!" Captain Tower cursed. This was his fault. If not for Sand Creek, peace had still been possible. Tower was always amazed over how the Cheyenne communicated, but he suspected that by now practically every separate band in all of Colorado knew about the massacre. Cheyenne warriors would be enraged, as he was certain those coming at them now were.

He dismounted and started digging his own trench. There was no time to make it deep enough, but he could at least crouch into it. He decided Craig's men were on their own. When he quickly looked around he saw them forming their own circle and frantically digging.

Once the warriors were in range, Tower shouted, "Fire!"

Rifles roared in unison. A few warriors fell, but in minutes the rest of the thundering Indian ponies were upon them, dust making it difficult to even see. The singing of arrows, the war cries, rifle fire, stinging dust, all were ways Cheyenne warriors had of creating confusion and bedlam. The soldier beside Tower began to panic and suddenly jumped up and ran.

"Private Anderson, get back here!" Tower shouted.

Someone cried out, and Tower kept firing, hitting several of the warriors. When the dust cleared for a moment, Tower saw a warrior driving a hatchet into Private Anderson's chest, over and over. Tower aimed and fired, killing the private's attacker, but it was obviously too late to save the young man's life.

The battle scene quickly became bloody and wild and chaotic. Tower had no idea how much time had passed when he shouted orders for those soldiers still unhurt to gather closer together. He ran out to help a wounded soldier who was trying to crawl back to safety. He knelt to grab hold of the man, then heard a wicked war cry from behind. He turned to see a painted Cheyenne warrior, hatchet raised, charging toward him. Tower had no time to reach for his rifle.

Suddenly a second warrior rode up behind Tower's attacker. The second warrior swung a war club, slamming it hard against the other Indian's skull, smashing in the side of his head and sending him sprawling beside the wounded soldier. The dust cleared, and Tower saw the second warrior. It was Two Wolves!

"Take him to the others!" Two Wolves shouted to Tower. "I will try to stop this!"

He turned his horse and began riding in a circle around the other warriors, shouting in their own tongue. To Tower's relief, they began backing off.

"Hold your fire!" Tower shouted to his men. "It's Two Wolves!"

Already Two Wolves and those he rode with were headed for Craig's men, who did not obey the captain's orders to stop firing. The warriors rode right into them, turning their full attention to Craig and his men while leaving Captain Tower and those with him alone.

They savagely landed arrows and lances and knives and hatchets into a good share of Craig's troops, while others of the volunteers either ran or hurried over to Tower's men, hoping to find help and protection. But more warriors followed, pulling only Craig's men from Tower's soldiers and killing them, some shot, some knifed or lanced.

Sergeant Craig aimed his handgun at Two Wolves, but he'd run out of bullets. Craig started to run, but Two Wolves charged into him, his horse knocking the man to the ground not far from where Tower stood. Two Wolves immediately dismounted and ran up to Craig just as the man was trying to get up. Two Wolves jerked him up from behind and wrapped a powerful arm around Craig's neck.

"I told you that you would one day feel my knife," Two Wolves growled.

Craig's eyes were wide with terror. "You stinking bastard!" he roared at Two Wolves.

"*You* are the one who stinks," Two Wolves answered. He kept his strong arm locked under Craig's chin and forced his head back, then sliced his hunting knife across the man's throat, then proceeded to ram the knife into his heart. He yanked it out and tossed Craig to the ground.

Craig lay there gurgling in his own blood.

"Now my wife's honor is avenged," Two Wolves told him. "And those who would kill innocent Cheyenne women and children are dead!"

He rose, raising his muscular arms into the air and letting out a piercing war whoop. He faced Tower then, and the captain was struck by what a grand specimen of man he was

"Tell Major Ansley that I tried to stop them, but the Cheyenne are furious over Sand Creek," Two Wolves shouted to Tower. "I cannot stop Cheyenne Dog Soldiers! For now, they will let you go, so go. Quickly! Our revenge is only for Sergeant Craig and his men."

He whirled and leapt onto *Itatane*, letting out another war whoop as the rest of the warriors rode away.

"Two Wolves!" Captain Tower shouted. "Where are you going? What about your *wife?*"

Their gazes held as Two Wolves rode closer. "Watch over her," he told Tower. "And tell her I will come home soon."

"But where are you going?"

"Probably to hell!" Two Wolves turned and rode out after the rest of the warriors.

Tower watched after them, stunned. Two Wolves had just saved his life, yet he'd deliberately killed Sergeant Craig as though killing a rabbit. He had no idea how to report this. Worse, what to tell Claire! As an Army scout, Two Wolves could be hanged for being part of an Indian attack on U. S. soldiers, as well as for deliberately murdering a Colorado volunteer. Right now, Peter Matthews was all Cheyenne, and Tower wasn't sure if he would ever be anything else.

Chapter Twenty-Nine

Mid-December 1864...

Claire helped Gertie fold some clothes. Her visits to the Becker house were always enjoyable and kept her from feeling so lonely. She'd been coming to the fort more and more often just to keep herself occupied.

"I'll have to go soon, Gertie. I told Klas to pick me up with the wagon at five, and it's nearly that late now. Besides, I've let Hubert and Klas run the store more than they should have to. I'd better stay home a little more–go over inventory and such. And when Peter comes back, it's more likely he'll stop at the store or the cabin before reporting in. I just hope he can make it by Christmas."

"Whatever is keeping him, it's for good reason, I'm sure," Gertie told her.

Just then Sergeant Becker came inside. "Claire, Captain Tower and his men are back."

Claire set down the towel she'd been folding and hurriedly took her coat from a hook on the wall. "Is Peter with him?"

The look in Harry's eyes changed from excitement to sadness. "No, Ma'am. I'm sorry. But I'm sure Captain Tower will know something. I can escort you over to Major Ansley's quarters."

Claire turned a helpless look on Gertie. "Where could he be?" she asked, as though Gertie would have the answer.

"I don't know, child. Go and talk to Captain Tower."

Claire fought tears of disappointment as she tied on a woolen hat. She finished buttoning her coat and walked out with Sergeant Becker.

She didn't notice that before turning to take her arm, Becker looked at his wife and shook his head.

Gertie turned away. "Poor child," she muttered.

Harry could hardly keep up the pace as Claire practically ran to Ansley's quarters. She saw men bandaged up, blood showing through the bandages. One horse drew a travois behind it. Claire's heart froze when she realized there was a body on the sled, completely covered. The way a dead man would be covered. She stopped and stared, noticing another man on a different travois. He was alive. Still, he looked badly wounded.

"Harry!" she exclaimed. "They've been in some kind of fight! Who is that dead man?"

"Don't you be worrying about that. It's not Two Wolves, if that's what you're thinking."

"Oh, my God!"

Claire hurried even faster then, walking into Major Ansley's quarters with no announcement. Standing in the room with the major was Captain Tower, and when he met her eyes, then closed his and turned away, Claire realized something was terribly wrong.

"Captain, where is Peter?" she asked right away.

"Sit down and let him explain things, Claire," Ansley told her. "I need a quick report, after which Captain Tower will have to tend to those wounded men out there."

Shaking, Claire took a seat across from Ansley's desk. Captain Tower sat down wearily beside her, and Sergeant Becker stood across the room.

"What the hell happened?" Ansley asked Captain Tower. "I didn't send you on to Chivington's camp to have you come back with dead and wounded men."

Captain Tower sighed deeply. "The Cheyenne are on a rampage, Major, and it's because of Sand Creek. You already know Chivington attacked Black Kettle's camp. Maybe you've already heard glowing reports about it." He glanced at Claire, then turned back to Ansley. "Major, I first went to the camp, like you asked me to do, to check things out." He paused, leaning forward and resting his elbows on his knees. "What I found isn't for a woman's ears to hear."

"I'm no wilting flower, Captain," Claire insisted. She sat up straighter and faced him, pretending she could handle whatever Tower had to say. "You said the Cheyenne are on the warpath now because of Sand Creek. What did you find?"

The captain looked from Claire to Ansley again. "We both know that Black Kettle was trying hard to keep the peace, and that he was camped at Sand Creek only because Major Anthony would not allow him and his people to settle closer to Fort Lyon for protection. He had every right to stay where he was and winter it out there. But Chivington ended all that. And he ended our chances for peace with the Cheyenne. There couldn't have been more than two hundred or so Indians there, but Chivington had upwards of seven hundred men along. And in his own words he told me it was a surprise attack. He meant to make sure those Cheyenne had no chance to fight back." He rubbed at tired eyes and ran a hand through his hair.

"And?" Ansley asked.

Captain Tower paused yet again. "I saw women and children sprawled everywhere, their –" He sighed deeply again and looked at Claire. "Are you sure you're all right? You're carrying. I don't want you getting upset."

"The only thing that upsets me is not knowing what's going on, Captain."

Tower looked at Ansley again. "A lot of the women had been stripped naked, their breasts cut off, their insides ripped out. I saw babies with smashed heads and little children all shot up. Some of them got away by running up the creek to where the banks were higher, but according to Chivington, his men found a lot of those, too. They shot them down where they sat huddled together.

Claire gasped and put a hand to her mouth. "Dear God!"

Tower kept his eyes on Ansley. "It was no battle, Sir, in spite of how Chivington describes it and brags about it. It was slaughter. I asked him about the women and children, and he said that nits make lice, and the only way to end what he called a scourge of Cheyenne, was to end their ability to find food, to survive winters, and end what helps their people grow in numbers. That would be the women who have the babies... and the babies he killed so they couldn't grow into warriors."

Ansley closed his eyes and shook his head. "That son-of-a-bitch," he grumbled.

Claire looked at Ansley. "Major, you said Peter ran off to chase after Chivington, that he wanted to warn Black Kettle."

"He must have been too late," Captain Tower told her before Ansley could answer. "And I'm sure he saw the slaughter. I think it affected him deeply."

"You *think* it did? Does that mean you saw him? Talked to him? Where is my husband, Captain?"

Tower clenched his fists, hating the fact that he had to tell Claire what he knew. He looked her over, thinking how beautiful and frail she looked, so small and alone. He wanted to hold her, but she belonged to Two Wolves. Still, he'd been ordered to look after her. And by their other short conversations, he was astounded to think that Two Wolves was practically telling him to take care of Claire Matthews forever if he didn't make it back.

"I truly don't know, Claire, but I saw him. In fact, he saved my life."

"Where and when?" Ansley demanded.

Tower turned his attention back to Ansley. "Chivington has set off a storm, Major. We will all regret what he did at Sand Creek. You know how word travels through the Cheyenne Nation. A lot of them are already on the warpath. We were attacked by about fifty warriors on our way back to Fort Lyon. Sergeant Craig and his bunch of volunteers were with us, but they didn't hunker down into trenches like most of my men did. It was a rough battle, to say the least. I have five men badly wounded and one dead." He turned to Claire. "Peter was with the warriors."

Claire's eyes widened. "No! He wouldn't attack soldiers."

"I said he was with them, painted up and letting out war whoops, the whole thing, but most of the warriors went for Craig and his men. Those who attacked us suddenly backed off because Peter risked his life asking them to do so. It's not easy going up against Cheyenne Dog Soldiers. We're lucky Peter was able to rein them in. I don't think he attacked any of our troops himself. I ran to pull in a soldier who'd been badly wounded. While I knelt over him, one of the warriors came at me with a hatchet. The next thing I knew, a second man smashed his skull with a war club before the first one could kill me. It was Two Wolves who wielded the war club. He stayed close and told me to gather the rest of the men and he would put a stop to the attack, but he didn't try to stop them from slaughtering Craig and his men. In fact —" He hesitated.

"My husband killed Sergeant Craig, didn't he?" Claire said calmly.

Tower closed his eyes and shook his head. "Yes, and he was pretty vicious about it. I heard him say that he'd promised Craig would feel his knife. Let's just say he kept his promise."

Claire covered her face. "God help him," she said softly.

Ansley rose from his chair. "Damn," he muttered. "Peter rode off with the other warriors, didn't he?"

"Yes, Sir," Tower answered. "I reminded him he has a pregnant wife waiting for him. He told me to look after her until he gets home." He glanced at Claire. "He does plan to come back. I'm sure of it. But when I asked him where he was going, his answer was 'probably to hell.' I'm not sure what he meant by that. I think he needs come kind of revenge of his own. He probably found his cousin at Sand Creek, the woman he said in the beginning he was going to try to find. She had a small son. From what we found there, it's likely she was one of those killed."

Claire rubbed her forehead. "Oh, Peter. Peter."

"We can only hope for the best," Ansley spoke up. "I think I know that man well enough that he'll stay with those warriors and keep trying to talk them out of making more war. He knows war will only make things worse."

"I'm just not sure he can talk them into any kind of peace," Tower answered. "From all I've seen and heard since I've been out here, I don't think the Cheyenne have ever committed the kind of slaughter Chivington and his men committed. Some of my men vomited at the sight. The worst most Cheyenne do to white children is take them captive. They seldom kill children outright. They don't consider that being brave. I've seen women killed, but not gutted like those Cheyenne women were. And most of the time women, too, are taken captive."

"I have a suspicion that Peter stayed with those warriors to make sure they understood he was one of them," Ansley said. "They won't listen at all if they think he's more white than Cheyenne and is just spying for our sake. He has to *be* one of them to have any chance of getting through to them."

"And if they believe differently, they could kill him," Tower put in. "And if he rides with them against Chivington or regular soldiers, he could also be killed. Either way, the real problem is the fact that a lot of those men out there watched him kill Sergeant Craig. He's an Army scout who's half Cheyenne and who deliberately killed a white man. That might be a big problem for him when he gets back."

"Craig would have willingly killed more women and babies," Claire spoke up. "He deserved to die. And so does Colonel Chivington!"

"Whether a man deserves to die or not, people don't forgive when an Indian kills a white man," Ansley answered.

"I'll stick up for him every way I can," Captain Tower told him. "He saved my life. You know how that feels. He saved yours once, too."

"But that time he was fully dressed and riding as an Army scout, not warring with Cheyenne Dog Soldiers."

"It doesn't matter. My men will all vouch for him. He's the one who called off the attack on us. It was Craig and his men they were really after. I have a feeling Two Wolves was watching us the whole time. He probably followed Chivington on his own after Sand Creek, then saw us and Craig's men catch up with him. When we left, he followed, because he had his eye on Craig."

"And now Craig is dead," Ansley said. "But Two Wolves didn't let it end there. He rode off with those warriors." He sat down again, taking a cigar from a desk drawer and lighting it.

"I'm sure it's what he thought was best," Tower answered. "He likely knows where a good share of the warriors will meet. He'll go there and try to talk them into peace. As far as Two Wolves being the one who killed Craig, if I tell those men out there not to let on about it, no one will know who did it. The man was simply killed in a battle with the Cheyenne. Names don't need to be tossed around."

Claire looked at Tower. He was sticking up for Two Wolves, but she knew that deep inside he was sticking up for *her*. He was trying to keep her calm.

"Thank you, Captain," she told him.

Tower looked at her, and Claire was surprised at what looked like love in his eyes. "How are you holding up?" Before she could answer, he turned to Sergeant Becker. "Can she stay the night here?" he asked. "Someone told me she was here visiting with your wife."

"Klas is coming for me with a wagon," Claire answered.

"Then Klas can also stay the night. You've heard some pretty upsetting things, Claire. You should rest and maybe eat some supper with Gertie and get some sleep before going back to the settlement. You have Hubert there to take care of things. Peter and I aren't the best of friends, but he did save my life and asked me to look out for you. I thought that was a strange request, but I intend to do what he asked, and I truly don't want him to come back to find you've lost that baby."

"I agree," Ansley added. He looked over at Sergeant Becker. "Take her back to your place, Harry. I, too, insist she stay the night with Gertie. Captain Tower and I need to go tend to the rest of the men." He looked at Tower. "What about Major Anthony? He was with Chivington. What happened to him?"

"By the time I reached Chivington, he'd sent Anthony and his men back to Fort Lyon with a few prisoners and a few of the dead–to prove they'd won the battle, I suppose, if you want to even call it a battle. They must have taken a different path returning to Fort Lyon because we didn't run into them. I'm sure he, too, will call Sand Creek a major victory. I'm hoping some of the men involved will eventually tell the truth. Out of almost seven hundred men, there had to be some who did not agree with that slaughter, maybe even held back. Something like what I saw can't help weighing on a man's conscience the rest of his life. It will weigh on mine, and I wasn't even a part of it. Some of those men will break, and when they do, the public will learn the truth, and Chivington will be driven out of Colorado. I sincerely hope that happens. Right now, I don't blame the Cheyenne for retaliating, but it's still our job to protect the settlers, so it's going to be a mess for a while." He looked at Claire again. "And I'm afraid your husband will be mixed up in all of it until he's done whatever it is he thinks he needs to do."

Claire couldn't help the tears that came then. "I don't want him to hang for killing Sergeant Craig. Craig was an awful man."

"He won't hang," Ansley replied. "Captain Tower and I will make sure of it. So will those men out there."

"We would have been killed to the last man if not for Two Wolves," Tower put in, "and they all know it. We were in the open with no cover. It's the Cheyenne's favorite way to fight. They circle you to keep you confused and raise a lot of dust and keep themselves moving targets, while we are forced to remain stationary." He rose and took hold of Claire's arm. "You need to get back to Gertie's and lie down. Don't be worrying about Two Wolves. After what I saw, it wouldn't be wise for any man to go up against him, Indian or white. He's in the world he understands best right now, and I have no doubt he's trying to do the right thing."

Claire rose, taking a handkerchief from a pocket of her skirt and dabbing her eyes with it. She looked up at Tower. "Did he look well?"

Tower grinned. "Claire, I have never seen a man in better shape. He was fine."

"And he really said he'd come back?"

"Of course, he did. Nothing can keep him from it. And I'll make sure every man out there says Peter was there only to look out for us—and they never saw who killed Craig."

Claire held his gaze. "He's a good man down inside, Captain. He's kind and gentle and caring."

Tower smiled rather sadly. "The man I saw in battle wasn't exactly kind and gentle and caring, but I've seen that side of him at times."

"You said he killed a warrior who was ready to plant a hatchet into you. Won't the rest of those warriors be upset with him for that?"

"I don't think they even realized what he'd done. They were too caught up in attacking Craig and his men. That man can take care of himself, Claire. I highly doubt he needs to worry about his own people turning on him." He walked her over to Sergeant Becker. "Take her back to your place, Sergeant."

"Yes, Sir. Gladly." The burly, broad-chested sergeant put a hand on Claire's shoulder to lead her out.

Claire turned to Captain Tower once more, grateful he wanted to keep Peter out of trouble. Still, remembering her conversation with her husband before he left still made her worry and wonder about the comments he'd made then. He didn't like the captain because he knew Tower had feelings for her, yet he'd told her the captain would be a good man to turn to if he didn't make it back. Both conversations made her wonder if Peter truly would return... And when? She had a feeling she'd be spending Christmas alone. Klas and Hubert would be there because she would invite them. Maybe she would even invite Captain Tower, and Harry and Gertie.

Before she met the Indian Two Wolves, she thought she was just fine all on her own. Now she had a lot of new friends, yet she felt more alone than ever. The massacre at Sand Creek had taken more than the lives of too many innocent Cheyenne. It had taken her husband from her.

Chapter Thirty

The crowd that gathered on the main street of Denver City consisted of just about every citizen there as well as a few outsiders. Businessmen and waitresses, laundresses and prostitutes, restaurant owners, livery owners, supply store owners, women and little children, miners and freighters, lawyers and doctors—all gathered to watch the grandest parade that ever took place in their town. The crowd waved American flags to show their support for Colorado statehood, something they still had not achieved. But today flags were also displayed in support of the brave soldiers led by Colonel John Chivington.

The Colorado volunteers had won a great battle. Rumors over how many Cheyenne were killed at Sand Creek abounded. One hundred. Three hundred. Five hundred. And most of those killed were Cheyenne Dog Soldiers, the most dangerous of the Cheyenne warriors. Only seven or eight of Chivington's men had died, a few more wounded.

According to the *Denver Post* hundreds of Cheyenne had been taken prisoner and sent to Fort Leavenworth. Surely now people could relax. Farmers and settlers, freight wagons, stage coaches—all would be safe. Soon Colorado would be rid of all its Indians. Those remaining would be rounded up and herded out of the state, or they would head south and join the Arapaho, or north and east to join the Northern Cheyenne and the Sioux.

Sergeant Sam Goodrich, dishonorably discharged by Chivington for refusing to participate in the slaughter of women and children at Sand Creek, stood now as a citizen to watch the parade. He was half drunk and leaning with his arm around the bare shoulders of Sally Coombs, a saloon girl. She turned and kissed Sam's cheek before she began waving her flag as Chivington and his troops came closer.

The crowd cheered. Flags fluttered.

Chivington rode past first, sitting tall and proud in his saddle, nodding arrogantly to people in the crowd. He didn't crack a smile.

"He's so dignified," Sally told Sam.

"Yeah, right."

"Oh, look!" Sally pointed to two little Indian girls, perhaps six or seven years old. They rode a horse together and wore ragged dresses. Their hair was long and stringy, their faces and hands dirty, their dark eyes wide with fright and wonder.

"Are they Cheyenne?" Sally asked Sam.

Sam eyed them with pity. "Chivington is using them to show off, maybe to prove how dirty and slovenly the Cheyenne are."

"I feel kind of sorry for them."

"You should. They've likely been ripped out of their mothers' arms and had to watch their mothers raped and slaughtered."

Sally frowned. "What?"

"I haven't said anything so far, Sally girl, but Chivington is no hero, let me tell you. Neither are any of the men with him."

A captain rode by holding up a stick with something hanging on it.

"See that? I've seen ovaries before, when cleaning out a dead deer or bear. I'm guessing what's hanging on that stick is some Cheyenne woman's ovaries."

Sally gasped and put a hand to her mouth. "You mean...?"

"Those soldiers ran down women and children—shot them point blank, bashed in the heads of babies, cut up the women, shot a lot of them in the back."

"But it was supposed to have been a brave battle."

Another soldier rode by and noticed Sam. He laughed and held something out. "How do you like my new tobacco pouch, Sam?"

It was obviously made from a woman's breast.

"Go to hell, Private!" Sam shouted back.

Troops continued riding past, followed by soldiers on foot, tipping or waving their hats to the cheering crowd. A few were still bandaged from wounds. A band marched behind the troops, drums, flutes, tubas, clarinets, proudly playing patriotic songs, some of the crowd singing the words. They shoved past Sam and Sally as they pushed along behind the parade toward a park where people could meet with the soldiers and congratulate them.

Sally turned to Sam. "Was that a breast I saw that man using for a tobacco pouch?"

Sam swallowed more whiskey from the flask he carried with him. "Sure, it was."

Sally sobered. "How do you know so much about all of this?"."

Sam leaned on a hitching post and studied the lovely young woman. "I was there. And it was seven hundred men against a couple hundred Cheyenne. I don't know, maybe there were more than that, but they didn't have a chance. That was a peaceful camp, full of mostly women and children. Chivington attacked them by surprise, with no real reason to do so." He took another swallow of whiskey. "I never told you I was there because I'm ashamed of it. I saw what those men were doing, and I refused to participate. Chivington stripped me of my sergeant stripes and discharged me, but I didn't care. I'm glad I walked away from it all."

"But, everyone says it was a hard-fought, dangerous battle."

"That's how Chivington and his men describe it, but it wasn't like that at all. And the citizens of Colorado shouldn't rest thinking there won't be any more trouble. What Chivington did will cause more trouble than ever. The Cheyenne will be at all-out war now. The Volunteers did unthinkable things to them at Sand Creek. They even ran down those who fled, and they just kept killing, shooting a lot of them in the back, cutting babies' heads off, defiling the women."

"Oh, Sam, sweetie, why didn't you tell me?"

Sam studied the woman's hazel eyes and laughed with a grunt. "Who'd believe me?"

"But there must be others who can attest to what happened."

"Oh, there are plenty, if they have the guts to do it. I'm just hoping when it registers with people what those soldiers kept for souvenirs, they might start wondering. I figure there are others like me who are having a hard time living with what they saw—a lot of them over what they did."

Sally took his arm. "Come on, Sergeant. Let's get back inside the saloon. There will be a lot of celebrating. My boss will want me getting men to buy drinks for me."

Sam stumbled, clinging to her as he did so. "Say, that's a pretty dress, Sally." He ran a hand over her breasts and the pink satin dress with black lace trim that covered them.

"Never you mind that, Sam. You'll have to *pay* for that pleasure, honey."

She smiled as she led Sam inside a saloon, where men were packed in to celebrate Colonel John Chivington's great victory over the Cheyenne.

Chapter Thirty-One

The night was unusually quiet and still, which made it seem colder. Two Wolves sat in a council circle inside a *tipi* with Black Kettle and some of his warriors, all huddled together around a central fire, staring at the flames, deciding what to do next. Wolves howled in the distant foothills, but in spite of being camped along the Smoky Hill River in Kansas Territory, there was no rippling sound of water. The river was frozen. Somewhere in another *tipi* a small child was crying, a remnant of the children caught in the Sand Creek massacre.

"Tell me what you saw, Black Kettle," Two Wolves asked in the Cheyenne tongue. He knew that in the *tipi* next to the one in which he sat, Black Kettle's wife lay suffering from nine bullet wounds.

Black Kettle sighed, tears in his eyes. "We just ran up the creek," he told Two Wolves. "The soldiers shot down many, most of them in the back, including my wife. I looked back, and I saw a soldier standing over her shooting her again and again, when she already lay there helpless. I could not believe my eyes. I managed to hide, and when the soldiers finally left, I went back for my woman."

The old warrior shook his head. "I could not believe she was still alive. My brother was taken captive, as was the half-blood Jack Smith. Other warriors tell me that later the soldiers shot Jack Smith in cold blood." He rested a look of sorrow upon Two Wolves. "Tell me friend, you know the white world. Why have they done this? I wear a medal of peace. I flew the American flag over my dwelling, and a white flag for peace. We were mostly women and children, and most were sleeping. We did not attack those soldiers. But they attacked us, and now I am ashamed that I told my people the whites want peace. Now their hearts are full of fury and revenge, and there will be no peace."

Two Wolves struggled with his own anger and hatred. "I wish I had an answer, Black Kettle. I can tell you that the soldiers I ride with want peace. Major Ansley and the rest of us were on our way to Sand Creek to give you protection if you wanted to go north to the Sioux, or south to the Arapaho. The Great Father in Washington gave us this permission, but the leader of the Colorado volunteers got there first. John Chivington is a man whose heart is bad and filled with hate for the Cheyenne. I wish that you would understand this is not what the Federal government wanted."

Black Kettle nodded. "I believe that. But now I will not be able to contain the young men whose hearts are filled with a need for revenge. I, too, was wounded at Sand Creek, and I still suffer. Some of us captured a few of our horses. We stayed in a ravine that first night, and it was so cold. We were driven out of our beds and so had little with us for warm blankets and clothing. It was a night of terrible suffering for the wounded. There was not even wood for fires. We made small fires from grass and put the wounded near them, covering them with more grass because that is all there was for some little warmth."

Two Wolves could hardly stand the ache in his heart over what his people had suffered. It made him ashamed to be white.

"We kept calling out," Black Kettle continued, "hoping to attract others who were scattered all over the prairie by the soldiers. I am sure some of them froze to death out there. By morning we were all so cold and sore we could hardly move. I have a bad hip, and now it is worse." He wiped at tears. "And it was all so bad on the women and children. We lost most of them."

"Soon Cheyenne and Arapaho from other camps on the Smoky Hill learned what happened," another old warrior named He Who Fights spoke up. "*Maheo* heard our prayers and our cries for help. They brought blankets and horses, cooked meat and supplies. We had many friends and relatives among them, and they came to help." He choked back tears. "I tell you, Two Wolves, that when we saw them coming, saw their lodges lit with warm fires, we all wept and fell into mourning because of how much we had lost. Fathers and mothers, sisters and brothers, sons and daughters and cousins. We are broken, but now the young men will not see that. They will be too angry and proud. They will continue the fight. Already there is talk of raiding the supply warehouses at Julesburg. I am sure there will be other raiding and warfare. The white man will regret what they have done."

Two Wolves nodded. "I am sure they will. I would advise you to urge the young men to stop making war, Black Kettle, but I know it would do no good."

"Already the pipe has been sent north to the Sioux, asking them to come and join us in a war on the citizens of Colorado," Young Brother spoke up.

To his relief, Two Wolves had found his young friend living among the survivors, and already he was painted for war and anxious to kill.

"The Arapahoe have agreed to join us, so we will be stronger in numbers."

"More of our brothers and sisters are coming from all over the land to join us in war," He Who Fights told Two Wolves. "Arapaho, Northern Cheyenne, Sioux, many Dog Soldiers. I think we will be many hundreds strong, maybe a thousand. Your soldiers will not be able to stop us. And I see in your eyes that you, too, are full of hate and feel a need to seek revenge for what happened to your cousin and her little son. Surely your Cheyenne heart feels this need. We ask you not to return to the soldiers. At least do not tell them what we plan to do. Chivington and his men surprised us. Now we will surprise those at Julesburg. There we will find all the supplies we need to be strong again—horses and blankets, food and bandages, cloth and things to cook with. It is the only way to survive the rest of the winter. We cannot survive on what little is left to us, and we need protection from the cold."

"Our young warriors are ready to do what is needed to help the women and old ones get through the winter," Black Kettle declared. "Are you with us?"

Two Wolves closed his eyes, his heart in pain. *Claire!* "I have a white wife at Fort Collins," he told them. "She is a good woman, and she carries my child. I want nothing more than to go home to her, but my

Cheyenne blood runs hot with a need to help all of you. I killed one of the Volunteers when I followed some of them after Sand Creek. It is possible I am already in trouble with the whites and with the leader of the troops I scouted for. If I go with you to Julesburg, I could be asking to be hanged as an Army scout who turned to the Cheyenne and took part in killing whites."

"It is a difficult world you live in," Black Kettle told him. "We know you are our friend. If we did not believe this, we would have to kill you for being a friend of the Blue Coats, but we know what you do is for our good, a desire for peace."

Two Wolves nodded. "*Aye*, this is true. Right now, my heart is more torn than it has ever been. I promised my wife that I would live the life of a white man once I married her. And I want nothing more than to be a father to my child. I do not want to break the promises I made to my family and to the leader of the soldiers. He has befriended me and called me son." He shook his head. "I will go with you to Julesburg. I will help raid for supplies and gather as many as I can. But I cannot kill innocent white settlers or women. This you must understand. If a white man tries to kill me, then I will kill him. But I will not kill those who stand back or hide. I will not go to Julesburg just to kill. I will go only to raid because it will help you survive."

He Who Fights nodded. "It is good that you would do that much. Our men will help protect you so that you can go back to your family in the north. And so that you can tell the major there that we still want peace—that we will raid and steal only because our women and children and old ones are dying from starvation and cold."

"You must make them understand that we have no choice," Black Kettle added.

Two Wolves nodded. "I will try." He stared at the flames, seeing in them Claire's bright red hair. *Claire, I love you so. I pray that our child still lives in you, and that you will wait for me and not give up and think that I have left you. I will come home. This I promise.* But first he would keep his promise to Black Kettle and the others. He would join them in a raid on Julesburg.

Chapter Thirty-Two

December 23, 1864...

Claire laid Peter's wrapped hair ornament under the small pine tree Klas and Hubert had dug up for her. They'd brought it inside in a wooden barrel. She wanted a tree with roots so that she could plant it outside the cabin after Christmas, as a memory of her and Peter's first Christmas. She'd strung the tree with the popcorn ribbons she'd made, and she hung tiny bells on it.

Her husband would like the bells. They were to celebrate his belief that bells drew good spirits.

"Please come home for Christmas, Peter," she said softly.

There were only two days left. A fresh-killed turkey, thanks to Hubert, was in her ice box, ready to be roasted Christmas morning and served with roasted potatoes. Tomorrow she would bake bread and pies. Klas and Hubert would be her guests, along with Major Ansley and Captain Tower, as well as a lovely young woman Klas had met in the settlement.

Claire smiled at the thought of how starry-eyed Klas and Sarah Kling were when they looked at each other. That's how she felt about Peter, her handsome, grand warrior.

She stood back to study the tree after tying a large red ribbon at the top, and just then she felt movement in her belly. Was the child all she would have left of him? Stories about the atrocities at Sand Creek were growing, horrors so awful she found them hard to believe. Major Ansley told her he'd learned an investigation was already underway. Meantime, the Cheyenne were hot on the warpath and for as many stories about Sand Creek, there were an equal number about Indian attacks everywhere. Was Peter a part of those attacks? Surely, he wouldn't kill white women and children, or innocent white settlers. She couldn't imagine that he would kill soldiers.

She touched her belly. The fact remained he *would* kill Colorado Volunteers if they attacked an Indian camp, or even white men who would threaten Cheyenne women and children. She'd already seen him do it, and Captain Tower had witnessed him kill Sergeant Craig. Maybe he thought he'd be arrested if he came home. Maybe that's what kept him away. Still, he'd promised, and Peter James Matthews was a man of his word.

Someone knocked at the door and she hurried to it. After what had happened at the store, she kept her door locked at all times. Heart pounding, she called out. "Peter?"

"It's Captain Tower, Claire," came the voice on the other side of the door.

Disappointment filled her again, but she did enjoy company. She opened the door and Tower stepped inside wearing a heavy wool Army coat that made him appear bigger than he really was. He looked quite handsome, his hair neatly slicked back, his face clean shaven.

"I know Christmas is only two days away," he told her, "but I did promise Two Wolves I would watch over you until he got back. I just came from helping Doctor Lane set a young boy's broken leg." He looked her over. "You all right, Claire?"

She closed the door. "I'm fine. Take off your coat, Captain. I'll get you some pie and coffee before you go back to the fort."

He smiled eagerly. "That sounds good!"

He removed his coat and hung it on a wall hook, then walked to where Claire had gone to retrieve a coffee pot from an iron rack over the fire. She took hold of it with the end of her apron and carried it to the kitchen table while Tower rubbed his hands together in front of the fire.

"It's so bitterly cold this morning," he told her.

Instantly Claire wondered if Peter was warm enough wherever he was. And what about the Cheyenne who'd fled Sand Creek? How many of them had frozen to death by now?

"I've had a really busy morning," Tower told her as he turned to sit down at the table.

Claire poured a cup of coffee. "What happened?"

"I delivered a baby," he told her. "For Mrs. Adeline Beeker. She had the cutest little tow-head you ever saw—a boy. She already has three little girls, and they all have hair as golden as real gold. I wanted to tell you because you might want to go see the baby and see what you're going to have yourself by spring."

Claire cut a piece of apple pie from where it sat near the sink and put it on a plate, bringing it over to Captain Tower. "Yes, I think I'd love to see the baby. I am beginning to feel more and more movement myself. I think this baby will be strong and healthy, like his father."

"You're still sure it's a boy, are you?" Tower asked with a smile.

Claire sat down to the table. "I'm sure."

The captain drank some coffee, then set it down and studied her eyes for a moment. "I've just realized how green your eyes are," he told her. "Peter once described them as green as prairie grass."

For a quick moment Claire caught the adoration in the captain's eyes before he looked away and cut into the pie.

"Where do you think he is, Captain?"

He waited a moment while he chewed and swallowed the pie. "I wish you would call me Edward," he told her then.

"It seems too personal for an Army officer. I know Major Ansley much better than I know you, but I still call him Major. And please answer my question."

He met her gaze again, sadness showing in his eyes. "My guess is that he's still with the Cheyenne and trying to talk them out of making war. They respect him a great deal. He's hoping they will listen, but from reports coming in, that's not working. He probably went looking for Black Kettle. That old chief is one of the few Cheyenne who might still opt for peace." He ate more pie. "This pie is delicious, by the way."

"Thank you." Claire waited until he finished the second bite. "Do you think Peter would join the Cheyenne in making war?"

Tower set down his fork. "I don't want to think that he would, but I honestly think he might. That day he saved my life, I could tell how angry he was. He'd seen the results of Sand Creek by then. And the vicious way he killed Sergeant Craig..." He shook his head. "I sure would never want to go up against him myself, I'll tell you that." He sighed. "Peter is his own man. He will do what is in his heart to do, and right now his heart is broken, and he probably feels as angry and vengeful as the rest of the Cheyenne, and I don't blame them."

"But Peter could be hanged or shot for joining them."

Tower set his fork aside and drank a little coffee, then leaned back in his chair. "Not necessarily." He looked her over again, his gaze full of adoration. "Claire, not one man at the fort is going to say your husband did anything wrong. He saved us from being wiped out. I'm sure he still wants to do the right thing. He saved my life and called off the attack, except for the one on Craig and his men. If worse comes to worse, we will just say that Craig was coming at Peter with a weapon and all Peter did was defend himself. Don't worry about what happens when he comes back. And he *will* come back. Whatever is keeping him, it's something important, or he would have come home by now."

Claire needed to hear those words. "Do you really believe that?"

Tower nodded. "I really believe it." He studied her eyes. "I have to admit that part of me doesn't want him to come back because I have deep feelings for you. You know that. But I don't want that to make you uncomfortable. I want you to feel free to call on me at any time, especially if you think there is a problem with that baby, understand? Peter would want that. His very words were for me to look after you, even though he knows I care about you. I think he believes I'll take good care of you *because* I care about you." He leaned forward, elbows on his knees. "I'll never overstep my boundaries, but I want you to remember me if anything happens to your husband. Don't try to live out your life alone."

"I can't even think about that," Claire answered. "There is only one man for me, Captain. I appreciate your concern and your help, but I don't want to talk about anything beyond that. I refuse to believe there is any possibility Peter won't make it back. But I am losing faith that it will be by Christmas." She fought tears at the thought.

"Are you sure you want all of us here Christmas Day? Don't overdo yourself."

"It's fine. It will help keep me occupied. I will otherwise be unbearably lonely." Claire rose to set the coffee pot back on the grate. "You should do more visiting among the settlers, Captain. There are several young women among them who are unattached. You're a good and able man, and because you are a doctor you will always do well." She set the pot on the grate and turned, smiling. "Any young woman would be overjoyed at the prospect of landing you for a husband."

Tower smiled sadly. "And if not for Peter, would you?"

"Of course, I would."

The room hung silent for a moment as they held each other's gaze. "Then I don't think I'll do too much searching among those settlers out there until I know your husband is or is not coming back."

Claire put a hand to her head. "You had better go, Captain. Thank you for checking on me, but I'm fine."

Tower picked up what was left of the pie and put the whole thing into his mouth, then washed it down with the rest of his coffee.

"You send for me if you feel sick or are worried something is going wrong with that baby. Promise me. I don't want Peter coming home to find out I didn't help you when I could have. I definitely do not want to have to answer to that man."

Claire couldn't help a smile. "I promise."

"He saved my life. I owe him. The situation irks me, but that's how it is." He turned and walked over to take up his coat. He pulled it on. "Thanks for the pie and coffee. I look forward to that turkey dinner, and I know Major Ansley does, too."

Claire folded her arms. "And so do I. I need the company."

Tower looked her over and nodded. "We are all glad to oblige. I'm sure your cooking will be a hundred times better than what the men will be served Christmas Day." He took hold of the door knob.

"Captain."

He hesitated and met her gaze.

"Let me know if you hear anything at all, good or bad, will you?"

He nodded. "I will."

"Are they still investigating what really happened at Sand Creek?"

"Yes. I'm hoping Colonel John Chivington ends up being ridden on a rail right out of Colorado."

"I hope the same."

Tower turned and left. When he closed the door, the breeze it caused made the bells on the Christmas tree tinkle, as though to remind her that Peter was with her in spirit. He was out there somewhere, and she sensed that he was longing for her just as much as she longed for him.

She heard the hooves of Captain Tower's horse as he rode off. She walked over to the little tree, and suddenly she felt a wonderful warmth, as though Peter was standing behind her and moving his arms around her.

Nemehotatse, Maeveksea.

Claire turned. She'd heard he words as surely as if he was really there. His spirit was strong. He was with her. The bells tinkled again.

"I love you, too, Two Wolves," she whispered.

Chapter Thirty-Three

January 7, 1865 ...

They were one thousand strong, and there was no stopping them. Visions of Claire haunted Two Wolves as he headed out of western Kansas with the huge contingent of Cheyenne Dog Soldiers, Northern Arapaho warriors and Lakota Sioux ... all hot for revenge. If he'd tried any harder to stop them they would have killed him. As it was, he knew he rode a dangerous trail. Any one of these warriors could decide he was only with them to spy, that he might break away from them at any time to try to warn the citizens of Julesburg—or the soldiers at well-fortified Fort Rankin—that the Julesburg way station was about to be ransacked.

Julesburg was a primary stop for travelers headed along the South Platte toward Denver. There was a stagecoach station there, stables, horses and cattle, a telegraph office, warehouses and stores. About fifty well-armed men manned the sod walls that surrounded the settlement. Two Wolves knew the place well. Many of the things Claire ordered from Omaha and Chicago for her supply store came through Julesburg. It lay in the northeast corner of Colorado Territory, almost straight east from Fort Collins.

He could try to sneak away, ride to Fort Collins and be with Claire, tell Major Ansley what was happening, but not only was it likely the warriors with whom he rode would kill him, but a part of him wanted to be here. A part of him still seethed with anger and sorrow over what he'd seen at Sand Creek. Most of the Cheyenne warriors with him now had suffered great losses —mothers and fathers, wives, daughters and sons, cousins and aunts and uncles. What happened would burn in their hearts and minds for years to come. It had left them depleted of supplies necessary to survive, and it had depleted them of feelings.

After Julesburg, many Cheyenne would keep heading north into Nebraska, Wyoming, Montana and South Dakota. Others would first go back south to the Smoky Hill in Kansas, where they would prepare women and children and the old to come with them. There the Sioux and Northern Cheyenne would give them shelter. They would be strong again.

The air was filled with the steam that came snorting out of the nostrils of over a thousand horses. Warriors huddled into heavy coats and capes made of animal fur. Their legs were covered to the knees with laced-up animal skin moccasins. Two Wolves was well aware that Christmas had passed. Claire had spent it alone. Or likely with Klas and Hans...and maybe Captain Tower. His feelings for Tower were torn. Part of him was grateful the man would very gladly look after Claire, and part of him wanted to land a hatchet into the man's skull for having a desire for her.

He wrestled with the agony of loving Claire and knowing he should be with her, the agony of knowing what these warriors were suffering. There was no excuse for what had happened. It was a pitifully sorry way to think peace could be had. Colorado's governor and the government in general had sorely underestimated the anger that Sand Creek would stir in the Cheyenne. They had thought the slaughter would bring the Indians to their knees. To Chivington and Governor Evans and the others, they thought proper "punishment" to all Cheyenne for atrocities only a few committed would make the rest of them come crawling, begging for help and forgiveness and shelter.

Looking around at the intimidating warriors now made him want to laugh. If only Governor Evans and Major Anthony at Fort Lyon and the president of the United States himself could see this—proud, strong, brave, determined warriors planning revenge.

This entire venture could have been prevented. Major Ansley and his troops should have been allowed to accompany Black Kettle and his camp north. There might have been a chance for peace.

Not now. They would attack Julesburg, and he would be part of it because he had little choice. Back at Fort Collins a beautiful woman pregnant with his child waited for him. Now he wondered if he would ever see her again, or ever see his son. He'd not planned any of this. And now here he was, getting off his horse and sneaking up a huge hill that overlooked Julesburg, calculating the best approach.

Young Brother crouched beside him. "They will be very surprised," he told his friend eagerly.

"Aye."

Secretly, Two Wolves was relieved to know there were few women and children below. Julesburg was a supply post consisting of nearly all men. About one mile to the west lay Fort Rankin. He looked down the hill to watch a Cheyenne warrior named Big Crow ride in that direction with ten other warriors. Their plan was to act as decoys to lure soldiers out of Fort Rankin and lead them on a wild chase that would distract them from what would be happening at Julesburg.

Another contingent of fifteen warriors headed out behind Big Crow. They would lie in wait for the soldiers Big Crow would lure from the fort, and they would attack and kill all of them they could, making it more difficult for those left at the fort to come and help the men at Julesburg. Those left would be afraid and would likely huddle inside the fort and do nothing while Julesburg was ransacked.

Two Wolves and the others snuck back down the hill and made ready. They waited, giving Big Crow time to distract those at Fort Rankin. It was not long before gunfire cracked into the still, cold air. It was then the rest of the warriors made their move. Cheyenne, Arapaho, Lakota Sioux—their war cries filling the air—rode in one fell swoop into Julesburg, lances and rifles raised, some using only arrows, knives and hatchets for protection. They began circling the settlement, ducking gunfire, charging their horses through gates and over fences and into warehouses.

Some among them had the duty of grabbing as much loot as they could. They would not fight. They would ride in behind the warriors, gathering blankets, canned goods, utensils, cloth and clothing, cans of fuel oil, tobacco, whiskey, guns and ammunition.

Two Wolves saw a man raise a rifle and aim it at him. He fired his revolver, and the man screamed as he went down with a bullet in his thigh. He could easily have killed him, but he'd promised himself he wasn't here to kill. Still, he was caught up in the attack now, the war cries and wild conquests around him bringing forth his own warrior blood. He saw that most of those defending the warehouses realized early on that they were greatly out-numbered. Most of them withdrew inside one large barn. Someone stuck a piece of white cloth tied to a stick out the barn door. Some of the warriors shot burning arrows into the building, while hundreds charged their horses right into the stores and warehouses, loading up blankets with supplies.

To Two Wolves' great relief, the battle, if it could even be called that, was over in a mere fifteen or twenty minutes, with few soldiers and settlers killed. As far as he could tell at first, no Indians had been killed, and hundreds rode off loaded down with plunder. He knew that those who'd ridden to Fort Rankin would try capturing a large herd of cattle kept there, giving them plenty of meat for their trip north.

Two Wolves turned to follow those who now fled with supplies. He would help distribute them and try once more to convince those waiting on the Smokey Hill to agree to a new peace treaty. They would leave behind the life they once enjoyed in their homeland and join with the Sioux, probably never to return to the land they loved. They could part from everything they once knew, but they would not be able to abandon the memories of Sand Creek.

It was then he saw Young Brother on foot. Somehow, he had lost his horse. Three men were chasing after him. One raised his rifle to shoot. Two Wolves took up his own rifle, aimed and fired. The man went down. The other two started to run back to shelter, and Two Wolves charged up to Young Brother.

"Get on my horse!" he shouted.

Young Brother obeyed. Then a shot rang out. Two Wolves winced at the initial sting in his side. Another rifle shot cracked through the air, and it felt as though someone had hit the side of his head with a rock. Another shot. He felt *Itatane* stumble. The horse fell to the ground, and Two Wolves' body sprawled across the snowy, muddy ground.

More shooting. War cries. Someone lifted him. Men were shouting in the Cheyenne tongue. In the next moment everything went black.

Chapter Thirty-Four

January 10, 1865...

Just as Hubert climbed down a ladder he'd used to re-stock kerosene lamps on an upper shelf, the door to Matthews' Supplies burst open and several men came inside. Claire turned from straightening bolts of cloth, both she and Hubert taken back by the anxious mood of the settlers, who all headed for an area where Claire kept a store of pistols and rifles.

"We're looking for ammunition, Hubert," one of them spoke up.

It was Albert Deeds, a huge, burly man who was the local blacksmith.

"is something wrong?" Hubert asked.

Claire moved closer, somewhat alarmed at how some of them looked at her. Most of the settlers accepted the fact that she was married to a half-breed, mostly because all they had heard was that Peter Matthews was an educated man who helped as an Army scout and had saved soldiers' lives. Claire had become more comfortable with those who came into her store, and she'd befriended several of the women, both in the settlement and at the fort. Still, she sensed something had changed.

"There sure is something wrong!" Tom Shuman answered. "We could be attacked at any time, and I aim to protect my farm supply."

"What's going on?" Claire asked boldly.

"Cheyenne attacked the supply post at Julesburg," Albert told her in his booming voice. "We don't know how many were killed, but they ransacked the whole place, took thousands of dollars in supplies, burned a barn, attacked Fort Rankin, stole a couple hundred head of cattle. I expect a lot of those supplies were headed here, so now we'll be short.

Word now is the Cheyenne have teamed up with Arapaho and Sioux, and war is breaking out everywhere, ranches burned, settlers killed. We sent some men into the fort to ask Major Ansley if more soldiers are coming out here. We need help! There aren't near enough Army personnel to protect the whole damn territory."

Claire faced all of them squarely. "This is because of Sand Creek. Every day we hear new stories about what Chivington and his men did there. The Denver newspaper says an investigation has begun. You can hardly blame the Cheyenne for retaliating. Most of those killed there were women and children, and they were not just killed. They were mutilated."

"The fact remains the Cheyenne are on the warpath stronger than ever," Albert shot back. "They say there were a good thousand of them at Julesburg. Some say they are building their strength somewhere on the Smokey Hill in Kansas. They gather there, and then they come into Colorado to do their dirty work."

"We intend to be ready for them," Tom spoke up. He was a man of small stature and usually quiet and friendly, but right now he was all bluster. "We need all the ammunition you have on hand, Mrs. Matthews, and some of these men want to buy extra rifles."

"At least *you* don't need to worry if they attack our settlement," Buck Lewis spoke up. A saloon owner, Lewis was one of the rougher men among the settlers, more out-spoken and sometimes a trouble-maker.

"What do you mean by that?" Hubert asked, moving closer to Claire.

Buck looked Claire over, his eyes resting on her now more-obviously bigger belly. "I mean the Cheyenne won't hurt Mrs. Matthews here." He looked at Hubert. "She's married to one of 'em."

"And he's an Army scout who would save your own hide if it came to that," Hubert answered angrily. "If there is going to be a fight, Buck Lewis, let it be between the Cheyenne and us or the soldiers. Do not do or say something that will cause hard feelings among our own!"

"And where *is* Peter Matthews?" Buck shot back. "He hasn't been seen since he first left with Major Ansley weeks ago! Ansley came back without him, and Captain Tower says he saw Peter fighting right alongside the Cheyenne who attacked him and his men and killed a whole company of Colorado Volunteers!"

"He also said that Peter saved his life that day," Hubert reminded Lewis. "You know that he would not attack soldiers on his own. It's his job to work among the Cheyenne and try to keep the peace."

"Well he sure hasn't been able to do that, has he?"

Claire turned away. Christmas had come and gone. Early January had brought bitter cold, and Peter was out there somewhere suffering right along with the Cheyenne. Now this! Julesburg! And other attacks all across the territory. Where was Peter?

"If Peter is not back yet, it is for a good reason," Hubert argued. "And if any of you says one more word to upset Mrs. Matthews, you can all leave without the guns and ammunition you came for. That is what you are here for, so go over to where we keep our supply and pick out what you need Just be sure Mrs. Matthews gets *paid*!"

The disgruntled herd of men exchanged comments about what each would do "if the damn Cheyenne dared to attack their settlement."

"At least we're close to Fort Collins," one of them said. "We're lucky we have soldier protection."

"Yeah, it's those out there farming and ranching on the open prairie who are most in danger, and all the small settlements scattered across the plains."

"That damn Chivington really started something," another grumbled.

Claire looked over at Hubert. "I'm going to find Klas," she told him. "I want to go to the fort and ask what Major Ansley knows."

"You be careful, Mrs. Matthews. Tempers are high. People don't think straight when that happens. You know that from the trouble you and Peter got yourselves into in Denver City a few months ago."

"I know." Claire went into a back room to get her coat. She bundled up and went outside to find Klas already hitching a wagon.

"I heard," he told her. "I knew you would want to go and see Major Ansley."

"You are too intuitive and too kind, Klas," Claire told him.

She waited for him to finish hitching the horses, then climbed onto the wagon seat with Klas' helping hand. Snow and sleet stung her face as they headed for the fort. Her heart felt heavy, and she shivered with loneliness. With every day that went by with no word from Peter, her hope dwindled more. She remained silent as the wagon clattered across frozen ground. Feelings of fear and anxiety seemed to fill the air. Claire saw some people nailing boards over their windows. Other store owners were bringing display items inside. They passed a small farm where the owner was herding horses into a barn. Small groups of people were gathered in various places, some turning to stare at her as her wagon passed them.

They finally reached the fort, where soldiers opened gates to let them in. Several nodded their greetings, tipped their hats. Some did not. She asked Klas to hitch the wagon in front of Major Ansley's quarters. Klas helped her down as a private went inside to tell the major he had a visitor. The private stood back and let Claire inside, Klas beside her. Ansley walked from behind his desk and gave her a fatherly hug, then led her to a chair.

"Sit down, Claire. I was going to come and see you, but it's obvious you've already heard."

"Yes." Claire sat down and removed her gloves. "Several men barged into my store looking for guns and ammunition. The whole settlement seems to be stirred up and scared."

"Word just came in about Julesburg and other attacks," Ansley told her. "I've sent Captain Tower to Fort Rankin. A good ten or fifteen soldiers were wounded there when part of the Indian band who attacked Julesburg also attacked the fort. The captain went there to help tend to them. I sent several men with him because right now we can't be sure where the Cheyenne will attack next. I'm sending a wire to Washington to ask for more troops."

Ansley took a seat behind his desk, and Claire faced him, almost afraid to ask.

"You know why I'm here, Major. Is there any word about Peter?"

Klas sat down beside Claire. "If Peter is out there with the Cheyenne, he would have known about Julesburg," Klas spoke up. "He would have come and warned you, or gone to Fort Rankin to warn *them*, ya?"

Ansley shook his head. "I've heard nothing. I'm hoping Captain Tower will learn something at Fort Rankin. I believe Peter is probably still in the south working with the Cheyenne down along the Arkansas. If he was as close as Julesburg or Fort Rankin, he would have reported in and would have come to see Claire and explain where he's been."

"Ya," Klas answered. "He will be coming back any day now, I am sure," he assured her. "The Cheyenne, many are going north now. If Peter can make peace in the south, he will be home soon."

Claire studied Major Ansley's eyes. He knew Peter as well as she did. "Unless he can't," she spoke up. "The mood the Cheyenne are in right now, they could easily turn on Peter. He knows that. As long as he's among them, he has to *be* one of them if he's going to help. And if that's not the reason he still hasn't come home, then he could be hurt. Or they might have already turned on him. He could be dead, couldn't he, Major?"

Ansley sighed. "Don't be thinking that way. Peter is a smart and able man."

"Or he could have decided to make war right alongside them because of Sand Creek. We already know he was with those who attacked Captain Tower and his men and that he killed Sergeant Craig."

"He also saved Tower's life," Ansley reminded her. "And he asked Tower to tell you he would be back. A Cheyenne man doesn't break his promises."

"Unless something has happened that he can't *keep* those promises."

Shouts came from outside Ansley's quarters then, men yelling about posting more soldiers in and around the growing settlement beyond the fort walls.

"Everyone is afraid," Klas told Major Ansley. "They think the Cheyenne will attack everywhere."

"It seems they *are* attacking everywhere, and with a war still raging back East, getting more men out here isn't easy," Ansley replied. "I feel lost as to what to do next without Peter's advice. He's our best scout."

"I felt it, Major, when my husband first left to help you find Black Kettle's camp and bring him north. I felt as though I was saying goodbye to him forever." She choked back tears. "Something just isn't right. Knowing Chivington was on the hunt the same time all of you left made me so uneasy. God knows how Sand Creek affected Peter. He had to be so torn."

"And he has you to keep him grounded," Ansley reminded her. "Don't give up hope."

She shook her head. "I try not to." She swallowed and took a deep breath. "Sometimes I feel as though Peter is trying to reach me, trying to get back to me, but he can't. I try to tell myself it's because he is working for peace and because to stay safe he has to convince the Cheyenne he is not their enemy. I don't like to think about the only other possible reasons he hasn't come home because I don't want to believe any of them. His Cheyenne blood might have won out after Sand Creek. He might stay with them until the last battle is fought. Or he could be hurt, or..."

"You have to stop torturing yourself, Claire. And I hate to say it, but some of those settlers out there might make life difficult for you back at the settlement. They're afraid, and they hate the Cheyenne and anyone who would have anything to do with them. You're *married* to one. I think you should stay here at the fort for a while with Gertie."

"No. I should be home tending to my store."

"Klas and Hubert can do that for you. Right now, I think it's dangerous for you to be there. You have that baby to think about. Until things calm down, I want you to stay here. At least wait until Captain Tower gets back. We'll know a lot more about Julesburg when he gets here."

"Ya, Mrs. Matthews, you can hear those men out there," Klas told her. "Some of those people will not be kind to you. You should stay here a while. We will take good care of the store."

Peter, where are you? Please, please come home! "I have to go back first and get some of my things," Claire told Klas. She looked at Major Ansley. "It seems like the whole territory is falling apart, and it's all because of Sand Creek and that horrible Colonel Chivington."

She rose, angry and confused and desperate to feel Peter's arms around her. How she loved the safety of those arms! "People need to know the truth, Major. They need to understand why the Cheyenne are on the warpath."

"I think most of them do, Claire. And with the investigation going on right now, it won't be long before the whole truth comes out. When it hits the newspapers, Chivington will be done in this territory. Personally, I think they should hang the man. Either way, once more is learned about

Sand Creek, people won't be so ready to blame the Cheyenne, but the fact remains they still don't like the idea of the Indians being on the warpath. And until Peter returns, you aren't so safe back at the settlement. I think most of the Cheyenne and Arapaho will end up in the north with the Sioux and Northern Cheyenne. Things will calm down then. Peter will come home, and you can get back to a normal life."

More shouts came from outside headquarters.

"I don't know what normal is any more, Major," Claire told him. "I just feel like Peter needs me right now, yet even if I could go to him, I wouldn't know where to begin to look. He could be on his way north, or with the Cheyenne we all know are gathering strength along the Smokey Hill, or clear down south on the Arkansas with the Southern Cheyenne. He could be anywhere."

"But he knows where *you* are, and your best bet at seeing him again is staying right where you are and taking care of yourself and that baby," Ansley reminded her. "Things are going to be dangerous wherever you go right now. The whole Territory is in a whirl of confusion over what to do next, and when people are upset and scared and angry, they do and say things they normally wouldn't, so you need to stay here for a while."

Claire turned to face him. "Just for a while, but I'm hoping you can find a way to send some men out there to inquire about Peter. Maybe some of the scouts from other Army posts can learn something."

"I already thought of that, but right now I'm going to have my hands full, and I don't want to have to add you to my list of things to worry about. You staying here will make my job a little easier, so please do me a favor and don't go back to the settlement, at least for the next few days until we learn more about Julesburg and until the Cheyenne calm down and stop the raiding and killing. If you hadn't shown up here, I would have come to get you."

Claire looked at Klas. "I'm sorry I have to keep asking you and Hubert to take care of things."

"It is our job, and Peter is our friend," Klas answered. "And he would want us to help you."

"Thank you. And I'm sure you're anxious to go back to the settlement anyway so you can look out for Sarah."

The Swede grinned. "*Ya!* I think in the spring we will marry."

Claire smiled through her tears. "Oh, I'm glad!"

"And by then you will have a new baby. Peter will be home and all this will be over, *ya*?"

How I pray you're right. "Ya," Claire answered, using Klas' accent in an attempt to cheer up the moment. "All of this will be over with."

She thought how strange it was that barely six months ago she was a young woman struggling alone in Denver City, trying to save her father's freighting business. She remembered standing on the street watching a procession of soldiers and Cheyenne come through town to talk peace with Governor Evans. One of those in the parade was an Army scout, a grand-looking warrior whose proud, handsome looks fascinated her as he rode past. He'd turned to look back at her, and their gazes held for just a moment.

That one look had captured her heart. And now here she stood, carrying that man's baby, not knowing if she would ever see that handsome warrior again.

Chapter Thirty-Five

Early February, 1865...

Peter awoke to the sound of a man's soft singing. He understood only some of the words. He lay there confused, trying to pinpoint the language.

Arapaho? Lakota?

He looked upward to see the dark-stained smoke hole of a *tipi*. He blinked when something passed over him, close to his face, then felt soothed at the sweet smell of the smoke that followed, drifting over his face and nostrils. The object swept past him again, and he realized it was a large feather.

Chanting. The smell of sweet grass. A feather fanning him. These were the acts of a shaman, but if it was a shaman who sang to him, why were his words not Cheyenne? He closed his eyes again and tried to think. A man's voice said something to someone else, and he picked up the word "awake." He recognized the Lakota tongue. Then came a woman's voice. She sounded excited.

Who were these people? Where was he? He fought to remember... remember... Sand Creek... riding with the Cheyenne... fighting soldiers... shooting someone. Who? Remember! Remember!

He tried to move, but pain ripped through him when he did so. He groaned. The shaman began singing again. More smoke filled his nostrils. The woman said something again, and the shaman answered.

Now Two Wolves remembered. Sergeant Millard Craig. He'd killed him—slit his throat. He enjoyed the memory of cutting into the man who'd murdered many innocent Cheyenne...the man who'd insulted a white woman. A *white* woman. He saw her now. Eyes as green as prairie grass. A smile as bright as the sun. Hair as red as canyon rocks.

Claire! It was Claire! Did the woman's voice he heard belong to her? The last he remembered now he was with the Cheyenne when they had attacked some warehouses. Where were they? Why was it so hard to remember? Why did his head ache so badly? Think! Think!

Julesburg. That was it. Julesburg. He'd helped the Cheyenne raid Julesburg so they could get badly needed supplies to help the pitiful survivors of Sand Creek. So many dead! He remembered the horrified looks on the faces of some of the dead there, looks of terror frozen in time. Mutilated bodies. Dead babies. Heads cut off. Insides cut open and ripped out.

Julesburg. Young Brother. He had to help Young Brother, who'd lost his horse. The whites would kill him if he couldn't escape. Two Wolves remembered now–remembered riding up to Young Brother to help.

Then he remembered nothing but pain. He had a vague memory of Young Brother telling him to hang on. Beyond that there was nothing. He opened his eyes and looked around, hoping to see Claire. A shriveled old man with thousands of lines in his face moved into view then. He grinned, showing only three or four teeth. He tapped the feather gently upon Two Wolves' face.

"*Wakan-tanka,* the old man said softly. He reached to something nearby, then took his thumb and rubbed something onto Two Wolves' forehead. He smiled and nodded, then stood up and left.

Wankan-Tanka. That was the Sioux word for the Great Spirit, just as *Maheo* was the Cheyenne word for God. He looked around the *tipi* again, studying the hand paintings on the skins that lined the inside of the dwelling. They were Lakota signs, not Cheyenne. Two Wolves could hear a harsh wind outside, and the sides of the *tipi* were sucked in and out by it. Snow made a soft swishing sound as it sifted under the edges of the *tipi* from where pegs were planted in the ground.

He could tell it was blizzarding outside. Yet it was very warm inside. He figured the *tipi* must be made of many layers of skins. More heavy animal skins covered him. Again, pain in his side made him cry out.

He managed to move a hand to where the pain stabbed at him. He felt bandages. He knew by their crusty texture that they were probably hard from dried blood.

Now he remembered more. The sharp pain at his side. Someone must have shot him when he was picking up Young Brother. He also remembered pain at the side of his head. Had he been grazed there by another bullet? He reached from under the heavy skins and touched the side of his head. His head was not wrapped, but he felt dried blood there. And pain.

What happened after Julesburg? Why was he lying in a dwelling belonging to a Lakota man or woman? He remembered that the Cheyenne on the Smokey Hill had meant to head north after raiding Julesburg, where they would meet up with the Sioux and Northern Cheyenne for strength in numbers, so that they could continue their revenge for Sand Creek.

Had they brought him north? How far was he from Fort Collins and from Claire? Did anyone know where he was? How much time had passed? Did Claire think he was dead? That he was never coming back?

Someone came inside the dwelling then. He wore a heavy fur robe against what Two Wolves realized must be wicked weather outside. The man came closer and sat on the ground next to the bed of robes where he lay. He threw off a heavy fur hood, and Two Wolves recognized Young Brother.

"Two Wolves!" the young man exclaimed in the Cheyenne tongue. "The Shaman came to tell me that you are finally awake! His wife will come back soon to bathe you and feed you."

Young Brother seemed greatly relieved.

"We feared you would never awake again," the young man told him, "that we had lost you to the world of the crazies, who lose their minds and go to sleep forever."

Two Wolves closed his eyes. "How long has it been? Where am I?"

"We are in the Black Hills of the Dakotas. It is the Moon When the Snow Hurts the Eyes. The Lakota call it the Moon of Heavy Snows. The Hunger Moon."

Two Wolves groaned. "*February!* It can't be!" He managed to sit up, wincing and crying out with pain as he did so. "I have to go to my wife!"

Dizziness overwhelmed him and a dull ache stabbed at his side, as though ribs were broken.

Young Brother reached out and grasped his arms. "You must move slowly, Two Wolves. Give yourself time. When you rescued me at Julesburg, you were shot. Twice. I managed to hang on to you as we rode away. You lost consciousness because one bullet hit your skull but did not penetrate. I took you to the Smokey River, and a Cheyenne Medicine Man took the bullet from your side, but you would not wake up. Many of us left for the north to join the Sioux. I made them bring you along because you are my friend. I was afraid that if you were left behind the Colorado Militia would find you and kill you or imprison you."

"You should have taken me to my wife at Fort Collins! She must be so afraid, wondering what has happened to me. Wondering if I am even alive."

"These are bad times, and Julesburg had been attacked. I feared that anyone who left us and tried to take you anywhere would be killed by angry whites. Julesburg was attacked a second time when we fled north. We took even more supplies and burned down all the buildings. Now there is safety only in staying together. We have joined Red Cloud and the Sioux, and we are strong! Very strong! Many soldiers and whites are coming into Red Cloud's country looking for gold. They are encouraged by a new soldier leader called Custer. He has long golden hair. Some call him Long Hair. Already he has attacked some Sioux camps for no reason, much like Chivington was doing to the Cheyenne. But now we are much stronger. Already Red Cloud has forced the closing of many forts along what the white man calls the Bozeman Trail. It is possible to win this time, Two Wolves. We have chased away many soldiers!"

Two Wolves studied the eagerness in Young Brother's eyes. He wanted to tell him what he knew was the truth. They would never win this war. There were too many whites back East, and when the war they were fighting there was over, hundreds of thousands more would come to this land to look for gold and to claim it as their own. He knew the white man much too well to think he would ever give up.

His heart shattered with the stark truth. Too many other tribes had already been forced from their homeland in the East and in the Southeast.

Now the Cheyenne were gradually being forced out of Colorado, and soon the Sioux would be starved out by killing off the buffalo and by sending more and more soldiers into the Black Hills to kill Indians. There would be one treaty after another, and all would be broken.

There was no future for the Indian. There would be more tragedies like what happened at Sand Creek. His own efforts at talking peace had failed, and now he'd been seen riding into war with the Cheyenne. Captain Tower had seen him deliberately kill Sergeant Craig. For all he knew he was wanted back home. Going there to be with Claire could mean his death. He had no future in either world–white or Indian. But whether he was wanted or not, he had to get home to her.

Had his child been born? Had Claire given up on him? Maybe by now Captain Tower had turned her eyes and heart away from her Indian husband and made her think she was better off marrying white, better off denying his love. Maybe she was angry with him for not coming home as he'd promised. By now she must think he was either dead or had permanently joined the Cheyenne in war. That he'd broken every promise he'd ever made to her.

For the moment he couldn't bring himself to destroy the Young Brother's hope. "I am glad you escaped unharmed, Young Brother–glad you are stronger now you have joined forces with the Sioux and Northern Cheyenne. But this is no longer the place for me. I have to go home to my wife." He fought the dizziness and grimaced as he got to his knees. "Help me stand."

"Give yourself time. Just for today at least. Sit up for a while and eat something solid. You have lost much weight because we were able only to get broth down your throat. You are very weak. If you get up too soon you will never make it to Fort Collins. And it is very dangerous out there. Soldiers everywhere will shoot you down when they see you."

"I have papers." Two Wolves sat back down, waiting for things to stop spinning around him. "I have proof I am an Army scout."

"They are lost. As we rode away, someone shot your horse. We fell, and two other warriors came and rescued us. We took you away quickly, leaving behind all of your extra supplies."

Two Wolves closed his eyes, feeling desperate now to get to Claire. "*Itatane* is dead? My papers are gone?"

"*Aye*. This is why it will be very dangerous for you to try to get back to Fort Collins. And my heart is sad that you wish to leave us. Will you turn and fight with the Blue Coats? Will you scout for them again?"

"No. My heart is too heavy. My journey there was to have been my last. I was to go back to Fort Collins, but what I saw at Sand Creek tore at my heart. I hoped to bring some kind of peace in spite of what happened there, yet I also wanted revenge, just as the rest of you wanted the same. I want you to know that my presence among the Cheyenne was always out of a desire for peace. Never have I fought against them or betrayed them. And I never will. I do not want you to ever see me as your enemy, but only as your friend."

Young Brother nodded. "I believe you. Somehow, when you are well and able to ride, we will find a way to get you back to Fort Collins."

Two Wolves felt agony and sorrow at the mention of home. He was not sure any more where that was. And he could tell it would take many days, maybe longer, for him to be strong enough to go anywhere.

The nearby fire crackled against a quiet calm all around. For now, there would be no fighting. The wind outside howled, as though voicing the weeping and groaning of those who'd suffered at Sand Creek. Snow was likely covering the dead and frozen bodies left behind. Children. Babies. The memory still brought him so much pain, and the anger it had stirred in him had brought him here to the Black Hills, so far away from Claire, wounded and unable to contact her. What was she thinking? Would she continue to wait for him?

The blizzard outside seemed to intensify. The Sioux and Cheyenne would huddle against the February snows for now, making plans for more fighting as soon as the weather cleared. Part of him wanted to join them, but there was a woman waiting for him at Fort Collins. *Maheo, help me.*

Perhaps soon the war back East would be over, but here in the West, it would rage for a long time to come.

Chapter Thirty-Six

Late February, 1865...

"I'm worried about Claire Matthews, Major." Captain Tower sat in a chair near the pot-belly stove at one end of Major Ansley's office. The only window in the room rattled from a cold wind that sent sleet *ticking* against the glass as though asking to be let inside.

Ansley puffed on a pipe, staring at the flickering flames that showed through holes in the stove door. "So am I. I've seen the hope fading from her eyes. I'm glad she's still staying with Gertie. I hate to think of her all alone in that cabin in the settlement, listening to the wind and wondering if she'll ever see Peter again."

"Let alone the fact that feelings against the Cheyenne are still pretty high."

"Nothing much will happen in this weather. Besides, a good share of the Cheyenne fled to the north."

Tower sighed and leaned forward, resting his elbows on his knees. "So, what do we do next?"

"We?" Ansley smiled. "Don't you mean *you*? You're falling in love with Claire Matthews, Major, and that is very dangerous–for you. You'll get your heart broken, because I know Peter, and I still believe he'll be back. There is some good reason he hasn't shown up. Maybe he's hurt. Or maybe right now the weather is keeping him away. And even if he doesn't make it back, it will be months, maybe years, before Claire Matthews will allow herself to care about any other man."

"I can't help hoping, but then I care for her so much that I actually want to see her husband come home."

"Peter was her first love, and he's a unique man whom a woman doesn't easily forget. He saved her life, more than once and became her friend, her safety, and then her lover. If he doesn't return, his baby will be all she has of him, and she'll devote all her love and attention to the child, not to another man. Even so, any man would have to go a long way to match Peter in her heart. So, you'd better protect your own heart and keep an eye out for some of the pretty, young, unattached ladies in that settlement out there. Surely you've met a few already when you've been called upon to go help Doctor Lane."

The captain ran a hand through his hair. "One in particular has caught my interest, but every time I visit Claire, I see what could be. Sometimes I think Claire and Peter fell in love with each other's bravery more than anything else." He looked at Ansley. "You must agree, Major, that the two of them couldn't be a worse match. By all rights Peter would have been happier with a Cheyenne woman, and Claire belongs with a white man. It's just natural."

"Is it?" Ansley shook his head and puffed on the pipe again. "Captain, Peter *is* half white, you know, and educated. He can be as white as Claire needs him to be, but it doesn't matter to her. It's Two Wolves the Indian she fell in love with. To her he's just another man and, Indian or white, she loves him dearly. And the Indian in Two Wolves, or Peter, I should say, will force him to keep his promise to come back to her. I'm telling you right now that something is keeping him. If he has any life in him at all, he'll find a way to return."

"And then what?" Captain Tower rose and walked to a window to watch a mixture of sleet and huge snowflakes whip around fence posts and wagons. "The fact remains that Peter killed a militia man, a *white* man, deliberately, and from what I saw, eagerly."

"And in the same fight he saved your life. Besides, you know damn well Craig deserved what he got. The man would slaughter a two-month-old baby if it was Cheyenne.

"The fact remains that a lot of soldiers and citizens believe Peter broke away and decided to side with the Cheyenne and fight right alongside them."

"He's done it before as a scout," Ansley reminded him. "You know that. The only way to know for sure how the Cheyenne are feeling and whether or not we can talk any kind of peace is to live among them for a while—get them to trust you. Peter is good at that."

"But he doesn't truly do it as a spy." Tower turned to face the major. "I think he does it because part of him *wants* to live and fight among them. Spying gives him an excuse to do what he really wants to do."

Major Ansley sighed and rose, wincing with the pain in his bad knee and thinking how glad he'd be to retire and go home to his long-faithful wife and be rid of the hardships of life out here. He walked up to the captain. "Listen to me. You want to believe that statement because it makes you feel better about caring for Claire. But she will never belong to anyone but Peter. He is her whole world."

"She's young, and I fear she has some hard lessons yet to learn."

"She's strong and brave, and she knows exactly what she's doing. You and I both owe our lives to Peter, so when he gets back here, and he will, we are going to fully support him. And *you* are going to keep your feelings to yourself and start making more visits to the settlement. You're just a young man who is lonely and in need of a woman. I might be old, but I know exactly how that feels, Captain. Just about every man here who doesn't have a wife along feels the same way, which is why, when they are on leave, they generally run to Denver or any other town close enough where there are whores to visit."

Tower snickered and turned away. "I'm not interested in that."

"Well I suggest you get interested in *some*thing <u>or *some*one</u> other than Claire Matthews."

Tower nodded. "She's just so beautiful. And so lonely. And she won't admit it, but I know she's scared. Peter became her safety. Her hero...her everything."

"That's right. Remember that. Look how happy Klas is with Sarah Kling. She has some very pretty young friends, and in a couple of months we'll be having a spring dance. So, save all your yearning for a woman's company for the dance and get yourself interested in someone else."

Tower shook his head. "I just hope that by the time of the spring dance Peter is here to dance with Claire. Mainly I just hope he's back before she has that baby. That means everything to her."

"That's only a couple of months away now. If he doesn't return by then I'll stage my own search for him. I'd start one now if it weren't for the weather."

The captain rubbed at his eyes. "Much as part of me hopes he *doesn't* come home, for Claire's sake I hope he does. In the meantime, I promised Peter I'd watch after her. He asked me to, and I think he knows how I feel about her, so he knows I'm the best one to take care of her if something *has* happened to him. That's part of the reason I'm having trouble not caring, Major, and having trouble thinking about someone else. What if I'm all she has left?"

"You can watch after her and still see someone new, Captain. I'm telling you that her whole world will be that baby and it will be a very long time before she will care about any other man, even if it's proven Peter is dead. And if that is the case, I'll take her and the child with me to Pennsylvania when I retire early this coming summer. My wife will be glad to take them in. She loves babies and we lost our own years ago. She never could have another child, so she'd welcome a youngster with open arms. Back East Claire might eventually find someone else. If Peter is dead, I think it would be best for her to get away from here all together. She can sell that business to someone from the settlement."

Tower held his gaze and nodded. "You're probably right. Staying out here will just mean taking her a lot longer to get over what's happened. The thought of her going to Pennsylvania with you makes me feel a little better. It's likely I'll be stationed out here for months or years to come. It would be better for her to just leave. She'll never be able to forget Peter if she stays here where everything happened."

Ansley puffed on his pipe again. "I'm glad you understand." He walked around Tower to watch the wicked weather outside.

Captain Tower took up his wool coat and put on his hat. "Speaking of Claire, I'm going to check on her. She's admitted having pains a time or two. If Peter Matthews is coming back, I don't want him coming back to find Claire lost that baby." He left.

Major Ansley turned to look at the door, then closed his eyes and walked to his desk to pull open a deep-bottomed drawer. He took out a small leather pouch he'd not shown to anyone. When a Lieutenant Mark Ambrose came to him a few days after the first attack on Julesburg to report what happened, he'd brought the leather pouch with him.

My commander told me to give this to you, Sir, the lieutenant had told him. *He wasn't sure how important it would be, but it apparently belonged to one of your scouts. It was taken off a dead horse after the raid on Julesurg. The horse had Indian paintings on its rump but some of its gear was army issue. My commander thought maybe it was just stolen by some Indian in some other battle, so he's not sure if this actually belonged to the rider or was stolen. It's stamped as gear from Fort Collins, so he told me to give it to you.*

Inside the pouch were Peter's papers proving he was an Army scout. *So, you were at Julesburg. Were you one of the raiders?*

Ansley shook his head and put the pouch back into the drawer. Peter could already be in a lot of trouble. Finding his papers at Julesburg only made things look worse. He'd decided not to show them to anyone just yet, not even to Captain Tower. And especially not to Claire. It would only upset her, maybe even cause her to go into labor. He'd decided he wouldn't show it to her until after she had the baby.

"Damn it, Peter, where in hell are you?"

Chapter Thirty-Seven

Mid-March, 1865...

Two Wolves dressed, wearing deerskin leggings and shirt, and over that, a buffalo coat and buffalo skin chaps, with knee-high beaver-skin moccasins. The weather was still bitterly cold here in Montana, where he'd been forced to migrate with Sioux and Cheyenne because he'd been too weak to leave them. Their quest now was to continue to keep the Bozeman Trail completely closed to white gold miners who kept trying to infiltrate Indian land. They felt relatively safe now, since they'd even forced the closing of several forts, at least for the winter.

He was stronger now himself. He'd gained some weight over the last three weeks, and the last few days he'd run around the huge camp several times a day as a way to build up his stamina. He had a long, lonely journey ahead. He was going home to Fort Collins... to Claire. Last night he'd sat in council with several of the elders, explaining why he had to leave and helping them understand it was not because he intended to join soldiers and fight against them. He was one of them, and he always would be. But he had a white wife who carried his child. No Sioux or Cheyenne man would abandon his wife or children. They understood.

He was given a sturdy horse, and weapons—bow and arrows, a war club, a hatchet, a spear—but not a rifle. Rifles were too few and too precious when fighting soldiers. The elders agreed that since Two Wolves knew the white man's tongue and had some of his education and was married to a white woman at Fort Collins, he should be safe. Young

Brother had reminded him that several of the single young women had an eye for him and that perhaps he would be better off choosing to stay with the Cheyenne and to take a new woman.

Your heart belongs with us, he'd reminded Two Wolves. *And now you and I are good friends. I do not want you to leave us.*

The young man's words left Two Wolves feeling guilty for leaving a people whom he knew were doomed to extinction or reservation life. But his guilt over leaving Claire was far greater. It was time to report back to Major Ansley, to return to the white world. To hold Claire again and be a proper husband to her. He hoped he could make it home before their child was born.

Suddenly there came an explosion. A strange silence. Another explosion, this one much closer. Then came the screams and shouts, followed by pandemonium and war cries.

Two Wolves charged out of the *tipi* to see several dwellings on fire.

"Soldiers!" one of the warriors shouted.

"Get the women and children to the Lakota camp to the west! There are many warriors there!"

There was no time to think, only time to act. Two Wolves grabbed two children who ran out of the *tipi* next to his and quickly lifted them to his horse as more explosions came from howitzers positioned on a nearby hillside. The children's mother ran to him. "Help me!"

Two Wolves lifted her also. "Go," he told her. "Take my horse."

"But you will need it to fight!"

"I will be all right. Go! Save your children." Two Wolves picked up a third child who seemed to be confused. He plopped the child onto the horse. "Take this one with you." He slapped the horse's rump. "Go!"

The woman looked at him with concern. "*Ha-ho!*" She thanked him before kicking the horse's sides. "*Hai! Hai!*" She clung to the youngest child with one arm while guiding the horse toward the distant hills, the other two young children hanging on for dear life.

Soldiers were charging toward the village now. It had been peaceful. None of those here were making war, but still the soldiers had chosen to attack, just like at Sand Creek. This time there were more warriors present, more men able to help a lot of the women and children escape. It was late enough in the morning that many of them were at least already up and dressed, This was a stronger camp.

The Sioux and Cheyenne had been wrong to think the soldiers would not attack in such cold winter weather. They had done the same thing at Sand Creek. He quickly helped guide more women and children to horses. A woman ahead of him took a bullet in the back and fell forward. Two Wolves grabbed up her two little girls and started running with them. He couldn't see Young Brother anywhere and hoped he'd managed to escape.

Part of him wanted to hand the girls over to someone else and turn and fight. He was carrying weapons, and this attack was uncalled-for. But this all had to end somewhere, at least for him. He could already be in enough trouble. He wanted to kill every soldier coming at them, but to have any chance of surviving this and getting back to Claire, he couldn't allow any of the soldiers to see him kill one or more of them.

Screaming and war whoops filled the air, along with the sound of vicious yelling by the soldiers, swords clanking, rifle fire, the snorting of frightened horses, more explosions from howitzers, the thunder of charging steeds. Two warriors rode up beside Two Wolves and demanded he hand them the two little girls. He gladly obliged, knowing that men on horses had a better chance of saving them. The woman who'd ridden off on his own horse had already disappeared.

So, this was how it would be for the Sioux and Cheyenne for weeks or months to come—constant attacks—always having to be on the alert and ready to run at any moment, each time losing valuable supplies and horses, which the soldiers would most certainly destroy. He grabbed a little boy and ran again, finally handing the child off to yet another fleeing warrior.

He wanted dearly to turn and fight, but he had no rifle. A war club and knife and even bow and arrows wouldn't be enough to save him against the soldiers charging at him now. He raised his arms, holding his bow high. Five soldiers surrounded him. If he chose to fight, he had a damn good chance of landing a hatchet and knife into at least three of them before he went down, but he didn't dare.

"I am not your enemy!" he shouted. "My name is Peter Matthews. I scout for Major John Ansley at Fort Collins!"

The soldiers all looked at each other.

"What the hell?" one of them commented.

"What were you doing here in an Indian village?" another demanded. "I saw you come out of a *tipi* like any other Indian, and you were helping some of these savages escape!"

"Just some of the women and children." Two Wolves seethed. "They cannot harm you. You need not hunt them down and kill them. Your fight is with the warriors, not the women and children."

At least fifty more cavalrymen charged past them, chasing down those who still fled. Two Wolves watched them go by with a desire to kill them all.

"He speaks good English," one of the soldiers commented. He pointed a rifle at Two Wolves.

"That's because I am half white," Two Wolves answered. "I am a scout from Fort Collins," he repeated. "I am only here because I was wounded, and the Cheyenne brought me here when I could not care for myself. Let me go so that I can report back to Major Ansley. I have a wife at Fort Collins. She was with child when I left. I must get back to her!"

"We don't give a damn about your wife and kid, Indian," another grumped. He deliberately rode his horse into Two Wolves, forcing him to defend himself by ducking out of the way. Two Wolves whirled and pulled the soldier from his horse.

"Get him!" someone else yelled.

A soldier grabbed Two Wolves from behind, and the man he'd pulled from a horse pummeled his middle, reawakening the wound there just freshly healed. Then came a fist to his face.

The man holding Two Wolves threw him to the ground.

"What are you doing here holed up with Cheyenne and Sioux, and dressed and decked out with weapons just like them?" another soldier demanded.

Two Wolves rolled to his knees. "I told you...I was...wounded." He grasped his middle, and his head spun from the blow of the other soldier's fist. "Let me speak to your commander. I will explain!" Two Wolves realized he couldn't say he was wounded at Julesburg. They would believe he'd deliberately fled with the Cheyenne and that he'd been part of the attack, which he had, but not for the reasons they would think. He wanted dearly to land into the man who'd hit him, but he knew that at the moment his only chance of getting back to Claire was to not fight back.

One of the soldiers dismounted and stormed up to him, jerking Two Wolves to his feet and opening the buffalo-skin coat he wore, searching for weapons.

"You don't look like any damn scout to me," the soldier seethed. "You look Cheyenne, and the fact remains that you came out of one of the *tipis* and helped some of the women and children escape. If you were a scout, you'd be on *our* side."

"I can explain," Two Wolves answered, grabbing at his side again. "Who is in charge here?"

"Colonel George Armstrong Custer!" another soldier replied proudly. "And he's no friend of the Indians. And if you *are* a scout, you'll be court-martialed just for being here and helping them, and you'll be hanged for deserting to the enemy."

"Where are your papers?" the soldier who'd searched him demanded. "If you're an Army scout, you would have papers proving it, and you should have an Army shirt with an insignia of crossed arrows."

Two Wolves closed his eyes, realizing his predicament. *Claire! I was coming home to you!* He couldn't tell these men he'd ripped off his crossed arrows patch in raging anger after what he'd seen at Sand Creek. "I lost my papers at—" He hesitated. He couldn't even tell them the truth about his papers—that he'd lost them at Julesburg. They would most likely would kill him on the spot if they thought he'd been part of the attack there. "I am not sure where I lost them. I told you that I was wounded. Somewhere in Colorado. I must have lost them then. Perhaps the Indians I was fighting stole my Army shirt and made off with it."

"And then they turned around and *helped* you and brought you clear up here to Montana? You aren't making sense!"

Two Wolves studied the man who'd made the statement. He was a young lieutenant, most likely inexperienced and out to prove he was some kind of great Indian fighter.

"Just wire Major John Ansley at Fort Collins," he told the man. "He will vouch for me."

"We aren't close enough to civilization wire *any*body," the soldier answered. "And I think you're *lying* about having papers and about how you ended up here."

"I do not lie! I am a scout for the United States Army. If you get in touch with Major Ansley, he will tell you it is true." Two Wolves glared at the lieutenant. "What is your name?" he demanded. "You will be in trouble when Major Ansley finds out how you have treated one of your own scouts."

"My name is none of your goddamned business, Indian! Put out your hands."

Two Wolves dearly wanted to slam a knife into the man, but he obeyed. For Claire. He was wounded. Fighting back would only mean dying and never returning to her. The lieutenant tied his wrists and dragged him over to one of the soldier's horses. He tied the other end of the rope to the pommel of the soldier's saddle.

"Take him up the hill and keep him there until we can straighten this out. He'll go down to Fort McPherson with any other prisoners we can round up. He'll probably end up sent to prison at Fort Leavenworth."

Still not totally recovered and now with his wounds battered, having to run uphill behind the soldier's horse left Two Wolves out of breath and bending over from the pain in his side. He collapsed and was dragged the rest of the way up the hill. Once at the top, he managed to get to his knees, then to his feet. He turned to see soldiers still chasing down villagers, heard more gunshots, saw *tipis* on fire. He looked around then, and farther in the distance on the same ridge where he stood he saw a man sitting straight and proud, blond curls spilling out from under his hat.

"Long hair," he said softly. He instantly hated Custer as much as he knew the Sioux hated him. Young Brother and others had said the man was not very different from John Chivington.

He closed his eyes and looked away, hoping the woman and children he'd helped flee had managed to get away. Still, in the distance he saw some of them plus a few warriors being herded together as prisoners and forced to climb up to where Two Wolves stood. Two of the warriors were shot down even as they obeyed orders to give up. Farther away soldiers continued to chase down others, while even more soldiers set fire to the rest of the *tipis*.

The lieutenant who'd forced prisoners together ordered them all to sit down, and for at least another two hours the fighting continued somewhere in the distance, most of it out of sight. Two Wolves could hear continued shooting and war whoops and screams. He watched two soldiers ride back to the village to an area where a herd of Indian ponies were roped off. They proceeded to shoot them down, one by one.

Finally, it all seemed to be over. He and the other prisoners were forced to their feet. Heading back to Fort McPherson meant going through the now-burned village because that was the direction in which they had to go. Two Wolves surmised the soldiers deliberately made them walk through the mayhem just to prolong he horror of what had just occurred. Far ahead of them George Custer led the procession.

Two Wolves and the others looked around at what was left of the village that just a couple of hours earlier had sat in total peace. That was when Two Wolves saw him. Young Brother. He lay with a hole in his forehead, his eyes still open and staring upward.

Chapter Thirty-Eight

Late March, 1865...

"Something's wrong! Something's wrong!" Claire writhed in pain and panic. The baby was coming, and too soon. It was only March. "Don't let my baby die! Don't let him die!" Where was Peter? He should be here! What if he came home only to learn their child was dead?

"We'll do everything we can, Claire," Captain Tower told her. He put a cool cloth to her forehead. "Doctor Lane is here with me. And I've asked every woman here at the fort to come and help. I've delivered babies before, but I don't know much about babies themselves, especially ones that are premature. The women might be a better help there."

"Where is Peter? I want Peter!"

"I'm sure that wherever he is he's trying to get home, Claire. You know that."

"He's dead! He must be dead!"

"Don't think that way."

"She's almost completely dilated, Captain," Doctor Lane told him. "This baby is coming, early or not."

"No! No, it's too soon!" Claire couldn't help tears of panic. Her weeping turned to screams as her contractions became deeper, as though the devil himself clawed at her insides.

"Peter! He always helps me. He takes away the pain. He should be here. He should be here!"

Another scream.

Gertie smoothed back her hair. "We'll get you through this, dear. This baby belongs to Two Wolves, so you know he'll be strong, even though he's coming a little early."

Sarah Flower rushed into the sergeant's quarters where Gertie lived. Emily Sternaman arrived at almost the same time.

"Robert is off duty today," she told the captain. "He can watch our baby."

Tower faced both women. "I need your help, not with Claire but with the child. It's coming almost a month too soon, and I don't know anything about how to treat a premature baby."

"Warmth," Emily told him. "The baby is used to the warmth of his mother's womb. And we'll have to help Claire begin nursing as soon as possible. New mothers sometimes need a little help at first." She turned to Sarah. "Heat some water, and lay out some blankets, but find a way to hang them near the fire to warm them up first. As soon as the baby comes, we'll clean him or her up with warm water and wrap it right away. And if we can get him or her crying, that will help clean out the lungs."

"Good idea," Tower told them. "I do know that most premature babies die from lung problems, mainly because their lungs aren't fully developed. Make him or her exercise those lungs."

"This child was fathered by Two Wolves," Gertie reminded all of them. "Do any of you know a stronger, more able man? This baby will be fine."

Claire grasped the woman's hand. "Gertie, don't let my baby die! I don't want Peter to come home and find out I lost the baby. It means everything to him!"

"Peter will be glad just to know *you* are alive, Claire. You can always have more children."

"But thinking about the possibility of having a son here waiting for him will keep him alive if he's hurt."

"*You* are his hope, Claire." The words came from Captain Tower.

Claire caught his gaze, saw the love there. He'd made no bones about how he felt about her, and he'd been at her beck and call all these weeks and months. "I'm...sorry, Captain. You've been...so good to me."

"Nothing to be sorry for. My only concern is keeping you and this baby alive."

The pain came again, this time much more intense.

"Push, Claire," Doctor Lane told her. "The baby is crowning."

The black pain engulfed her now. The room became a whirling maze of Doctor Lane telling her to push again, Captain Tower joining him in telling her to push, telling her she was doing fine and that her baby looked fine. Gertie soothing her. Emily and Sarah assuring her they would take the best care possible of the child.

Pain. Black pain.

Then a weak cry.

Was it her baby? *Peter.* The weak crying grew stronger. "Captain... Is it my baby?"

"Give him to me—quickly!"

Was that Emily's voice? She'd said "him." A boy! A son for Peter?

The crying faded.

"My baby!" she cried out.

Someone massaged her belly, and she felt more pain as something was expelled from her insides.

"We need to get the afterbirth," Doctor Lane told her. "Not getting it could cause an infection that would make you very sick.

"My baby! Is it alive? I don't hear it crying!"

She felt Captain Tower leaning close. "It's a boy, Claire, and he seems quite healthy and a decent size considering he's premature."

"He's alive?"

"Emily and Sarah have him," Tower told her. "They're cleaning out his nose and mouth, and they'll wash him up and wrap him in nice, warm blankets for you. Gertie will help us clean you up, so you'll be ready to hold him and nurse him. He'll need lots of nourishment right away. Understand?"

Claire couldn't stop her tears. "Thank you," she told Tower. "Don't let him die."

"Doctor Lane and I will do our best to make sure he doesn't. I promise."

"Find Peter. Tell Major Ansley to find him, please!"

"We've tried. You know that, Claire. And if he's alive, he'll do everything he can to get back to you."

Claire closed her eyes and lay still, feeling weak and spent. Gertie washed her and packed her private area with soft cloths. Someone picked her up while Gertie changed the sheets. Claire could tell she'd been put into a chair and someone removed her soiled nightgown and put a clean one on her. Someone lifted her and put her back into bed. A baby's crying came closer, and she opened her eyes to see a tiny, tiny infant beside her. She couldn't help a smile at the fact that he had a head full of straight, black hair. His skin was still a ruddy red, his eyes black as coal.

"He eseems really strong for being so tiny," Emily told her. "And look at that hair! He's Peter's son, all right. And he has strong lungs. That's important. Sarah and I will help you learn the right way to nurse him. He'll need plenty of his mother's milk."

"Yes, I have to make him stronger and keep him alive," Claire told them. Tears slipped down the sides of her face. "Thank God. I didn't want Peter to come home to find out his baby died."

"Do you have a name for him?" Captain Tower asked.

Claire studied her son, the way his little fists flailed in the air. Strong. Yes, he was strong, like Peter! "*Okohm*," she replied. "That's the Indian name my husband wanted for him. It means coyote. His English name will be John, for my father and for Major Ansley. I think his middle name should be Peter. John Peter Matthews. And they're both Biblical names, just like his father, Peter James."

Captain Tower knelt beside the bed and touched a finger to the baby's fist. *Okohm* opened his tiny fingers and grasped the captain's little finger.

"Oh, my goodness!" Claire exclaimed. "He's hardly any bigger than your hand."

"Yes, but he'll grow fast enough from your love and nourishment," Tower told her with a smile. "And he has a strong grip." He met her gaze. "Just like his father."

Claire put a hand over the captain's. "I love him so, Captain. Please, please try to find him."

He studied her sadly. "Claire, between bad weather, the war back East and now raging Indian attacks practically everywhere out here, it's impossible to send troops out just to find one man who can very well find his way home when he is able. I don't mean to sound uncaring. It's just a fact. Major Ansley is sending wires to every fort he can reach, asking about Two Wolves, so it's not as though we're doing nothing at all. The only trouble is, the Sioux and Cheyenne have cut down a lot of telegraph lines everywhere, so it's hard to reach some places. You know Ansley will keep doing his best. You just take care of yourself and this baby, so you're both here for Peter when he makes it back. We all still believe he will."

"Promise me you'll let me know the minute you hear anything."

The captain smiled softly, then leaned closer and kissed her forehead. "You know the major and I both will. You just remember I'm here for you if the news isn't good, all right?"

"I'll remember."

Tower rose and faced the other women in the room. "I'll leave things up to you now. I'm going to let Major Ansley know about the baby. If any problems arise, get Doctor Lane."

"We will," Emily told him. "Thank you, Captain."

Tower nodded, glancing at Claire and the baby once more before leaving the room to wash up in the kitchen.

Claire couldn't take her eyes from her son. "He's beautiful," she said softly. "Just like his father. Peter is the most handsome man I've ever set eyes on."

"He is all of that," Gertie told her with a chuckle. "Just don't forget that's what got you into all this trouble."

All the women laughed, but Claire's heart ached with a dread she didn't want to voice. Her beautiful son might not ever get to see his handsome father.

Come home, Two Wolves, and see your son. Come home and hold me again... hold us both.

The baby opened his eyes and looked into hers, and there she saw him— Two Wolves. He was with her now, in the spirit of this tiny being who was making a little "o" with his mouth and who grasped at a ruffle on the front of her gown. Strong, amazingly strong. Oh, yes, he was his father's son.

Chapter Thirty-Nine

Mid-April, 1865...

The wire came on a sunny day. Outside in the fort assembly yard men marched in drills, their boots squishing into slick mud from melted snow and thawing ground. At times a soldier would slip and fall, bringing laughter to the others and sharp reprimands from their sergeants to shut up and stay in line.

Major Ansley watched from a window, enjoying the heat of the sun as its rays came through the glass.

"Major! We got a wire about Two Wolves!"

Ansley quickly turned to see Captain Tower walk up to his desk. He handed out the piece of yellow paper. Ansley took it eagerly. "Is it good news, or bad?"

"Not good, but at least he's alive, and we might be able to help him."

Ansley scanned the wire.

RECEIVED YOUR INQUIRY. STOP. A MAN NAMED PETER MATTHEWS HAS BEEN PRISONER HERE SINCE EARLY MARCH. STOP. ALSO KNOWN AS TWO WOLVES. STOP. FOUND IN RAID ON SIOUX CAMP IN BLACK HILLS. STOP.

Ansley looked at Captain Tower with raised eyebrows. "The Black Hills! That's clear up in the Dakotas!" He squinted to read the rest of the message.

HEARING IN ONE WEEK FOR DESERTION TO THE ENEMY. STOP. IF YOU HAVE KNOWLEDGE OF THIS MAN OR

EVIDENCE OF HIS INNOCENSE YOU MUST ATTEND THE HEARING. STOP. HIS SENTENCE COULD OTHERWISE BE DEATH. STOP.

The wire was from a Lieutenant Frederick O'Toole at Fort McPherson in Nebraska. Ansley looked wide-eyed at the captain.

"Jesus! We have to wire back right away! Tell them we most certainly do know about Peter Matthews and that he is one of our best scouts. They have to delay that hearing until we can get there. Tell them if they sentence Peter to death without hearing our testimony, heads will roll."

Captain Tower nodded. "This will hit Claire hard."

"Don't say a thing to her until we get a reply. If we can at least tell her they'll put off a hearing until we get there, that will soften the blow a little."

"You know Claire. She'll want to go with us."

"She can't. It's too dangerous out there now. With warmer weather and melting snows, the Sioux and Cheyenne will be on the rampage again all over Kansas, Nebraska, the Dakotas, Montana—you name it. They've burned down or closed half the forts up in there. Some new man, George Custer, I think he's called, has started a lot of trouble by broadcasting that there is gold in Montana. The damn fool is a high-ranking soldier. You'd think he'd know better than to practically invite thousands of men into Indian country! That land was promised to the Sioux and Cheyenne and Crow in the Laramie Treaty in 1851. Now white settlers and the government are breaking every single promise in that treaty, and this Custer is making it all worse!"

"Can you honestly name one treaty that *hasn't* been broken, Major? Broken treaties have been one of the things Peter has had to fight in order to keep the Cheyenne calm. Broken promises make him crazy, and he's probably half crazy right now from being held prisoner and not being able to keep his own promises to Claire."

Their gazes held, both wondering the same thing. "How in hell did he end up clear up in the Black Hills?" Ansley said aloud.

"Good question. The only answer is that he must have joined the Cheyenne and ridden north with them to continue making war."

Ansley shook his head. "No. I don't believe that. It's something else."

"Either way, it got him into a lot of trouble. I'll send that wire and we'll head to Fort McPherson. I'll bring some of the men with me who were involved in that battle when Two Wolves—Peter, I should say—saved my life. They can vouch for him, too."

"But they also saw him kill Sergeant Craig."

Captain Tower frowned. "There isn't one man out there who will testify to it. They knew the kind of men the Colorado volunteers were. The newspapers have been filled with the truth about Sand Creek, and Chivington is on his way out. Between that and how much they all like Peter and Claire and that new baby, they aren't going to say anything to get Peter hanged."

Ansley thought about the leather pouch in his desk, found at Julesburg. Peter had definitely been there. How could that be explained?

"Jesus," he muttered, looking at the wire again. "We need to leave right away and get over there to help Peter. We could be held up by an Indian attack or the weather. Anything could happen. We'd better take plenty of men."

"I'll start getting things ready, Sir."

Major Ansley handed him the wire. "I am also going to send a wire to a senator from Pennsylvania whom I know well. We actually grew up together. Maybe I can get this taken care of through some kind of orders from Washington that would put an end to all of this."

"It certainly would save a lot of headaches," Tower answered. "I'm anxious to tell Claire we have found Peter, but I hate telling her the circumstances." He looked down at the wire. "I'll, uh, I'll send a wire right away to Fort McPherson and let you know their answer." Tower saluted the major before turning to leave.

"Captain," Ansley called to him.

Tower stopped and turned.

"*I'll* tell Claire about this. You just go send that wire. It's time for you to let go of feeling so responsible for Claire. It isn't good for you *or* her. And didn't you tell me that young lady whose broken arm you set a couple of weeks ago brought you cookies yesterday and looked at you with such adoration it almost made you blush?"

Tower faced the man with a sly grin. "Her name is Susan Elsner."

"Ah, so you remember!"

"Of *course*, I do. I had to set her arm. She's barely eighteen, Major."

"Old enough to marry. In the meantime, Claire is taken, heart and soul. She'll be so excited about finding Peter that we're going to have trouble making her understand she can't go with us to Nebraska. We might have to tie her to a post or something."

Both men smiled at the remark.

"You might be more right than you think," Tower suggested.

"You just remember that when we get back here we'll be having that spring dance we talked about. I'm sure Miss Susan Elsner will faint dead away when you ask her to go with you."

Captain Tower smiled and shook his head. "I haven't asked her yet. And since when do ageing Army officers play Cupid?"

"I guess it's time I did retire," Ansley answered. "I've been out here too long, and I've let myself become too involved in the lives of some of my men."

Tower left and Ansley sat down behind his desk. He pulled out the drawer again and took out Peter's leather pouch with his papers inside. He would have to write up new papers for him. He couldn't use these without explaining where they had been found. To tell the powers that be in Nebraska that Peter had been at Julesburg wouldn't help his case one bit.

"I'm getting a little tired of keeping your neck out of a noose, Peter," the major muttered. He put the pouch back and walked to where his wool coat hung on the wall. He had to go tell Claire her husband had been found.

Chapter Forty

Claire took fresh-baked bread from the oven. Hubert and Klas would be by soon to each pick up a loaf, something she did for them every time she baked more. She was happy for Klas, who beamed with delight whenever she brought up his engagement to Sarah Kling. It would be a summer wedding, and the whole settlement looked forward to a reason to hold a big cookout and enjoy the relative peace they had known through the winter. She could only hope Peter would be here to join in the celebrations.

She set out the rest of the bread, fighting the dwindling belief her husband would come home. The Cheyenne had calmed down in this area, but in the north, so she'd been told, and for the rest of Colorado, things were worse than ever. She'd cried so much over Peter not seeing his beautiful son that it seemed there were no more tears left in her. She felt lost and homeless, even though she was back in her own cabin next to the store, and even though most of the settlers had warmed up to her again, mainly because she was a new mother with no husband and no help. They saw how she struggled to take care of her little son and also help run her store, her only livelihood.

Nothing seemed real. What did her future hold? Major Ansley had told her once that when he retired he would take her with him to his wife in Pennsylvania, where she could start a new life. If Peter returned, he would be able to find her there. *You'll be safer there, and people will be kind to you,* he'd promised. Claire appreciated the man's big heart and fatherly attitude, and she knew he was just as concerned about Peter as she was. He'd taken a personal interest in her, something Army officers seldom did, and certainly not toward Indian scouts, who many of them didn't even trust.

She walked over to the cradle Klas had made by hand for little *Okohm*. In the three weeks since he was born, he'd taken his milk well and had actually gained a pound. Yet he still seemed so tiny. His eyes were bright, and sometimes she could see Peter there, his spirit reaching out for her. He'd shown little baby smiles, and he was so good. He seldom cried, and he cuddled against her so sweetly when she fed him. Sometimes they would share a look that made it seem like her son actually realized something was missing.

She reached down and gently touched his silky shock of hair. "Your *daddy* is missing," she said softly.

The pain that brought to her heart had been almost unbearable at times. There were moments when she just crumpled to the floor and sobbed, so unsure where to go from here, arguing with herself that she should not give up on Peter.

Someone knocked on the door then. She put an extra blanket over *Okohm* to protect him from drafts. "Who is it?"

"Major Ansley. Claire, I have news."

Claire almost lost her breath. She flung open the door to let the major inside. "What is it? Have you found Peter?" She closed the door.

"Just calm down and go *sit* down," he told her as he removed his heavy wool coat and a beaver hat. "It's almost warm enough that this winter wear is too heavy," he commented. "I'll be glad to hang up that heavy coat for good." The major looked down at his feet. "I stomped off as much mud as possible. I think I can walk to the table without leaving a messy trail."

Claire was already sitting, feeling crazy with both excitement and dread. "I don't care about that! Sit down, Major. Tell me what you know. Is Peter alive?" Her insides ached at the possibility of bad news.

Ansley hauled his hefty frame to the table and took a chair, sitting down with a heavy sigh. "Yes, he's alive," he answered. He took the telegram from a shirt pocket and handed it to her.

"You don't look very happy, Major," Claire told him as she hesitantly took the telegram from him.

"Well, it's good news and bad news. We can only hope for the best."

"Oh, my God," she nearly whispered, her eyes filling with tears. "Peter! He's alive! Oh, God, thank you! Thank you!" She held the telegram with a shaking hand. "Thank God you found him! All your inquiries paid off." She met Ansley's gaze, tears streaming down her cheeks. "I was just talking to the baby about his daddy." She swallowed back a lump in her throat. "How bad is the bad news?" she asked. "Is he hurt?"

"I don't know. Just read the telegram. Then we'll talk about it."

Claire wiped frantically at her tears so she could see better, then opened the small piece of paper. Her blood ran cold as she read the message. *"Desertion to the enemy."* She looked up. "He wouldn't do that, Major! You've got to help him!"

"I already wired them and requested an extension in case Captain Tower and I can't get there in time for the hearing. We'll have to take some of the men with us who were there when Peter saved Tower's life, plus a few extra troops. It will be a dangerous trip."

Claire struggled with mixed emotions. She'd suspected herself that Peter might turn to his Cheyenne blood and fight with them, but surely, he wouldn't do that, knowing he could be branded a deserter, that he might never see his son. "I have to go with you. I have to see him. And he should see *Okohm* before he ... I mean ... if he dies never seeing his—"

Claire couldn't finish. Her whole body shook at what could be happening. Ansley grasped her hands.

"You hang on, Claire Matthews. We already received an answer. They will postpone the hearing two extra weeks. That gives me and Captain Tower more time to get there to defend Peter. But you can't go with us."

"I *have* to! I have to see him. I'm all right now, Major. I can make the trip."

"Absolutely not! *Think* about it, Claire. You have a son who was born premature and is lucky to be alive. That baby can't make a trip like that. You know damn well that this time of year a wicked blizzard can barrel over those mountains on any given day. We could get buried in a snowstorm, and your son would freeze to death. Or, if something happened to you, he'd *starve* to death! If we can get Peter out of this, that little boy will mean *everything* to him. Your job is to stay right here and take care of that baby, and keep yourself healthy, so that Peter can come home to a *family*. And it's not just the weather we'd have to worry about. Any kind of travel beyond this settlement, especially between here and Fort McPherson, is dangerous. The Sioux, Crow, Cheyenne—they have banded together and are on the war path. It's so bad that the government has had to close some of the forts along the Bozeman Trail. It's no place for a white woman and a baby. You absolutely cannot go with us."

"But what if he's convicted and hanged?" Claire covered her face. "He'd never get to see his son," she sobbed. "And I'd never get to see Peter again."

"You listen to me. He is *not* going to be convicted—not once Captain Tower and I testify on his behalf. And if he *is* convicted, I'll do everything in my power to get permission to bring him here first. He'd have to come as a prisoner, but at least he could see his son and have a chance to see you again. If we have to..." He hesitated, hardly able to bear the thought of it. "If he's supposed to be hanged, I'll take him to Fort Rankin. There isn't one man here at Fort Collins who would want to see that."

Claire groaned, still holding her head in her hands. "No! No! We can't let that happen. You'd have to let us run away together...somewhere...anywhere. You can't let him die, Major!"

"I'm going to do everything in my power to keep that from happening. I have connections in Washington. I grew up with a man who is now a senator from Pennsylvania. I've wired him. I'll do everything I can to stall any kind of execution until I can get some kind of pardon for Peter. But it's possible none of that will be necessary. I think once we testify, they'll let him go. I'm sure this is all a big misunderstanding. Peter might have good reason for having made it clear up to the Black Hills with the Cheyenne, something beyond willingly joining them. I know how much he loves you. He wouldn't have left Colorado and gone clear up there without at least seeing you first and explaining why. The captain and I are leaving right away—first light—and come hell or high water, I'm coming back with Peter, understand? Whether the sentence is good or bad, I'm bringing him home to you. That's a promise."

Claire took a handkerchief from the pocket of her apron and blew her nose and wiped at her eyes. "Thank you for anything you can do, Major," she half sobbed. "You've been so good to me and to Peter."

"I care about both of you. And if worse comes to worse, you're coming to Pennsylvania with me when I retire, understand? You'll need to get out of Colorado and all things familiar."

All things familiar. What was familiar was Peter's arms around her in the night...the majestic Rocky Mountains and the cry of wolves...a powerful Cheyenne man saving her life...his kisses...the feel of him invading her very soul...his handsome smile...his voice...his promises...spring wildflowers...the shrill call of elk in the fall.

"I *need* to be near familiar things," Claire told the major. "Colorado is home to Peter. So much has happened to me here that I don't think I could ever leave. It would be like leaving a piece of my heart behind."

She pulled away and rose, walking to the baby's cradle and looking at her very Indian son.

"Sand Creek did this," she said sadly. "Peter must have seen the terrible things that happened there. The newspaper reports are finally bringing out the truth. Some of the men who were there and refused to take part in that awful slaughter are talking, and it's hideous what happened to the women and children. I hope they tar and feather Chivington before running him out of Colorado."

"A lot of people feel that way, but right now we need to concentrate only on Peter and on getting him back here." Ansley rubbed at his eyes in frustration. "Don't you give up, Claire. At least your husband is alive and has a chance to come home. He needs your prayers more than anything else, and for that baby to be kicking and healthy the first time he sets eyes on him. He will understand why you didn't come with us. It's far too dangerous. He would probably even be angry with us if we brought you along. We'd be risking your life and the baby's."

"I suppose. If it was just me I wouldn't care. But you're right about the baby. He's still so tiny." She wiped away another tear and faced the major. "But he's all Peter, isn't he? He's strong for being early, and he's gaining weight. His hair is black as coal, and I see his father's spirit in his eyes. He'll be a warrior, just like his father—a warrior for peace."

"Maybe so. But if he's just like his father, you'll have your hands full raising him. He'll be spirited and daring, full of spit and vinegar and difficult to discipline."

Claire couldn't help a smile. "I expect you're right." Their gazes held, and she saw the same worry in his as she knew was in hers over how this would end. "Go and get Peter, Major Ansley. *Okohm* and I both need him."

The major rose. "I'll do my best, my dear. So will Captain Tower." He walked over to take a look at the baby. He shook his head and smiled. "Peter will be so proud." He walked to the door and put on his hat. "The weather's warmed up so much that I think I'll just carry my coat back to my quarters. I hope it holds, and we don't get buried in a sudden snow storm on our way to Fort McPherson. In the meantime, you take care of yourself and that baby, and we'll get Peter back here as soon as we can."

"Thank you, Major." Claire hurried up to him and hugged him. "You've been a good friend."

Major Ansley patted her back. "You've stolen my heart, Claire Matthews. I want to see you and your husband together and happy again. I did warn you, though, that it wouldn't be easy to be married to a man like Peter." He pulled away and leaned down to kiss her forehead.

"I know, but I love him, and there is no way to stop feelings like that."

"Then God be with you." Ansley sighed and turned to the door. "I've got to go get things ready to leave in the morning. Take care of yourself and that baby."

Ansley left. Claire closed the door and leaned her back against it. She noticed that the yellow telegram still lay on the table, and it hit her with full force. Peter was alive! But he could end up shot or hanged.

No! It couldn't end that way. The tears came again, tears of joy that her husband was alive and would get to see his son mixed with tears of terror that he could be put to death.

Chapter Forty-One

"Major!" Two Wolves rose from the wooden bench that was the only furniture in the small, dirt-floored cabin where he'd been kept for weeks, his ankle chained to a large post in the middle of the room.

The private who had let Major Ansley and Captain Tower into the tiny dwelling that served as a prison room handed Ansley a lantern and started to close the heavy wooden door.

"Leave that door open!" Ansley commanded, noticing how Two Wolves blinked and turned his head when a shaft of sunlight filled the area. It hit the major right away that there were no windows in the room, and he spotted a chamber pot in one corner. "Has this man been kept here in the dark all this time?"

The private swallowed and backed away a little. "Yes, sir."

"And can you tell me *why?*"

"N-no, Sir. Those were my orders, and that's all I know."

"And someone's fucking head is going to roll for this," Ansley fumed. "*Leave* us. And leave that damned door open. And send someone in here who can unlock that chain and get this man's foot out of that ankle cuff."

"Sir, he's a Cheyenne warrior. He might kill someone or run."

"He's in no *shape* to run. You can damn well see that. And I know this man well enough to tell you he'd never deliberately kill a soldier just to try to get away. Now go find someone who can get that chain off him!"

The private nodded and hurried away.

Major Ansley looked at Two Wolves, who was not the robust, healthy man who'd left with him months before to go to Fort Lyon. "My God, Peter, what have they done to you?"

"I was wounded," Peter answered. "I had healed enough to try to get home to Claire, but then we were attacked, and they took me away as a prisoner. They beat me and have brought me little food." He put a hand to his side, still obviously in some kind of pain. "I thought to try to escape, but I held on to the hope you would find me. It is only because of Claire that I did not run. I am glad to see you, Major." He looked at Captain Tower then, and the two men shared the same thought.

"My wife. Is she well?"

"She had the baby," Captain Tower told him. "You have a son named *Okohm*. He was born early, but he's doing fine. Claire knows we've found you, and she's waiting for us to bring you home."

Two Wolves closed his eyes and walked over to sit down on the bench.

"Claire," he groaned. He looked at Tower again. "I tried to get back to her, but a head wound knocked me out for days, maybe weeks. I don't even know how long it was. I suffered the injury at Julesburg. When I awoke, the Cheyenne had brought me up here. They saved my life, but now I am accused of desertion."

"We know all that," Ansley told him. "We have a lot to talk about, Two Wolves. But right now, I'm going to get that damned chain off you, and we'll get some hot water in here and get you cleaned up. I brought you a clean Army uniform. That will help when you face whoever will be at your hearing. It's one of your shirts with the crossed-bows insignia on it. Claire gave it to me. I've arranged for the hearing to take place tomorrow, so we can get you out of here as fast as possible. I'm going to speak to the commander and finish arrangements for your release, whether guilty or not. I promised Claire I'd bring you back to Fort Collins no matter what, so you could see her and the baby before—" Ansley didn't finish.

"Before they hang me?" Peter ran a hand through his hair, hating the fact that it wasn't clean, hating for Captain Tower to see him this way. He valued cleanliness as part of his personal pride, and now here he sat, thin and filthy. Heaven only knew what life was like for the other prisoners who'd been brought here with him. All of them had been sent to a reservation somewhere. It sickened him to think what proud, beautiful people the Cheyenne and Sioux were, and how that pride had been broken, how shamed they were now.

Part of him wished to be with those who still rode free and made war and fought proudly. But he knew that could not last forever. The way of life for the Indian would one day be no more. His heart ached over it, and every night he saw Young Brother, the excited young man who thought the Cheyenne could win this fight, lying on his back with a hole in his forehead.

"No one is going to hang you," Ansley told him. "I'm waiting for a wire from a senator friend of mine, giving me permission to accompany you back to Fort Collins, where you'll be free to decide what you will do with your life."

"You can't guarantee that."

"I'm going to do my best. I wired everywhere about you most of the winter. But there were times when the Sioux had cut down the telegraph lines up here and closed a lot of the forts. I couldn't always get through. Thank God I finally did. You just get yourself cleaned up and let Captain Tower look at your wounds. I'm leaving for a while, but I'll be back."

Ansley left, and Captain Tower walked closer, setting his doctor's bag on the bench, then sat down beside Peter. "What can I do for you? How badly were you wounded?"

Peter rested his elbows on his knees. "Bad enough to be unconscious for a long time. My people took care of me and kept me with them all the way up there. I am grateful to them for that. I was also shot in the side. When the soldiers found me, they kicked and hit me there. It has been very painful ever since."

"Do you want me to look at it?"

"Maybe later, after I have cleaned up."

"What about the head wound? Have you had any seizures? Headaches? Any lapses of memory?"

Peter shook his head. "No. I just... woke up. Sometimes I do get a headache, and I do not sleep well, but I think maybe it's over my worry for Claire." He faced Captain Tower. "Is she still mine?"

Tower raised his eyebrows at the question. "What the hell kind of question is that?"

"You know what I mean." Peter looked away. "I broke my promise to her. She must be very discouraged and lonely. I did not mean to do that to her."

Tower sighed. "If you are asking if there is anything between me and your wife, Peter, there most certainly is not. Do you really think I'd want to answer to you for something like that? Besides, a team of horses couldn't pull that woman away from you. All winter long she pestered the hell out of Major Ansley to try to find out what had happened to you. He even had to argue with her to keep her from coming up here with us. She thought she should come, but it's too damn dangerous around here for a white woman, let alone the danger it could be to your son. You can't count on the weather in Colorado and Nebraska in the spring, to say nothing of Indian attacks."

Peter remained silent for the next several seconds. Tower frowned with concern. "She's doing fine. So is the baby. You have a son. He was born too soon, but he survived and he's thriving, mostly due to his mother's unending love and attention. He is all she has of you, and she knows it. The best thing that could happen to her is to have you with her again. Ansley will find a way to get you out of this."

Peter nodded. "You delivered the baby?"

"With the help of Doctor Lane, the settlement doctor. Several women from the fort also helped—mainly in saving the baby. I can deliver them, but I'm no expert on how to treat a newborn, especially when it's premature. Claire had been staying with Bertie for the winter. Ansley insisted on it. So, she had plenty of immediate help when the baby came."

"Good." Peter stood up. "I let her down. Perhaps she will not want me back."

"That's foolish talk, Peter. She knows about Sand Creek and what that must have done to you. Never once has she given up on you coming home. It's all she talked about the whole time you were gone. She kept saying you must have a good reason, and she was so scared you were hurt. It turns out she was right." Tower also rose. "She understands you better than you think... the Indian side of you. I imagine it's because that's who you were when you first met and rescued her. Two Wolves. That's how she always thinks of you. And she knows you are hurting because of Sand Creek and everything else that is going on out here. She was so scared she might lose the baby. She kept saying the baby was what would bring you back."

Peter met his gaze. "*Aye*, they are all I have thought about. Claire and my son." He smiled sadly. "At least what I supposed would be a boy." He closed his eyes. "Nothing worked out the way I thought it would. I tried more than once to get back to her, but part of me couldn't leave my people just then. Things happened that were out of my control, things that make me look guilty of the very thing they want to hang me for."

"Ansley won't let that happen."

"He is a good friend, but I fear he doesn't have the power it will take to get me out of this." Peter winced with pain and put a hand to his side again.

"Peter, let me help you."

He shook his head. "Not until I am clean. They gave me this filthy shirt and pants and have not allowed me to bathe. I think I had one or two broken ribs that did not fully heal. It will just take time." He looked out the door at sun and grass. A horse trotted past, the ground squishing under its hooves. "Would you have stayed and loved her if I did not come back?"

Tower turned away. "Jesus," he said softly. "That's a dangerous question, Peter."

"It is an honest one. I need to know, in case they hang me."

"Peter, it doesn't matter. She wants no one but you. No one. She already agreed that if the worst happens, she'll go with Major Ansley and live with him and his wife in Pennsylvania until she gets on her feet and knows what she wants to do with her life. She needs *you*. Yes, I could love her, but I never pushed it because there would be no future in it. You are the air she breathes, and that's that. You have a beautiful, loyal, devoted wife who needs you, and Major Ansley and I are going to make sure that happens."

Claire! They had not even been together a full year, yet now it seemed they couldn't live without each other. "She is a good woman. I knew it the moment I set eyes on her. She is very much like my mother—strong and determined and loyal. Back in Chicago my mother fought for me with bravery against those who scorned both of us. She made sure those people let me go to school and that they treated me like any other child, even though they saw me as different because I had Indian blood. Claire will fight for our son that way."

"Yes, I'm sure she will. And so will you. But you need to make that choice, Peter. You need to stay in her world. I hope you understand that."

Peter nodded. "I understand. Life as they knew it will soon be over for all those with Native blood. It lies heavily on my heart, Captain."

"I know it does." Captain Tower walked closer to him. "Peter, you're an educated man. There might be things you can do to help the Cheyenne without going to war with them. That has to end because it leads nowhere. You already know that. Maybe you can travel to Washington and speak for them. Major Ansley knows people there. And maybe you and Claire could move your supply business closer to a reservation and serve the outside settlers and also the reservation–kind of keep an eye on things on behalf of the Cheyenne. Maybe Ansley can pull enough strings to make you an Indian Agent."

Peter faced him. "I see you have been giving this a lot of thought."

Tower held his gaze boldly. "I want to see both of you happy. I care very much about Claire, and I owe you my life."

"It is a good thing I see you as an honorable man, Captain Tower, or I would not have saved your life that day."

Tower smiled. "Do you think I don't know that?"

Peter put out his hand. "I am glad you are here, Captain. I was losing hope."

The captain grasped hold and they shook hands firmly. "Peter, I didn't want to have to answer to you if anything happened to Claire, and now I don't want to have to answer to Claire if anything happens to *you*. We'll get you out of here."

Ansley returned then with a soldier who looked at Peter fearfully before stooping down to unlock his ankle cuff. He pulled it off, then rose and backed away as though he thought Peter might attack him. Peter looked at Ansley.

"I could escape now," he told the major with a grin.

"After all I've done to find you, if you mess this up by trying to escape, I'll shoot you myself," Ansley told him.

Peter folded his arms. "I believe you would. But you would not get the chance. I would take you down first. You have grown fat and slow."

Ansley chuckled. "Your days of fat and slow are coming.'."

"I do not doubt that. For now, I thank you, Major. You are a valuable friend."

"More valuable than you think. The reason I took longer than I should have is because before I found that man to unlock your chain, someone told me a wire had come for me. I had to go to the telegraph office to pick it up." He handed a piece of paper to Peter.

Peter took the paper and walked closer to the sunlight to read it.

TO MAJOR JOHN ANDREW ANSLEY. STOP. REGARDING YOUR SCOUT CALLED TWO WOLVES, A/K/A/ PETER JAMES MATTHEWS. STOP. YOUR JUDGMENT IS HIGHLY TRUSTED, MY FRIEND. THE PRESIDENT HAS DECLARED PETER MATTHEWS NOT GUILTY OF ANY CRIMES AGAINST THE UNITED STATES ARMY OR THE GOVERNMENT OF THE UNITED STATES. HE IS FREE TO GO BUT MUST ABSTAIN FROM ANY WARLIKE ASSOCIATION WITH THE CHEYENNE. HIS WORK AS A PEACE MAKER IS WELL KNOWN. ANYTHING BEYOND THAT COULD BE CONSIDERED UNLAWFUL. YOUR FRIEND IN SERVICE TO THE UNITED STATES, SENATOR JOSEPH PRIESTLY.

Peter looked at Ansley. "I am free? No hearing?"

"No hearing."

Peter closed his eyes. "If only it could be that way for my people and the rest of the tribes."

"I know, but there is no going back and undoing Sand Creek, and no way to stop the West from filling up with white settlement, which means this thing with the Indians will only get worse before it gets better, and you can't stop it."

Peter scrunched the paper into his hand as he shook his head. "I do not know how to thank you, Major."

"You can thank me by going home to Claire. She's dying to see you. I'll send her a wire to let her know you've been pardoned, so she won't worry about what's happening up here."

"I am grateful."

Ansley put out his hand, and Peter grasped it with both of his.

"For the rest of my life I will not forget you, or Captain Tower," Peter told the major. "You in particular have been like a father to me. May *Maheo* bless you forever. You will always be in my prayer offerings."

"Then I'm a safe man."

Peter held his gaze. "I will explain to you where I have been on our way back to Fort Collins. I have much to tell. What I saw at Sand Creek built a great anger in my heart." His eyes teared, and he took a deep breath against his sadness. "I rode with the Cheyenne, but not to make war. When they attacked Captain Tower I was not there to kill soldiers. I was there to kill Sergeant Craig and any Colorado Volunteer that I could kill. If Craig had not been with the captain and his men, I would have urged the warriors with me not to attack the soldiers. And Julesburg was something I could not stop. Either way, I had little power to stop them, especially the Dog Soldiers. The Cheyenne are too angry, and deep inside they are too afraid. They do not know how to keep their land and cling to their own way of life without fighting back."

"The captain and I both understand that. We don't need any explanations."

Peter let go of the major's hand and turned away. "At Sand Creek I befriended a young warrior called Young Brother. He escaped but lost his whole family. He and I both saw what Chivington's men did to the women and children there. I liked Young Brother and understood his anger." He faced the major again. "After the soldiers beat and arrested me, they forced me to walk through the village they had just destroyed. I saw Young Brother lying dead with a bullet in his forehead. He was perhaps only seventeen, a young man who held much hope of defeating the white man. That same hope was in the hearts of many of the Cheyenne, but it has been dashed. It is sad to see the light go out of a young person's eyes. I cannot forget what I saw, Major. It broke my heart to see my young friend lying there dead."

"Of course, it did. But soon the war in the East will be over, and a lot more soldiers will come west, along with a flood of new settlers. And that will be the end of it. You have to understand that."

Peter nodded. "*Aye.*" A tear slipped down his cheek.

"Claire will help you there, and that new son of yours," the major reassured him. "And from the looks of you, you could use several loaves of Claire's fresh bread. You need to put some meat back on those bones."

Peter smiled. "My wife's cooking would fatten *any*one. I think maybe she has been feeding *you* a lot."

All three men laughed, but inside Peter still wrestled with rage. His only calm came in thinking about Claire. Soon he would hold her again! In her, he would find his peace. And once he held his son in his arms, he would know his place in this world. But Young Brother would never know that, never know the joy of a wife and children, never live out a long and good life. Of all the things he'd seen and been through, for some reason the loss of Young Brother hurt the most. Perhaps it was because he seemed to represent all the Cheyenne had lost and would never get back.

"Someone will be here soon with some hot water, Peter," Ansley told him. "I'll get the clean uniform I brought along. Let's just get you home. It's time you saw your son. That beautiful boy will go a long way in healing your heart."

Peter nodded. "Yes. Thank you."

Ansley and Tower left, and Peter stared at the open door, realizing he could walk out a free man. But the Cheyenne would one day never ride free again. He walked over to the bench and sat down, putting his head in his hands, and wept for Young Brother, something he had not allowed himself to do until now.

Chapter Forty-Two

Claire drove the two-seater buggy herself. Little *Okohm* lay snuggled into pillows and blankets on the floor behind her seat. It was a beautifully warm spring day, and she hated the fact that the buggy's wheels were smashing down some of the sea of red and yellow and purple wildflowers that cascaded down the foothills and across the plains outside of Fort Collins. The sun actually felt a little hot against her shoulders.

She wore a soft green calico dress she knew Peter liked, with a square-cut bodice trimmed in lace and cut just low enough to reveal an enticing cleavage. She wanted to be beautiful for him. She had her figure back, and her hair spilled in long, loose red curls. That's how her husband liked it, undone and tangled by the wind. Her heart pounded with anticipation, but it also ached for the things Ansley had told her about what her husband had been through, and over the fact that he'd been wounded and was still healing.

Peter did not come into the fort when they returned, nor did he come straight to their cabin. He was waiting in the foothills beyond the settlement. He wanted to meet with Claire alone first, just her and the baby. Major Ansley had ridden alongside her for safety until Peter came into sight, then left so they could be alone. Claire slowed the buggy now as she drew closer.

There he stood, Two Wolves! That was how she would always see him. Major Ansley had told her that on their way back that Peter had visited with some peaceful Cheyenne camped outside Fort McPherson. He'd traded blankets and an Army coat for deerskin leggings and a shirt, as well as feathers, moccasins and hair ornaments. All his own

Indian clothing and supplies had been taken from him when the soldiers arrested him, but he wanted to be Two Wolves when he first saw her. Two Wolves, the Cheyenne Indian with whom she'd fallen in love. There would always be that part of him that needed to *be* Cheyenne, and Claire understood that more than ever now. She also knew he would teach their son the Cheyenne way, and that was fine with her.

Now there he stood, next to a bay mare with only a blanket on its back instead of a saddle. Her heart swelled with love at the sight of him standing there amid the wildflowers, a gentle wind blowing his long hair across his shoulders. He wore the feathers and hair ornaments in his hair, small feathered earrings, fringed buckskin leggings and shirt. It was not Peter she was coming here to meet. It was Two Wolves.

She drew closer and halted the horse. Two Wolves grabbed hold of the bridle and said something softly to the horse in the Cheyenne tongue to steady it. For a moment he just stood there, looking her over, still so handsome in spite of being so much thinner than when he left.

What had they done to him while he was imprisoned? She could hardly stand the thought of the horrors he'd seen at Sand Creek. What he'd suffered after the raid on the trading post. In spite of his lost weight, he was still her handsome warrior, and that Cheyenne pride shone in his dark eyes.

"You are so beautiful," he told her. "And I am so sorry. I did not keep my promise to come back soon, my promise to live as a white man and not ride with the Cheyenne."

Claire fought tears. "Two Wolves, it doesn't matter. I understand. I thought...I was so scared you might be dead."

He shook his head. "I love you, Claire. That has not changed. But if you have lost your love for me, if you think you should be with a white man, I will not blame you, as long as I can see my son."

Her heart ached at the remark. "How can you even *think* I would ever stop loving you? I have waited faithfully, and not so much for Peter James Matthews, the white man I married, but for Two Wolves, the Cheyenne warrior who stole my heart the minute I saw him ride past me in Denver City. And if you don't come over here and help me down and hold me right now, I just might pass out from the joy of seeing you standing there in one piece!"

Two Wolves walked over and reached up. Claire leaned down and threw her arms around his neck. In the next moment she was fully in his arms and weeping uncontrollably at the feel of his strength, the familiar smell of him as she buried her face into his neck.

"*Maeveksea!*" He groaned her name. "*Nemehotatse!*"

"Don't let go, Two Wolves. Don't ever let go of me again!"

"I will not. I will never leave you again for so long. I am so sorry. I have so much to tell you—"

"It's all right. I know what it must have been like for you at Sand Creek. It's been in all the news. People know the truth, and Chivington has left Colorado in disgrace."

"I rode with them, Claire. For a while I was a true warrior and considered staying, but the thought of you and our child kept me from joining them fully. I was coming back to you when I was wounded at Julesburg, and they took me away with them."

"I know what happened. Major Ansley told me. I am just so glad to be in your arms again." She moved her lips across his cheek, to his mouth, and he kissed her so deeply, wildly, passionately. Claire could hardly believe any of it was real. He left her lips and kissed her over and over, her hair, her forehead, her cheeks, her neck, holding her to him with her feet off the ground the whole time. She could feel him shaking as he crushed her close.

"Tonight, I will share your bed again," he groaned. "I will be inside you, and I will love you forever and live your way. We will stay here in Colorado and find ways to help my people, but I will never leave you again. This I promise."

Their lips met again in a delicious, long kiss of reunion and joy. Finally, he lowered her, and she rested her head against his chest. "Two Wolves, you never broke your first promise. You did come back. I did not fear that you would stay with the Cheyenne. I only feared that after Sand Creek you would join them in war and get hurt. I need you so. I only feel safe when I am with you."

"And we will always be together now." He let go of her slightly, putting a hand to her face. "At night I saw you, your flaming hair and your eyes green as grass. I felt you with me, and I ached to have you in my bed." He studied her lovingly, running a hand into her tangled hair. "Major Ansley said you were hurt by men who looked down on you because of me. I am so sorry, Claire. That will never happen again. I will always be here to protect you. I am so sorry for all you have been through."

"It's all right. I shot one of those men myself, and Hubert shot the other two. While you were a warrior with the Cheyenne, I was being a warrior here." She smiled through tears, and Two Wolves smiled in return, that wonderful, handsome smile that always melted her a little.

"So, you are a warrior woman, like some of the Cheyenne women." His smile faded as he wiped her cheeks with his thumbs. "No one will ever hurt you again. This I promise." He glanced at the buggy when he heard a little cooing sound coming from the back seat. He looked back at Claire and kissed her once more. "You brought my son. I was not sure—"

"Of course, I brought him! He was born early, but he survived, and he's gaining weight every day. He's still so tiny, though. He needs his father's love and strength." Claire pulled away and reached into the floor of the back seat, pulling little *Okohm* from the blankets. She kept one blanket wrapped around him as she handed him to Two Wolves.

Never had she seen such pride and joy in a man's eyes as when Two Wolves took the boy into his arms. The baby looked up at his father, and a tiny smile crossed his lips just before he stuck a fist into his mouth and sucked on it.

"He is beautiful!" Two Wolves told her. "My son!" He held him close, kissing the child gently on the cheek. "He is so perfect. And look at all that hair!"

"He is all you, Two Wolves. Maybe someday we will have a son or daughter with my red hair. They would make quite a pair."

"*Aye*, it would be something to see."

"I want him to always be proud of his Cheyenne blood," Claire told him. "You will teach him that pride. I insist on it."

Two Wolves gently stroked the baby's cheek with his finger. "I wish that my mother could have known him." He looked at Claire. "And you. She would have liked you very much." He pulled the blanket away a little more and studied the boy's eyes as the baby gazed at him as though he looked into his soul. Two Wolves could not help the tears that formed in his own eyes.

"I befriended a young Cheyenne man" he told her. "He was not even twenty. He was eager and brave and lost his family at Sand Creek. He wanted to fight back because that was the only thing that would make him feel better, and he had such hope that if all the Cheyenne banded together they could win the battle against soldiers and white settlement. I tried to explain it is a war that cannot be won, but he was so full of hope."

Claire's heart broke with sorrow for him when a tear slipped down her husband's cheek and dripped onto the baby's cheek. "The day the soldiers found me and arrested me, the camp where Young Brother had taken me was attacked, and when they took me away, I saw him lying dead, shot in the forehead."

Claire touched his arm and kissed it. "I'm so sorry."

Two Wolves breathed deeply for self-control. "I knew then that it is over. There is a new man now in the north, a new leader of soldiers who is not so different from Chivington. His name is Custer. He and his men are the ones who attacked Young Brother's camp." He met Claire's eyes. "For every Chivington who dies or is cast out, there is another to take his place. I want to raise our son to be proud but to understand he will have to live the new way, and we have to protect him from the Chivingtons in this world."

"We will."

The wind blew Two Wolves' hair across his face, where it stuck against his tears. Claire reached up and pushed it away.

"Stop blaming yourself for what is happening, Two Wolves. You have tried to stop it. But you are one man, and you can't do it all by yourself. It's time to let others try. Time to stay home with your son now and raise him to be a wonderful man like his father is. God saw to it that you were pardoned, and He allowed you to come home for a reason."

Two Wolves clung to his son as he leaned down to kiss Claire's lips gently, lovingly. "And He brought us together for a reason. Captain Tower suggested we could move our supply store closer to a reservation, where we could do business with soldiers and settlers as well as make sure the Cheyenne and Sioux and whatever other reservation Indians are there are well supplied. I am thinking it is a good idea. I could teach the younger ones about the white world and teach them about reading and arithmatic while you run the store. Perhaps Klas or Hubert would come with us. Major Ansley will leave soon for Pennsylvania, and we could go there. But I think it is best we stay here and that I help my people in a way other than war."

Claire smiled. "I think that's a wonderful idea."

Two Wolves handed her the baby and pushed some of her red curls behind her ears. "For all my abilities as a warrior, *you* are my strength, *Maeveksea*. You suffered because I was not here for you, and I suffered in my need for you. I will not let that happen again." He pulled Claire and the baby close, looking out over the vast prairie. "It is such a big country. How sad it is that the whites cannot learn to share it. There is enough room for all, and once the Cheyenne roamed all of Colorado Territory and parts of Kansas and Nebraska and Wyoming and Oklahoma. Now they will be squeezed onto small reservations. The buffalo will be killed off, and the railroad will come, and it will never be the same again."

Claire breathed in his scent. "The old ones will never accept that, but the young ones will learn a new way. You can help them. Your mother would be proud of you, Two Wolves. And so will Major Ansley."

A gust of wind swept across the wildflowers, making them wave wildly as though rejoicing. To Claire it was a celebration of having her husband back. But Two Wolves was sure he heard whispers on the wind, the spirits of so many who had died. He heard drumming and chanting... and war cries.

"I was not hostile to the white man. Occasionally my young men would attack a party of the Crows or Arickarees, and take their ponies, but just as often, they were the assailants. We had buffalo for food, and their hides for clothing, and we preferred the chase to a life of idleness and the bickerings and jealousies, as well as the frequent periods of starvation at the Agencies.

"But the Gray Fox (General Crook) came out in the snow and bitter cold, and destroyed my village. All of us would have perished of exposure and hunger had we not recaptured our ponies.

"Then Long Hair (Custer) came in the same way. They say we massacred him, but he would have massacred us had we not defended ourselves and fought him to the death. Our first impulse was to escape with our women and papooses, but we were so hemmed in that we had to fight.

"Again the Gray Fox sent soldiers to surround me and my village; but I was tired of fighting. All I wanted was to be let alone, so I anticipated their coming and marched all night to Spotted Tail Agency while the troops were approaching the site of my camp. Touch-the-Clouds knows how I settled at Spotted Tail Agency, in peace. The agent told me I must first talk with the big white chief of the Black Hills. Under his care I came here unarmed, but instead of talking, they tried to confine me, and when I made an effort to escape, a soldier ran his bayonet into me.

"I have spoken."

[The words of Crazy Horse, given to Major H. R. Lemly, who was stationed at Fort Robinson, where Crazy Horse was stabbed as soldiers tried to confine him to prison. He did not die right away. Lemly took down his words, and later the Major wrote: "In a weak and tremulous voice, he broke into the weird and now-famous death song of the Sioux. Instantly there were two answering calls from beyond the line of pickets, and Big Bat told me they were from Crazy Horse's old father and mother, who begged to see their dying son. I had no authority to admit them, and resisted their appeal, piteous as it was, until Crazy Horse fell back with the death-gurgle in his throat."]

From the Author...

The previous statements from Crazy Horse and from Major H. R. Lemly are from a book called *Touch the Earth*, compiled by T. C. McLuhan, Promontory Press, NYC, 1987.

Dear readers,

Black Kettle did not die at Sand Creek, but four years later, almost to the exact date, late November, 1868, he died on the Washita River, when the village where he stayed was savagely destroyed in a surprise early morning attack much like Sand Creek, an attack led by George Armstrong Custer and the 7th Cavalry. In 1876, Custer himself was killed at the Little Big Horn, but that was the last great battle waged by what was left of the Plains Indians. Their way of life vanished, as did a great many Cheyenne, whose population dwindled with each broken treaty. They were not recognized by the United States government as a separate tribe and culture and given their own land until the 1930's.

Made in the USA
Middletown, DE
19 March 2018